# FROM LADLE TO GRAVE

# FROM LADLE TO GRAVE

Amy Patricia Meade

**SEVERN HOUSE**

First world edition published in Great Britain and the USA in 2021
by Severn House, an imprint of Canongate Books Ltd,
14 High Street, Edinburgh EH1 1TE.

Trade paperback edition first published in Great Britain and the USA in 2022
by Severn House, an imprint of Canongate Books Ltd.

severnhouse.com

*British Library Cataloguing-in-Publication Data*
A CIP catalogue record for this title is available from the British Library.

ISBN-13: 978-0-7278-9056-6 (cased)
ISBN-13: 978-1-4483-0594-0 (trade paper)
ISBN-13: 978-1-4483-0593-3 (e-book)

*All Severn House titles are printed on acid-free paper.*

Typeset by Palimpsest Book Produ
Falkirk, Stirlingshire, Scotland.
Printed and bound in Great Britain
TJ Books, Padstow, Cornwall.

# ONE

'Mmm.' Julian Davis, Channel Ten newsman and occasional bartender, moaned with obvious delight as he stood before the industrial-sized stainless-steel refrigerator. With his right hand, he extracted two bags of ice from the lower freezer compartment and placed them on to an awaiting trolley. With his left, he crammed a *Harriet the Spy* tomato sandwich into his mouth. 'Although my mama . . .'

At the mention of Julian's mother, Tish Tarragon, owner of Cookin' the Books literary café, rolled her eyes. She had heard her best friend's tomato-sandwich tirade three times since devising the dish as the passed hors d'oeuvres for the Junior League 'Women of Literature'-themed fundraising dinner. With 150 guests about to arrive and a Sylvia Plath-inspired crab and avocado first course yet to plate, this was no time for a fourth.

Julian, however, felt no such pressure. 'My mama, who, if you recall, was Miss Alabama, would say this, with its toasted brioche and bacon mayonnaise, is more a BLT than a traditional Southern tomato sandwich.'

'Well, I could hardly slather some Duke's on a slice of Wonder Bread, slap a slice of beefsteak on top, and call it a day, could I, Jules?' Tish argued. 'Not while charging the Junior League fifty dollars a head. Then there's the whole vegan menu—'

'Vegan? How do you make this thing vegan?' he asked before scoffing the last chunk of sandwich.

'With an olive-oil country bread and vegan mayonnaise flavored with a splash of soy sauce and a generous dash of smoked paprika for that savory bacony hit,' she explained.

'Clever,' he replied. 'Well, the sandwich is delicious and I'm sure the ladies will love it – both versions. All I'm saying is that if my mama were here, she'd say it's not authentic.'

'I see the lack of authenticity hasn't stopped you eatin' none,' Celestine Rufus, Tish's employee and star baker, remarked as she recreated Calpurnia's fried chicken from *To Kill a Mockingbird* for the dinner's main course. 'You ate three of the test sandwiches last week and you've already eaten two tonight.'

Jules threw his exquisitely coiffed chestnut head backward and laughed. 'Have you been keeping count, Celestine?'

Celestine nodded, sending her dangling earrings dancing against her short-cropped, cherry-red hair. 'You bet I have. The more you ate, the more brioche I had to bake. You're like my grandkids. Leave 'em alone a few minutes and they eat me out of house and home.'

'Speaking of which,' Tish started, 'that plate of sandwiches is for the church ladies who volunteered to wait tables tonight – I've promised them dinner in exchange for all their hard work. St Jude's Episcopal has been extremely gracious to donate the use of their hall tonight. They were also kind enough to provide me with a key so I could shuttle supplies here after the café closed last night and set up in between today's breakfast and lunch crowds.'

'Don't worry,' Jules assured her. 'I'm about to roll this cart of ice out into the hall and set up the bar, so I won't be taking food away from the church ladies.'

'What drinks are you makin' tonight?' Celestine asked.

'In addition to the usual wine, beer, and soft drinks, I have a rhubarb and raspberry cordial that pays tribute to *Anne of Green Gables*. I used to love that television show as a kid. Remember Gilbert, Tish? He may have been my first crush,' Jules gushed. 'Anyway, I made the cordial from the first of the summer raspberries and the last of the May rhubarb. It can be mixed with soda water for a refreshing non-alcoholic beverage or combined with white wine for a fabulous spritzer.'

'Sign me up for one of those,' Celestine directed.

'Soda water or wine?'

'If I ever get away from this deep fryer, I'll have one of each.'

'Sure thing. Although you might want to wait until you hear about the second drink before you finalize that order, because I'm whipping up a giant bowl of Southern Lady Porch Punch from my mama's 1983 Junior League cookbook.'

Celestine peered over the top of her reading glasses. 'Porch Punch? What's in it?'

'The first of this year's peaches pureed with sugar, lemon juice, and mint and then mixed with vodka and soda and served on ice,' Jules explained.

'Hmm, sounds tasty, but if I get even a sniffle of hard liquor, I need a nap. I'll stick with the spritzer.'

Jules nodded. 'And you, Tish?'

'If there's any punch left at the end of the night, I'll have that,' Tish replied as she began halving and de-seeding avocados and squirting them with lime juice. 'Until then, I need to be completely sober if we're going to get these meals on the table in time.'

Jules, dressed in his bartender ensemble of white dress shirt, gray vest, red bow tie, and dark trousers, wheeled the trolley of ice toward the kitchen door. 'If I have any time before the guests arrive, I'll come on back to lend a hand.'

'Just so long as that hand ain't goin' to your mouth,' Celestine shouted, half-jokingly, after him.

An hour later, the doors to the church hall opened to guests, just as Tish placed a scoop of crab salad into the last avocado, garnished it with watercress and chopped chili, and placed it on a chilled plate. Celestine, meanwhile, had finished frying and had placed the trays of cooked chicken into a warm oven while she stirred the pots of mashed potatoes and collard greens.

'That's strange,' Tish noted. 'I'd have thought our servers would be here by now.'

'Maybe they got caught in traffic,' Celestine suggested.

'All seven of them? In a small town like Ashton Courthouse on a weeknight? I'm going out there to see what's going on.' Tish removed her dirty apron to reveal a fitted black T-shirt and capri pants and stepped out into the church hall to investigate.

Gathered around the bar was a flock of middle-aged women dressed completely in black. They took turns standing near Jules, smiling as he held a cellphone aloft.

It was the missing serving crew. And they were taking selfies with their favorite television weatherman.

'Who's next?' Jules asked the ladies congregated around him. 'Marge? Marge, did I get a photo with you yet? No? Well, get over here and pull in close.'

Tish didn't want to spoil the volunteers' fun, but she also had to round them up fairly quickly if they were going to pass trays of tomato sandwiches to guests as they arrived. She cleared her throat. 'Um, Jules?'

'Tish! I'm so sorry I didn't make it back to the kitchen, but these ladies are fans of mine and, well . . . how could I turn them away when they've been so kind to volunteer this evening? Would you be a lamb and take a photo of all of us together?' Jules handed her a phone in a pink, rhinestone-studded case and waved the servers to flank him on both sides. 'One shot together, everyone, and then it's show time. If you didn't get an individual selfie with me, let me know at the end of the dinner.'

Tish took two shots of the group to ensure at least one of them turned out well and then returned the phone to its owner, a tall woman with shoulder-length silver hair.

'You're so lucky,' the woman told Tish. 'It must be exciting to have a friend like Mr Davis.'

Tish eyed the lengthy queue that had formed at the bar while Jules had been chatting with the volunteers. Although she cherished Jules and his friendship, 'exciting' wasn't exactly the word she'd use to describe him. Spontaneous, unpredictable, unconstrained, and sometimes infuriating, but exciting?

'It's never the same day twice,' a diplomatic Tish answered with a smile before joining Jules behind the bar. Once there, she grabbed the ladle from the punchbowl and helped Jules serve beverages until the crowd was under control.

When they had finished, Jules expressed his thanks.

'No problem. I'll have one of the servers bring out more ice. It's warm in here – you don't want to run out.' She looked up to see a petite woman with short blonde hair and wide, expressive eyes staring back at her. She was in her fifties and dressed in a green, knee-length day dress and a pair of canvas sneakers.

'Who's that?' Tish inquired of Jules with a tilt of the head in the woman's direction.

'Hmm?' Jules glanced up from the bar. 'Oh, the ladies said she's some gypsy woman who tells fortunes.'

'She doesn't look like a gypsy, Jules.'

He shrugged. 'I'm just telling you what the church ladies told me. The woman donates free card readings to be auctioned off for charity and other church events. She's kind of a regular at these things.'

'OK, but why is she staring at me?'

'She probably remembers your picture from the news or something. You're both in the same business.'

'We're not at all in the same business,' Tish said.

'Yes, you are,' Jules maintained. 'She talks to dead people. You find out who killed dead people. It's all pretty much the same thing.'

Tish was once again prompted to roll her eyes. 'Never the same day twice,' she murmured to herself.

Before she could make her way back to the kitchen, a member of the Junior League stepped up to the microphone that had been positioned at the front of the room. Tish had been advised that the event would start with announcements, during which she would be introduced, so she waited at Jules's side.

'Good evening, everyone, and welcome to our annual summer fundraising dinner and auction. Before we start dinner, I'd like to thank everyone for being here. I'd also like to thank our event organizers without whom this evening would not be possible. We've gone with a theme this year – Women of Literature – and Ms Tish Tarragon and her team from Cookin' the Books Café are here to dish up a wonderful menu inspired by scenes in books written by female authors. If you haven't visited Cookin' the Books Café in Hobson Glen, you need to do so. I've been there for both breakfast and lunch and it's terrific.'

Jules leaned toward Tish. 'Better double next week's egg order,' he whispered.

'Also, joining Ms Tarragon is everyone's favorite weatherman, Channel Ten's Julian Pen Davis,' the woman continued as Jules waved and bowed. 'In addition to tending bar, Mr Davis is offering us the chance to have a selfie taken with him. Selfies are five dollars each, with all proceeds to benefit the Junior League.'

As the room broke into thunderous applause, Tish shot Jules a questioning glance.

'What? It wasn't my idea. The Junior League people asked me to do it,' Jules explained through a pasted-on smile. 'Don't worry. I'll still manage the bar just fine.'

The woman at the microphone waited for the applause to die down before she spoke again. 'Finally, as most of you know, many of our playground improvement and other projects would never have transpired if it weren't for the generous support of the Honeycutt Foundation. This year the Honeycutt Foundation has pledged to double that support. Here to present us with a check is foundation chairperson, Priscilla Maddox Honeycutt.'

Priscilla Honeycutt, red and flustered, emerged from the unused coat room where, given the immaculate state of her bright lipstick, she had clearly been freshening her make-up prior to making her grand entrance.

Before Ms Honeycutt could take the podium, Tish snuck back to the kitchen, where she prepared her volunteer wait staff to serve the first course. While they shuttled dishes of crab-filled avocado into the church hall, Tish and Celestine dished up the main course. Plates piled high with crispy, golden fried chicken (fried okra for vegetarians) with a mouth-meltingly tender interior were filled to groaning with early green beans simmered with ham hock, sweet pickled cucumbers with dill, Tish's family potato salad, and a fluffy angel biscuit slathered with honey butter.

The menu was a success, for the network of servers brought back nothing but compliments and empty plates. After loading the industrial dishwasher for the first cycle of the night, Tish rolled out a gigantic crystal bowl of ambrosia salad to ladle to guests who might find themselves still peckish during the auction.

A sweet, creamy fruit salad beloved by Southern families, Tish's ambrosia was made lighter with the addition of fresh local strawberries and fresh pineapple and by replacing the heavy sour cream and whipping cream with vanilla yogurt and a scattering of chopped mint. No one seemed to mind the modifications as they allowed more room for the Nora Ephron's *Heartburn*-inspired Key lime pie that rounded out the evening.

In the end, the event was a rousing success for all concerned. Nearly five thousand dollars – three hundred of it from Jules's selfie scheme – was raised to benefit the Junior League's children's literacy projects within the Ashton Courthouse and Hobson Glen neighborhoods and over a dozen people had requested Tish's business card to discuss potential catering jobs of their own.

'If business keeps up like this, you'll have to think about buying a van instead of just renting one,' Jules noted.

'I'm not sure I'm ready to buy a van, Jules,' Tish replied as she slid open the side door of the Ford Transit cargo van she'd rented for the evening and loaded in a crate of glass stemware. 'My business is still in its infancy and I already paid out a sizeable amount of cash converting the old storeroom into an office/bedroom.'

'Office/bedroom? Is that what you call that space? It's more like a jail cell. It doesn't even have windows.' Jules slid two boxes of dishes into the van alongside the crate of glassware. 'You should come stay with me. I have an extra bedroom with a queen-sized bed and I'd be happy to clear a shelf in the medicine cabinet for your toiletries.'

'A whole shelf, huh?' she teased. 'That's generous of you, Jules, but I like living at the café. Plus the living arrangements are only temporary. Once Mary Jo gets back on her feet and is able to rent a place of her own, she and the kids will move out and I'll have the upstairs apartment to myself again.'

Jules examined a well-manicured fingernail. 'Well, until then, *mi casa es su casa.*'

'If I feel I need a break, I'll take you up on your offer,' she promised.

'You can stay with me, too,' Celestine offered as she placed two cases of flatware atop the dishes. 'With Lloyd gone, there's plenty of room. Also, when you are finally ready to buy a van, let me know. Lloyd purchased plenty of vehicles for his plumbin' business, always through the same guy. If you're a friend of Lloyd's, he might give you a discount.'

'I'll keep that in mind.' Tish ran her hands through her wavy, bobbed hair and assessed the contents of the van. 'Chafing dishes, racks, serveware, utensils, glasses. Looks like we've got everything.'

'The church hall was empty when I left,' Jules asserted, using the glow of the June moonlight to check his hair in the van's side-view mirror.

'The kitchen, too,' Celestine added, as she untied her apron from her ample figure and fanned herself. 'I've got the leftover condiments and sauces in a cooler in my minivan. I'll bring 'em to the café when I do breakfast in the morning.'

Tish nodded her blonde head in approval.

'Hey.' Jules spoke up. 'It took longer than anticipated to clean up tonight. You don't think someone's locked the gate and trapped us in here, do you?'

'Not a chance,' Tish replied. 'The groundskeeper who's looked after this place for the past thirty years has two hard and fast rules. One, he goes to bed at nine thirty and therefore will not take on any tasks after nine p.m. – this includes locking the gate or any of the church buildings. And two, he mows the grass every Wednesday, whether it needs it or not.'

'Oh, thank goodness. I'd hate to have to spend the night here. Graveyards are so creepy.'

Tish was about to point out that they could stay in the church hall, but she was too tired to debate the point. 'I'll do a final check of the hall, lock up, slip the keys under the door, and we'll head back to Hobson Glen.'

As was customary, the nineteenth-century brick church was built facing east and was encircled by the parish cemetery. Sometime in the middle of the twentieth century, a freestanding parish hall structure had been built behind the church and to the northwest, on an adjacent property that had been purchased by the parish. And, more recently, a paved parking lot was added just outside the graveyard to the southeast. The two new additions were linked to the church and each other via a single winding gravel path.

A fatigued Tish gazed at the path, her feet throbbing. Although the walkway was lined on either side with solar-powered foot-lights, the quickest route to the church hall was a direct line through the cemetery, beneath a canopy of mature yew trees.

As the church clock tower had just chimed eleven and Tish was eager to get home to a cold shower and a moderately soft bed, she chose the shorter trail of the two. Picking her way between the tombstones, she wended her way along the 300-yard trajectory that separated the parking lot from the front door of the church hall.

The evening was warm and clear, and the moon nearly full, but the dark shadows cast by the yew trees obscured Tish's course. She felt in the pocket of her apron for her phone so that she might switch on its powerful flashlight. Finding the pocket empty, she then recalled having left the phone on the driver's seat of the van so as to avoid it falling out of her pocket while packing up for the night.

Shaking her head at her own lack of forethought, she pressed onward, treading carefully through the damp, fine fescue of the graveyard toward the hall. The prize was nearly in sight when the toe of Tish's right foot struck something hard, sending her tumbling, face forward, to the ground.

After the shock of the fall wore off, Tish hoisted herself to her feet and assessed the damage. Aside from an ache in her right ankle, which she must have wrenched when she tripped, she felt none the worse for wear.

*Well*, she thought to herself as she dusted the dirt from the front of her clothing, *if I was going to twist an ankle, better to have done so after the Junior League dinner than before it.* Thankful for this small saving grace, Tish continued her journey to the church hall, but not before taking a backward glance to identify the cause of her tumble.

Expecting to see a rock or a tree root, she was shocked when her eyes met what appeared to be a shoe. Stepping closer, she bent down so she could better see the item in the dim moonlight.

It was a shoe. A man's shoe.

And it was attached to a man's body.

# TWO

Julian Davis and Celestine Rufus sat on the hood of the van and watched as Sheriff Clemson Reade pulled his black SUV into the church parking lot and stepped out from behind the driver's wheel. He was tall, fortyish, ruggedly handsome, and, with his spiky hair and traces of stubble, more reminiscent of a rock musician than a civil servant.

'Hey, Ms Celly. Jules,' he greeted. 'You guys OK?'

'Yeah, we're fine. I can't speak for Tish, though. We were waiting for her to lock up the church hall when all of a sudden she came running back screaming,' Jules explained.

'She's out there now with Officer Clayton and someone else from your office.' Celestine gestured toward a section of the graveyard that had been illuminated by an LED lamp similar to those used by highway repair crews.

Reade gazed out across the cemetery. 'Did either of you see or hear anything suspicious before or after the discovery of the body?'

'No,' Jules replied. 'Before the discovery, we were busy cleaning up from the Junior League dinner and loading the van to go home. And after . . .'

'Aside from Tish shoutin' and hollerin', it's been as quiet as . . . well, as quiet as a graveyard,' Celestine added.

'And you saw no one else in the neighborhood?' Reade checked.

'While we were waitin' on your people to arrive, a car came down the road all slow like,' Celestine explained. 'But they just kept on goin'.'

'That's right,' Jules confirmed. 'It was a dark-colored car, black maybe, and we thought the driver might stop to ask us what we were doin' out here. Hell, if I were the driver I'd be wondering what we were doing standing out here in a church parking lot late at night. But like Celestine said, they just continued along the road. Aside from that car, we saw no one else.'

'OK. Why don't you two head home?' the sheriff suggested. 'No sense in all of us losing sleep. I'll type up your statements when I get back to headquarters. If I need anything else, I know where to find you.'

'Oh, but I drove here in the van with Tish,' Jules explained. 'I was going to help her load the refrigerated items back into the café and pick up Biscuit.'

Biscuit was Julian's adopted Bichon Frise and dress-alike companion. Since dogs were not permitted at the Junior League dinner, Biscuit had spent the evening at the café with Mary Jo and her two teenage children.

'You can get a ride with me,' Celestine offered.

'What about the food? We can't leave it here much longer.'

'Take the van. I'll see to it that Tish gets home,' Reade said before setting off to examine the body in the churchyard.

Celestine clutched at her lower back as she rose from the van fender. 'Can't say I'm sorry to be leavin' this place. You need me to follow you to the café, honey? I can give you a hand loadin' in.'

'Thanks, but I'll be fine, Celestine. You go get home and get to bed,' Jules instructed. 'You know, I hate to sound like a ghoul, but I'm kinda happy there's another case for Reade and Tish to work on.'

'If you're a ghoul, I am too because I was thinkin' the exact same thing.'

'It's been awful, hasn't it? Three months of those two awkwardly flirting and neither of them making a move.'

'Honey, you should be at the café in the mornin',' she said with a chuckle. 'It's downright painful. Clem's given up his usual breakfast sandwich and now orders whatever Tish recommends. And Tish – she who always kept recipe development top secret – has been consulting with Clem to find out what flavor combinations he likes so she can create new menu items.'

'Get out!' Jules exclaimed. 'In all the years I've known Tish, she's never once asked me about my flavor palate. How much more of a signal does the sheriff need?'

'How much does Tish need? A man who wouldn't even look at the menu starts asking for a recommendation each morning like the café is some Michelin-starred restaurant,' Celestine observed. 'When I called Clem this spring and told him he should come back to Hobson Glen, I thought he and Tish would ride the freeway of love like a Maserati sports car. Instead, they're like a station wagon full of nuns drivin' on the shoulder with their hazard lights flashin'.'

Jules laughed. 'That does kinda describe – wait. What? *You* told Sheriff Reade to come back?'

Celestine blushed bright crimson. 'Now don't go tellin' Tish.'

'Why not?'

'Because I don't want her to think I'm interferin' in her love life.'

'What love life? Tish has been divorced for three years and the only relationship she's had in that time was an eight-month stint with Schuyler Thompson. Since that ended, she's been living out of a room off the kitchen of her café and sleeping in a twin bed. The girl could use some interference.'

'As a mother and a grandmother, I know when a little meddlin' is in order. I also know that the most important thing about meddlin' is that no one knows you're doin' it.'

'OK,' Jules capitulated. 'I won't say a word to Tish. But—'

'How did I know there was going to be a "but"?'

'I want the scoop. Why did Reade leave town like he did? Why didn't he say goodbye or tell anyone where he was going?'

'He did say goodbye – to me. It was Christmas Eve and he stopped by the café on his way out of town. I was outside watching the grandkids play in the garden and happened to spot him. He was going to say goodbye to Tish, too, but then he saw Schuyler givin' his speech and thought better of it.'

'Why?'

'Because Clem's in love with Tish. I saw it when he saved her life at the fair.'

'I knew it!' Jules exclaimed. 'I knew it! When we were catering that function at Coleton Creek, Reade changed up his hairstyle, started wearing aftershave, and he started to get a brooding, smoldering Heathcliff-on-the-moors thing going on.'

'You've been watchin' BBC America again, haven't you, honey?'

'I have,' he confessed. 'You should give it a try, Celestine. You'd probably enjoy it.'

'Are you kiddin'? At my age, all that smolderin' is likely to catch my drawers on fire.'

'Oh, come on. You're not that old.'

'Don't let the hair color fool you.' She patted her cherry-red head. 'I'm not that young, either. Nah, with Mr Rufus gone, my smolderin' days are over. Give me a romance where the man cleans the woman's kitchen. Now *that* I can appreciate.'

'So, Reade,' Jules prompted. He wasn't about to let Celestine forget their deal. 'If he's in love with Tish, why would he leave like that?'

'Because Tish was in a relationship with Schuyler,' Celestine explained.

'I understand, but why didn't he tell Tish how he felt and let her decide?'

'Because Clem's a gentleman. He's not the type to make a move on a woman who's already in a relationship. He also felt guilty for Tish's shooting – like he hadn't done enough to protect her.'

'What did you tell him to bring him back?'

'I told him Tish had solved a case on her own while he was away, so he'd better quit actin' like a boob and get back and help her.'

Jules cackled with laughter. 'You didn't.'

'I did. And then I told him that Tish and Schuyler had broken up and she was livin' at the café. Worked,' she said with a smile. 'He was back here before the week was out.'

'Good job,' Jules praised. 'But what now? It's been three months since Reade's return and all they do is chat in the morning over breakfast. Obviously Tish is happy to have the sheriff back and the sheriff . . . well, we know how he feels. What do we do to push them past the awkward phase?'

'I can't think of anything. We just gotta hope that station wagon full of nuns shifts into a higher gear. Otherwise, you and me are gonna have to try and push it uphill.'

'Are you all right, Tish?' Sheriff Reade asked with a gentle squeeze of Tish's forearm.

'I'm OK,' she replied. 'You'd think I'd be used to this sort of thing by now.'

'I'm not sure this is the sort of thing you ever get used to.' Reade gazed down at the body sprawled before them.

The victim was male, approximately six feet tall, and with neatly trimmed gray hair that was thinning on top. He was dressed in a perfect summer ensemble of Hawaiian print shirt, khakis, and a pair of loafers; however, the tangle of blood, hair and matter at the back of his head indicated that his sunny day had ended with a particularly violent death. He lay upon a wide cemetery plot, which, according to the etching on an adjacent tombstone, belonged to a family named Honeycutt.

Reade knelt beside the body to take a closer look.

'The deceased died from blunt force trauma to the back of the head,' twenty-four-year-old Officer Jim Clayton announced. 'Deceased's age estimated to be in his late sixties.'

'Seventies,' Reade corrected. 'The victim was in his mid-seventies.'

Clayton was nonplussed. 'Really? How did you—? Oh, I guess I'm not a very good judge of age.'

'Relax, Clayton. Your estimate was fine. I happen to know this man. It's Gadsden Carney. He was sheriff when I first joined the department. I was about your age when I started and Sheriff Carney taught me everything he knew.'

'I'm so sorry, Clemson.' Tish expressed her condolences.

'Sorry, sir,' Clayton echoed.

'Not as sorry as I am.' Reade stood up. 'Especially to find him here of all places.'

'The cemetery?' Tish asked.

'Daisy Honeycutt's grave.' He gestured toward the headstone.

Beneath the Honeycutt name, three plaques had been affixed:

*Daisy Dupree 1990–1996, Delilah Dupree 1959–1999*, and *Benton R. 1946–2019.*

'The Honeycutt case,' Tish breathed as the details of the case slowly returned to the forefront of her memory. 'You know, there was someone from the Honeycutt Foundation at the dinner tonight.'

'Really? Who?'

Tish shook her head. 'Oh, I can't remember now. I went back into the kitchen when she arrived – but there was a name. A woman's name. I'd recognize it if I heard it again. I never thought to connect the foundation with the case.'

'What's the Honeycutt case?' Clayton asked.

Reade looked up at his assistant. 'That's right. It's been twenty-five years. You weren't even born yet, were you?'

'No, sir,' the rail-thin officer replied with a self-conscious clearing of his throat.

'Daisy Honeycutt was the six-year-old daughter of Senator Benton R. Honeycutt and his wife Delilah. Daisy was found murdered in their garage shortly after the family's annual Fourth of July barbecue. After several months of investigative work, the girl's mother finally came forth and confessed to the crime. Delilah had tried to get Daisy inside the house for a bath before bedtime. When the little girl refused, Delilah lost her temper and struck her daughter on the head repeatedly. Daisy's injuries were similar to Gadsden Carney's.' Reade gazed down at the body of his former colleague. 'Carney was sheriff at the time the murder occurred. He was in charge of the case.'

'What was Carney doing here at Daisy's grave?' Tish wondered aloud. 'It's only a few weeks until the anniversary of Daisy's death. Do you think he might have been paying his respects?'

'I don't know. Gadsden was never the sentimental type, but I suppose a case like that must stick with you.'

'Did he ever discuss the case with you?'

'No, I didn't arrive at the sheriff's office until six years later. By then, the case had long been closed. Delilah Honeycutt had died in prison of cancer, Benton had remarried, and Gadsden had announced that it would be his last term as sheriff, allowing him to retire just before his fiftieth birthday.' Reade drew a deep breath. 'It seems like a lifetime ago.'

'For some of us, it is,' Clayton remarked in a clear attempt to inject some levity into the situation.

Reade flashed a wan smile. 'You know, come to think of it, I do remember asking Gadsden about the case once. Just once. It was one night after work, when a bunch of us went over to the bar and grill for a couple of beers. I finally worked up the courage to ask him what it was like to work on such a high-profile case. He looked me straight in the eye and said the day he got the call about Daisy Honeycutt was the single worst day in his life. That was it. That's all he said. I didn't question him any further. Seeing him like this, I wish I had.'

The three of them stared at former Sheriff Gadsden Carney's body in silence.

After several seconds had elapsed, Reade spoke again. 'I just can't believe any of this. Once their two daughters were grown, Gadsden and his wife moved to Florida. I get their annual newsletter every Christmas with photos of them at the beach or on a cruise or visiting the grandkids. And now . . . what was he even doing here?'

'We'll find out, Clemson,' Tish assured him. 'We'll find out what happened. I'll help in any way I can. I'll help you find whoever did this to your friend.'

'Thanks, Tish.' Reade glanced meaningfully in her direction. 'I'd like that.'

Clayton spoke up. 'I'd like it, too, actually. Not only did you pretty much solve the bake-off case on your own, but looking into the murder of someone who investigated a case that's older than I am is going to be mega-weird. Having you around to help would make it less weird, if that even makes sense.'

'It does,' Tish replied.

Clayton nodded. 'Do you think this might be related to the Honeycutt case, sir?'

'Too early to say,' Reade sighed, 'but at first glance it appears it's either linked to the Honeycutt case or the killer wants us to believe it is.'

Tish stared at Delilah's name plaque. 'Which raises an even bigger question. If Daisy's killer has been dead for over twenty years, who else connected with the case could have killed Gadsden Carney?'

# THREE

Tish sat in the passenger seat of Reade's police-issued SUV and watched as the familiar, moonlit scenery of the post road that linked the communities of Hobson Glen and Ashton Courthouse whooshed past her window.

'Are you sure you want to come with me?' Reade asked as he steered the SUV back toward Hobson Glen. 'I can drop you off at the café if you're tired.'

Tish was more than tired, but she felt that Reade shouldn't have to break the news to Gadsden Carney's widow alone. She also wondered if Mary Lee Carney might be able to shed some light on why her husband was in the cemetery in the first place. 'No, I want to go with you. I don't think I'd be able to sleep now anyway.'

'Well, I appreciate the company. It's not going to be easy telling Mary Lee and the family. I'd have brought Clayton along but I didn't think the kid needed to be exposed to the grief. He'll see enough of it eventually. Leaving him in charge of the crime scene while I'm gone will be good experience for him.'

'How'd you find out Mary Lee was here in town?'

'Gadsden stopped by the sheriff's office this morning. It was my day off, so I missed him, but he told our desk sergeant that he and Mary Lee were in town visiting their younger daughter and her family. I had no idea Kathleen had even moved back to Hobson Glen. It must have happened since the last newsletter.'

Reade pulled the SUV into the driveway of a remodeled Cape Cod home with gray vinyl siding. From inside the house, light filtered through the drawn blinds of the front right picture window, indicating that someone in the household was still awake.

Tish and Reade followed the stone path that led from the driveway to the brick front stoop. Before Reade could even ring the bell, the door swung inward, revealing a woman in her late thirties with shoulder-length brown hair and a fearful expression. She was barefoot and clad in a white, fitted camisole and pink plaid cotton pajama pants. 'Reade!' she exclaimed. For a moment she appeared quite happy to see him, but then, realizing the purpose of his visit, her heart visibly sank. 'You must be here about my father.'

He nodded. 'This is my associate, Ms Tarragon.'

The two women exchanged murmured hellos. Although Tish wanted to be supportive to Reade while he delivered the bad news, her civilian status made her feel like a voyeur.

Reade quickly rectified that situation. 'Ms Tarragon does some consulting work for us. Is your mother here?'

'Yes, she – I – my husband went out to look for my father. Dad went out and still hasn't come home, so we were here waiting . . . waiting for one of them to call us.' She stepped back to allow Reade and Tish admittance and led them past the stairs to the second floor to a moderately sized but well-furnished living room just to the right of the tiny foyer.

There, upon a leather-upholstered sofa, sat a woman with chin-length bobbed hair. She was dressed in a white terrycloth bathrobe and matching slippers, and although significantly older, her face was identical to that of the woman who opened the door, both in appearance and expression. 'Officer Reade. It's been such a long time. So long that you're probably sheriff by now.' She struggled to her feet to greet him.

'You're right, I am sheriff. And this is my associate, Ms Tarragon.'

Mary Lee nodded in Tish's direction before gushing over Reade's accomplishments. 'Oh, Gad's going to be so proud when he hears you've followed in his footsteps. He had you pegged as sheriff from the start – oh, but that's why you're here, isn't it? It's Gad. You've found him, haven't you?'

Reade took Mary Lee's hands in his and gently eased her back into her seat. Kneeling before her so that he could maintain eye contact, he told her, 'Yes, we found him, Mary Lee. Unfortunately, Gadsden wasn't alive when Ms Tarragon discovered him. I'm so very sorry, but your husband is dead.'

Mary Lee Carney broke into sobs and was soon joined on the sofa by Kathleen, who, despite crying herself, sought to console her mother.

'W–w–where did you find him?' Mary Lee asked.

'The churchyard in Ashton Courthouse,' Tish replied.

'How I've feared this day,' she wailed.

Kathleen pulled her mother close and the pair cried in silence, both demonstrating genuine grief, but neither displaying much in the way of surprise.

'I've been dreading this day for over two months now,' Mary Lee blubbered.

Reade rose to his feet and exchanged questioning glances with Tish. 'You've been anticipating Gadsden's death?'

'Ever since the doctor's diagnosis nine weeks ago. Malignant brain tumor.'

'I had no idea Gadsden was ill.'

'No one did. Because he didn't want you to know. He didn't want anyone to know.' She sniffed. 'The doctors gave him five months, but we both knew it could happen sooner.' Her voice disintegrated into sobs.

Reade waited until she quieted down before he spoke again. 'This is going to be difficult for both of you to hear, but Gadsden didn't die from his brain tumor. He was murdered.'

Mary Lee and Kathleen stopped crying, their tears replaced with expressions of shock and horror.

'Murdered? My husband was dying – why would someone murder him?'

Reade wondered the same thing. 'He was found at the Honeycutt family plot. Do you have any idea what he might have been doing there?'

Mary Lee drew a hand to her forehead as if in a great deal of pain. 'That case. That damned case!'

'A few months before his diagnosis, my father started to re-examine his files regarding the Daisy Honeycutt murder. It's one of the reasons my mother, my sister, and I decided he needed to see a doctor,' Kathleen explained.

'He didn't just re-examine his files,' Mary Lee amended. 'He became obsessed with the case all over again. The spare room in our house became crime scene headquarters. Show them, honey.'

Kathleen got up from the sofa and retrieved a cell phone from the cherry-finish dining table in the adjacent room. After touching the screen several times, she passed the mobile to Reade.

Tish peered over Reade's shoulder and watched as he scrolled through photos of the guest room in question. Every inch of wall space had been covered with crime scene photos, newspaper clippings, and diagrams, and the double bed was stacked high with books, folders, and paperwork.

'Did he say why he felt the need to revisit the case?' Tish asked.

'Gad said there were some things he needed to set right,' Mary Lee stated. 'What those things might have been, he never said. He never told me exactly what he was doing or what he hoped to find. I assumed it was all part of his illness, this sudden obsession with the past.'

'Were delusions or an altered view of reality symptoms of his disease?' Reade inquired.

'No, headaches, mood swings, nausea, and blurred vision were part of daily life, but apart from the evidence room he created and the time he spent there, Gad always seemed to have a firm grip on reality. Personality changes, however, are very common in patients with brain tumors, so when Gad went from not wanting to discuss the Honeycutt case to obsessing over it, the doctor and I put it down to that. A personality change.'

Kathleen nodded. 'You knew Dad, Reade. He was a stickler for detail and order, but obsession wasn't his thing. He always balanced his work with family life. No matter what was going on at work, he always made time for my sister and me. Always.'

'I know. He even found time as sheriff to mentor a scrawny New York transplant and welcome him to Virginia.' A wistful Reade stared down at the carpet and took a moment to compose himself. 'Did Gadsden tell anyone that he was re-examining the Honeycutt case?'

Mary Lee shrugged her shoulders and sank back into the sofa. 'I don't know. Gad's been spending ten to twelve hours a day in the guest room, examining evidence, and then, at night, he's been going out for either a drive or a walk, depending on his vision. In the meantime, I've been busy making sure he takes his medications on time, planning his meals and experimenting with different herbs so that he can enjoy eating again, despite initial chemotherapy treatments destroying his taste buds, and battling with insurance companies who've been refusing to pay for Gad's treatment.'

'I'm sorry, Mary Lee. I know Gadsden had an excellent caregiver in you.'

Mary Lee flashed a sardonic smile. 'I'm not so sure about that. I'd get so angry that he was spending his time alone, instead of with me, that sometimes I'd lash out at him. Say things I didn't mean. It wasn't pretty.'

'That's why my parents came here, Reade. To get my father out of the house, give my mother a rest,' Kathleen shared, 'and let them spend some quality time with their grandson. But now . . .'

'Who could have done this?' Mary Lee asked. 'Why?'

'That's what we're going to find out,' Reade promised.

'Well, I did hear Gad talking on the phone from time to time. Who he was talking to and whether he told them what he was working on, I couldn't say. You could probably check his phone. He always carried it with him.'

'We didn't find a phone at the scene,' Tish disclosed.

'That's impossible. He carried it with him everywhere. He always did, but especially now, what with his illness. I wanted Gad to retain some level of freedom and autonomy for as long as he possibly could, but I made it clear he wasn't to go anywhere without a means of contacting me or nine-one-one. He always kept his phone in his front right pocket. Always.'

'Ashton Courthouse is seven miles from here,' Reade noted. 'How did Gadsden get there?'

'I gave him the keys to my car,' Kathleen answered. 'He and Mom flew here and we picked them up at the airport, so they have no vehicle, and Dad's vision seemed good all day, so I let him borrow mine. I also knew my dad probably wouldn't be able to drive much longer, so I figured he should enjoy it while he still could.'

'Give me the color, make, model, and license plate number of your car and I'll have my people look for it. Your father's phone might be inside.'

Her eyes full of tears, Kathleen complied and provided the necessary details. 'Wasn't it parked in the church parking lot?'

'No, the only cars there belonged to Ms Tarragon and her staff. There was an event going on this evening. The lot would have been full and your father may have parked along the road. It happens often there. Do you know why he may have been at the churchyard?'

Mary Lee shrugged. 'In Florida, Gad would drive to the beach and walk by the shore. He liked walking somewhere scenic.'

'That's probably what he did tonight,' Kathleen proposed. 'He parked the car and took a stroll by the churchyard. The grounds there are pretty this time of year.'

Tish nodded in agreement, even though the notion that Gadsden Carney just 'happened' upon Daisy Honeycutt's grave while enjoying the early-summer scenery seemed exceedingly unlikely.

Sheriff Reade also remained silent on the matter. 'Is there someone looking after your house in Florida, Mary Lee? Someone who has a key to the place?'

'Yes, our neighbor, Jeanne, is taking in our mail and watering the plants,' Mary Lee replied. 'Why?'

'Because I want to see your husband's files on the Honeycutt case. I'm going to contact your local police and ask them to send someone over to pack up the evidence and ship it here.'

'Gad's death has something to do with the Honeycutt case, doesn't it?'

'I'm not certain, but I think it's entirely possible,' Reade allowed.

'Possible? No one else would have wanted to murder Gad. No one. It has to be that case.'

'I can't draw any conclusions just yet. Now, if you could tell me where you both were this evening.'

'We were here,' Kathleen answered, 'at the house.'

'The entire time?'

'Yes, we'd been at the park in the afternoon, watching my son's little league team, but we were back home in time for dinner.'

'What time was that?'

'A little after six. By the time we put some steaks on the grill and finally sat down to eat, it was around seven.'

'Then what?' he prodded as he tapped notes into a tablet in a black leather case.

'Is all of this necessary?' Mary Lee demanded. 'My husband's murderer is out there somewhere and you're wasting time asking us when we ate dinner. We told you we were here all night waiting for Gad to return. Isn't that enough?'

'I understand your frustration, Mary Lee, but this is part of the investigative process. It's essential that I know when Gad left the house and what time he may have arrived at the cemetery. As the wife of a former sheriff, I'm sure you understand.'

Kathleen squeezed her mother's hand. 'Mom, please. We need to answer Reade's questions.'

Mary Lee quietly capitulated, but her discomfort with the situation was still palpable.

Reade continued with his questioning. 'When did your father leave the house?'

'When my son came in to get ready for bed. Eight fifteen . . . eight thirty. I can't remember exactly. It's tough to get a nine-year-old to bed when there's less than a week left of school and it's still light outside.'

'And your father left as soon as your son came inside?'

'Yes, I . . .' Kathleen swallowed hard. 'I didn't get to say goodbye to Dad because I was busy making sure Oliver took a bath. God, if I'd only known, I would have – I would have stopped him.'

Mary Lee patted her daughter's knee. 'You mustn't think that way. None of this is your fault.'

Kathleen pushed her mother's hand aside. 'But I . . . I let him take the car keys. I told him to get them from my purse before I went to make sure Oliver took a bath.'

'You can't hold yourself responsible,' Tish told the young woman. 'It's not fair to you. Although I didn't know your father, I'm sure he wouldn't want you spending your time wondering "what if."'

'Tish is right, Kathleen,' Reade agreed. 'Not only would your father not want you to take responsibility for his actions, but he was a very determined man. If he wanted to go out, you weren't going to stop him. Not even if you barricaded the door.'

Kathleen slowly nodded. 'I suppose you're right. I just feel like we're in the middle of a nightmare.'

'I understand. I only have a few more questions and then we'll leave you both in peace.'

Kathleen nodded again.

'At what time did your husband go out to look for your father?'

'My husband . . . oh, I'd better call Michael and tell him what happened,' she said, suddenly remembering. 'Um, Michael went out after we tried calling my father. It was getting dark and we were worried that it might impair his vision and he'd be unable to drive home.'

'So this was at sunset or after?'

'After. It was dark when Michael left.'

'Sunset was at nine forty, so closer to ten?'

'Yes, that sounds about right.'

'And you haven't heard from your husband since he left?'

'No. While Michael searched, Mom and I kept trying to call my father.'

'One final question for you both: can you think of anyone who may have wanted Gadsden dead?'

'No,' Kathleen answered. 'Everyone we know loved and respected my dad, except maybe the few people he put in jail while he was sheriff. Maybe one of them came out looking for revenge?'

'Don't be silly, Kathleen,' Mary Lee chided. 'Your father was found dead at that child's gravesite. It's the Honeycutt case that's to blame. That damned case nearly drove us apart all those years ago. Now it's finally finished the job.'

Reade drove into the café parking lot with the SUV's headlights dimmed. 'I'm sorry to get you back so late. I know you have a busy morning ahead of you.'

'Tomorrow's senior Wednesday, so, yeah, it will be busy, but nothing overly complicated. Just lots of orders for discounted coffee and egg sandwiches. Oh, and muffins and pastries to be shoved into jacket pockets and handbags to be eaten later in the day,' Tish noted with a chuckle.

'My grandmother elevated restaurant food hoarding into an art form. Her purse was filled with a filing system of re-sealable plastic bags the likes of which I'd never seen before and have never seen again. There was one bag for baked goods, another for sugar packets and sweeteners, another for those little packs of jam and maple syrup, and yet another for halves of sandwiches that she couldn't finish.'

'Wow, I thought my grandma was organized, but yours was a pro.' She laughed.

'Yeah, she was hardcore.' He smiled.

It had been more than six months since Tish and Reade had engaged in conversation away from the listening ears of café patrons. Now that she was alone with him again, Tish realized just how much she had missed their discussions. 'W–would you like to come in for some coffee? We could talk – I mean, if you're up to it. I know Carney's death must have hit you hard.'

'I would love to come in, but I should probably get back to the church and see how Clayton's doing.'

'Yeah, we shouldn't risk waking Mary Jo and the kids, anyway. Not this week.'

'That's right; it's finals week, isn't it?'

'Yeah, for Kayla. For Gregory, it's his last week as a high school student – forever. I can't believe I'm going to be the godmother of a college freshman.'

'Well, if it makes you feel any better, you don't look like the godmother of a college freshman.'

'Thanks. It's weird, some days I feel as though it wasn't very long ago that *I* was a college freshman. Other days, it feels like that was over a hundred years ago.'

'Time seems to get away from all of us, doesn't it?' he asked rhetorically. 'But let's not let that happen to us, huh? How about a rain check for that coffee?'

'You bet. I'll be here first thing in the morning with a full carafe at the ready.'

'That's great, but I, um, I was thinking of a different kind of rain check. Like maybe we could grab some dinner tomorrow night and discuss the case?'

'Oh.' Tish tried unsuccessfully to disguise her surprise. 'Yes, that would be – that would be great.'

'Great,' Reade repeated. 'I want you to know how much I appreciate you coming with me to see Carney's family tonight.'

'Well, I said I'd help in any way I can. Not that I did very much,' she dismissed.

'Just your presence alone was beneficial. But, then again, you're always there, aren't you? I couldn't have solved the Broderick, Shackleford, or Inkpen cases without you. And then there's the bake-off case – you cracked that one single-handedly.'

'Oh no, Clayton was in there just as much as I was. So were

Jules and Mary Jo. It was more like a sleuth-squad effort than a single-handed one.'

'Regardless, you were the driving force behind that squad and I want you to know that your work isn't taken for granted.'

'I never feel that it is. You've made your appreciation abundantly clear,' she reassured him. 'And if I ever think you're being ungrateful, I'll just put a one-cup limit on your coffee order.'

He laughed. 'Before it comes to anything as drastic as that, just know that I wasn't putting on a show when I introduced you to the Carneys as my associate.'

Tish wrinkled her nose. 'What do you mean?'

'I mean that the sheriff's department has a budget allocated to the hiring of consultants. Earlier this week, I completed the paper-work to have your name added to our list of investigative experts.'

'Wait. Are you saying that I'll be working for the sheriff's department?'

'Only when you want to. And when it doesn't interfere with you running the café. I know how much your business means to you. It's your dream. It's who you are. But if there's a case you feel you can help with – that you want to help with – and you can spare the time, then I'd, um, we'd love to have you.'

'Well, I'd like to help you with this case. I'd like to help you find who murdered Gadsden Carney – when I'm not busy with lunch or breakfast and when Mary Jo or Celestine can cover for me, of course. Will I be working for you?'

'No, you'd be working *with* me, like we usually do. Except that now you'll be getting paid for your time.'

'That's – I . . . I don't know what to say. That's very generous of you, Clemson.'

'It's not generous. It's what you deserve. Your time is just as valuable as anyone else's.'

'Perhaps even more valuable when it's spent baking cheddar pecan scones,' she teased, knowing the baked good was the sheriff's favorite.

'That's a close one to call,' he considered with a broad grin. 'Seriously, though, you've done a lot for this town and for the sheriff's department. It's high time you were recognized. I only wish we could afford to pay you more, but that would mean getting a new budget approved by the mayor.'

Schuyler Thompson, Tish's ex-boyfriend and landlord, had been sworn in as Hobson Glen's new mayor at the beginning of May. Since then, she had tried, twice, to offer him congratulations – once when he stopped by the café to collect the month's rent and another when she ran into him at the local Piggly Wiggly. Each time, she was rebuffed. 'Yeah, I'm fairly certain that wouldn't go over too well. Besides, whatever you pay me will be fine. The café has been doing a steady business and we're in the busy season for catering – all those strawberry socials, graduations, and weddings – so my consultant money is gravy, actually. I'll probably put it aside for a new vehicle.'

'Is your car OK?'

'It's fine. Purrs like a kitten, but Jules has been on me to buy a van in order to cut down on the rental fees. I can't even think about it right now, but if I can bank the money from your office, I might eventually save up a nice down payment.'

'Good. As I said, it's the least I – I mean, my office – can do.'

'And I'm grateful.' Tish stared at Reade in awkward silence for several seconds before announcing, 'Well, I'd better get inside and let you go.'

'Yeah, I should get back to Clayton before he wonders where I am,' Reade said, although his body language indicated he was reluctant to leave. 'See you in the morning?'

'Absolutely. I'll put on some extra coffee for both of us.' She opened the passenger door and stepped one foot on to the gravel lot. 'Goodnight, Clemson.'

'Goodnight. Oh, and Tish?'

She looked over her left shoulder. 'Yes?'

'I promise to keep you safe this time.'

Tish leaned back in her seat. There was no reason for Reade to feel responsible for her shooting, yet she knew it was pointless to argue with him. 'And I promise to make your job easier by not jumping in front of bullets.'

Her lighthearted approach worked, for Reade's face broke into a wide grin. 'Deal.'

She stepped out and closed the door behind her.

'Be sure to lock your doors,' he called after her. 'And set the alarm.'

Tish issued Reade a mock salute before climbing the front porch steps of the café and letting herself inside. Unsurprisingly, the sheriff waited until she had locked the front door and engaged the security system before pulling out of the parking lot.

Tish waved a brief farewell from one of the café's jalousie windows and wended her way behind the counter and through the kitchen, to the former storeroom she had converted into a bedroom/ office. Switching on the light, she kicked off her shoes and peeled off her black trousers. The café air conditioning was cool and refreshing, but Tish still felt clammy and buggy from waiting outside for the police in the damp mosquito-laden night air.

Unfortunately, the only shower on the premises was in the apartment upstairs, where Mary Jo and her children were fast asleep. Slipping into a camisole, a baggy pair of boxer shorts, and a pair of slippers, she padded out of her room, and into the small lavatory reserved for café patrons.

Grabbing a wad of paper towel from the wall dispenser, she wet it under the cold water tap and gave herself an ersatz sponge bath. With her toothbrush and toothpaste upstairs, brushing her teeth wasn't an option, and she was far too tired to even bother to try to remove her makeup without proper soap and a washcloth, so she splashed some water on her face, tidied the sink, and flopped into her single bed just as the clock on her phone turned one.

As she closed her eyes and tried to forget about Gadsden Carney, a warm, furry body jumped on to the covers and snuggled beside her with a loud purr. 'Tuna,' she whispered to the black-and-white long-haired cat who, in the past three months, had become a cherished pet rather than a stray who begged for his namesake. 'What are you doing out of your bed?'

Tuna had no answers, only head butts and purrs.

Tish sighed wearily. 'Goodnight, Tuna.'

# FOUR

As it did every morning the café was open, Tish's alarm rang at six a.m., prompting her to pull back the covers with a groan. She couldn't remember the last time she'd stayed out so late, but she was reasonably certain that previous outings hadn't resulted in her feeling as tired as she did now.

Attempting to pinpoint the precise moment in her life when one a.m. had become 'late,' Tish rose from her bed and trudged into the kitchen to feed Tuna, brew some coffee, and preheat the industrial-sized Viking oven for the morning bake.

Tending to the cat and coffee first, she had only just finished switching on the three Bunn automatic drip brewers when Celestine let herself in the back doorway. 'Hey, sugar,' she greeted.

'Hey,' Tish replied. 'You're here early. Couldn't sleep?'

'Nah, slept fine. Given what happened last night, I thought you might need a hand this mornin'. Looks like I was right.' Celestine gestured toward Tish's face.

'Oh, I didn't take my makeup off last night,' Tish explained. 'Do I look like Alice Cooper after a thunderstorm?'

'A little. What time did y'all get back here?'

'A little before one. I went with Clemson to notify the victim's family. Clemson was friends with the poor man. He was a former sheriff.'

'You don't say. I've lived in this town nearly all my life. Which sheriff was it?'

'I guess I can tell you. Just don't tell a soul until Clemson's announced it.'

Celestine responded by making a crossing motion on the upper left part of her chest.

'It was Gadsden Carney,' Tish revealed.

'Sheriff Carney?' Celestine repeated in surprise. 'Thought he retired and moved away years ago.'

'He had. He was in town visiting his daughter and her family.'

'I can't imagine how they must feel. Losing him suddenly is bad enough, but knowing that someone intentionally took his life . . .' Having lost her husband to a heart attack in March, Celestine was not unacquainted with sudden loss. 'How's Clem takin' it?'

'He's pretty shaken up. He's coming here this morning, as usual, and then tonight we're having dinner.'

'Dinner?' Celestine's head snapped up so quickly that her earrings jangled.

'Yes, to go over the case.' Tish turned the oven to 350 degrees

Fahrenheit and extracted two plastic-wrapped baking trays of pastries from the refrigerator.

'Oh,' Celestine sounded in disappointment.

'Clemson has asked me to be—'

'Yes?' Celestine's earrings again jangled in her excitement.

'A consultant for the sheriff's office – when I can fit it around the café schedule, of course – which means I'll be paid for my time.'

'Oh, that's nice. Clem isn't gonna be your boss, is he?'

'I wondered the same thing, but no. We'll be working together, side by side, like we've always done.'

'Well, I guess it's a start,' Celestine muttered under her breath.

'What?' Tish questioned.

'Where are you going for dinner tonight? Somewhere nice?'

'I don't know. We'll probably discuss it when Clemson comes here for breakfast.'

'Well, why don't you go get cleaned up and leave me to the bakin'? You know Clem gets here right when we open.'

Tish frowned. 'That's right, he does, doesn't he? I'd better go get dressed and wash this makeup off.'

'No, go take a shower. Do your hair. The whole kit and caboodle. You had a helluva night. Start today fresh.'

There was a thud from upstairs. 'That's Mary Jo and the kids. They're on an early schedule this week due to finals. I'll take that shower after we close for the day.'

'Honey, you must still be sticky from last night. That church hall wasn't air-conditioned. Take my house key.' She pulled a keyring from the oversized purse she hung on the coat rack near the back door. 'Go on over and freshen up.'

'That does sound good,' Tish conceded. 'But I don't want to impose.'

'You're not imposin'. My house is empty and I have a great big, brand-new water heater and a rainforest shower head, so get your buns over there and luxuriate.'

'All right,' she capitulated. 'Are you sure you're OK doing the morning bake?'

'Absolutely. I'm even good servin' for a while, so take your time,' Celestine assured her.

'Oh no, I won't be that long. I want to talk to Clemson before the café gets too busy and he has to leave for work.'

'Then you'd better get goin'.'

Tish dashed to her bedroom to gather up some belongings.

'Hey,' Celestine called after her. 'It's gonna be a hot one. Why don't you wear that cute little green dress you wore last week?'

'Really? I was going to wear it Sunday while serving lunch.'

'Nah, wear it today,' the baker urged, recalling how Sheriff Reade had admired Tish the last time she wore it. 'It's your first day as an official police consultant. You should look and feel the part.'

'It *is* a comfortable dress, too.'

'See? Perfect for someone who has a busy day of cookin' and crimefightin' in store.'

'Thanks, Celestine.' Tish grabbed a bag of clothes and toiletries and dashed out of the door of the café. 'See you in a bit!'

Celestine placed the trays of pastries into the oven to bake and watched as Tish pulled her car out of the café parking lot. 'Oh, Jules.' She sighed. 'This is harder than pushin' a station wagon uphill. This is like pushin' a cement mixer.'

Tish returned to the café at quarter past seven, looking refreshed and lovely. Reade was already seated at his usual spot at the counter.

'The lack of sleep clearly didn't do you any harm,' he remarked as Tish approached.

'Makeup. Lots of makeup,' she joked, although she didn't mind the compliment. 'You're here early.'

'Sorry, Tish, but I felt badly leavin' Clem outside for twenty minutes until we open,' Celestine said. 'Especially seein' as I knew he'd need his coffee this mornin'.'

'Sure. It also gives Clemson and me more time to review the case.'

'That's what I thought,' Reade said, echoing Tish's sentiment.

'Great minds. What can I get you for breakfast?' Tish asked as she donned a black apron.

'I'm already on it,' Celestine announced. 'I'm whipping up some scrambled eggs.'

'Ooh, you're in luck, Clemson. Celestine's scrambled eggs are a poem.'

'I'll whip some up for you too, honey,' Celestine suggested.

'You didn't eat much at last night's dinner and you haven't eaten anything today.'

'OK, if it's not too much trouble.'

'Just as much trouble to make a double batch as it is a single. You know that. Now you two get on with your work – this place will be packed before you know it.'

Tish followed Celestine's orders and poured herself and Reade a cup of coffee. 'Did you get any sleep last night?' she asked upon presenting him with the hot beverage.

'Couple of hours. I kept thinking about Mary Lee and the girls. All they wanted was to spend time together as a family.'

'What a terrible shock. How are you doing?'

'Meh. Trying to stay sane by focusing on the case.'

She nodded. 'Anything new?'

'Gadsden was definitely murdered. Preliminary results show his occipital bone was lodged in the back of his brain, meaning that he was struck with a blunt, heavy object.'

'I think we knew that from looking at the body, but it's nice of the coroner's office to actually name the bone for us,' she remarked, her voice dripping with sarcasm.

'Yeah, I know. We also found Kathleen's car earlier this morning. It was parked on the road, just a couple of blocks from the church. Forensics is looking it over now, but there was no sign of a struggle.'

'Did you find his phone?' she asked as she poured some skim milk into her cup and passed the pitcher to Reade.

'No.' Reade added a splash of milk to his coffee and then a packet of sugar before stirring the beverage with a spoon. 'We put a trace on it, but came up blank. Someone must have destroyed it. We did, however, have the Carney's phone records emailed to us. Mary Lee's phone called local Florida numbers – doctors, hospitals, people I'm assuming were friends – and their daughters. Gadsden's phone records for the last six months show that he used his phone exclusively to call out-of-state numbers, most of which were here in Virginia.'

'Did any of those numbers align with the Honeycutt case?' she asked, moving around the counter and sitting on the stool beside him.

'All of them did.'

Tish swallowed her mouthful of coffee. 'All?'

'Over the course of the past six months, Gadsden began contacting everyone who was at the house the day Daisy Honeycutt was murdered, as well as a few other people linked to the case.'

Celestine had returned with two plates of silky scrambled eggs and toast. Reade's plate featured the addition of a generous helping of hash browns. 'I know you're cuttin' down on carbs,' she noted to Tish.

'I am. Thanks, Celestine. It looks amazing.'

'Yeah, thanks, Miss Celly. This looks like just what the doctor ordered,' Reade said.

'I heard y'all mention the Honeycutt case,' Celestine stated. 'I remember the whole thing like it was yesterday. Cypress Hollow, the Honeycutts' ranch, is right near the county line, but it's only five miles from here as the crow flies. We all watched our kids like hawks, thinkin' there might be some crazy child killer on the loose. Then, as the case moved on, and it became clear that someone in the house did it, we were glued to our TV screens. I tell ya, for a mother to murder her own child, she would either have to be crazy or have ice water in her veins.'

Reade and Tish didn't respond, prompting Celestine to draw a hand to her mouth. 'Sorry, I shouldn't have gone on like that.'

'No,' Reade replied. 'It's good to hear about it from someone who lived here at the time and wasn't involved in the case. I remember the whole country was shocked, but living here . . . I can't imagine.'

'Yeah, it was a game-changer all right. Between the press and the gawkers stoppin' by, things took a long time to get anywhere near back to normal.'

'And Sheriff Carney? How did he handle things?'

'He was never an extremely talkative man, but he was even less so after the case was closed. Used to come in here back when Cynthia Thompson – Schuyler's mother – ran it as a bakery. I'd work the counter, and he'd come in every mornin' for coffee and a blueberry muffin and ask me how Lloyd and the kids were. The minute Delilah Honeycutt confessed, I was lucky to get a "good mornin" out of him. He was a changed man, but I suppose something like that would do it to ya.'

'Yeah, it probably would,' Reade agreed.

'Mmph,' Celestine grunted. 'Well, I'll leave you two to your breakfast. I'm goin' to spend these quiet few minutes with my coffee and a book. Let me know if you need anythin'.'

When Celestine had retreated back into the kitchen, Tish leaned into Reade and whispered. 'I have a confession to make. I told Celestine that the body we found last night was Gadsden Carney.'

Reade smiled. 'No need to confess. I don't consider sharing stuff with Celestine as spilling the beans. I've done it myself on occasion.'

'You have?'

'Yeah.' He colored slightly, as if uncomfortable with the question. 'A few times.'

'Oh, good.' Tish sighed and helped herself to a forkful of scrambled eggs. She hadn't realized how hungry she was. 'So,' she segued when she'd finished swallowing, 'you said Carney had called everyone who was involved in the Honeycutt case. Guess we should start looking there. What have we got?'

Reade took a bite of toast and pulled his tablet closer. 'Well, first a little background to refresh our memories. Daisy Dupree Honeycutt, aged six, was reported murdered in the family garage at approximately seven o'clock in the evening on July fourth, 1996. Cause of death was blunt force trauma to the back of the head.'

'Just like Gadsden Carney,' Tish noted as she nibbled some toast.

'The Honeycutts had hosted an Independence Day barbecue that afternoon. In her initial statement, Delilah Dupree Honeycutt, Daisy's mother, said that at the end of the party she went in search of her daughter so she could give her a bath and get her ready for bed. That's when she claimed to have discovered the body. It was only months later that Delilah confessed to the crime. She had, in fact, caught up with Daisy in the garage. When the little girl refused to get ready for bed, Delilah lost her temper and murdered her. Delilah pleaded guilty by reason of temporary insanity – she and the senator were having marital trouble,' Reade added, aside. 'The jury convicted Delilah of second-degree murder and she was sentenced to twenty years in prison with no chance of parole. She died three years later, in prison, of cancer.'

Tish felt a chill run down her spine. 'Ugh, brutal. However, it sounds like an open-and-shut case.'

'Yeah, it does. So much so that if Gadsden weren't dead right now, I'd wonder if his fixation wasn't a side effect of his illness.'

'I agree, and yet he was found dead at the Honeycutt family plot. The two cases must be linked somehow. We need to follow up on those phone calls and find out what, if anything, Gadsden uncovered from all those years ago.'

'The case is twenty-five years old, Tish. Unless the senator or someone else was guilty of terrorism or war crimes, I can think of only one thing Gadsden could have uncovered that might have gotten him killed,' Reade asserted.

'There is no statute of limitations for murder,' Tish said, comprehending the full meaning of Reade's words.

'Exactly. I don't have his files yet – they're arriving this afternoon – but Gadsden must have thought he put away the wrong killer.'

'Meaning that whoever killed Daisy Honeycutt also killed Gadsden Carney. We'd better look into those calls, Clemson. Who's at the top of the list?'

'Well, not the senator for a start. As you know, he's buried in the family plot beside Delilah and Daisy. He suffered a stroke back in 2018 and was paralyzed from the neck down for months before finally succumbing early the following year.'

'Taking his secrets with him,' Tish remarked.

'His death leaves Walker James Honeycutt, Daisy's older brother, as the only surviving member of the immediate family. He was ten years old at the time of the murder.'

'That excludes him as the murderer, doesn't it? A ten-year-old couldn't have murdered Daisy.' She sipped her coffee and hoped it took away the chill she felt.

'I wouldn't go that far. Children are just as capable of serious crimes as adults are. According to the housekeeper and her husband, the groundkeeper, Walker had tried to hit his sister on the back of the head with one of his golf clubs two weeks before she was murdered. Gadsden Carney called Walker James no fewer than five times during the past six months.'

'You think the two might have arranged a meeting while Carney was in town?'

Reade devoured a large forkful of scrambled eggs and hash browns. 'The thought definitely crossed my mind.'

'Who's next?' Tish asked as she, too, tucked into her plate of scrambled eggs.

'Family-wise, we have Delilah's sister, Dixie Dupree, on Gadsden's phone records.'

'Did she live with the Honeycutts?'

'No, but she might as well have. She had a room both at the Honeycutts' ranch at Cypress Hollow and their home in Georgetown and stayed with them often. I did a cursory review of the records we have on file at the sheriff's office, just to reacquaint myself with the basics of the case. According to what I read, Dixie arrived at Cypress Hollow Wednesday evening for the barbecue that Thursday afternoon. She had planned to stay for the long weekend.'

'Again, an aunt killing her niece?'

'No more horrifying than a mother killing her daughter,' Reade pointed out as he slathered his toast with strawberry preserves and took a bite.

'I suppose,' Tish allowed.

'Also, Dixie and Delilah were lifelong rivals. Benton Honeycutt was actually engaged to marry Dixie before he met Delilah.'

'Hmm, that's cozy. We'll need to find out more, but add her to the list of suspects.'

Reade nodded. 'Next up is Priscilla Maddox Honeycutt, Benton's second wife.'

'Priscilla! That's it – that's the name of the woman who came to the dinner last night. She was there to present a check to the Junior League on behalf of the Honeycutt Foundation.'

'So she can be placed at the scene of both murders. Interesting.'

'*Both* murders?'

'Yes. Priscilla was an intern in Benton's office at the time of Daisy's murder and was present at the barbecue. According to witnesses, she and Benton were having an affair.'

'Which is why Delilah cited her marital problems as the reason for her temporary insanity,' Tish surmised. 'We should speak with Priscilla right away.'

'Priscilla is a high-ranking member of the state legislature and rumor has it she's eyeing a congressional run, so it might be tough getting through the gatekeepers, but I'll see what I can do.'

'Who's next on Gadsden's call list?'

'Reverend Ambrose Dillard. According to friends of the

Honeycutts, Delilah wanted to save her marriage and had sought counseling with Reverend Ambrose Dillard, then head of St Jude's Episcopal Church of Ashton Courthouse – where your dinner was held last night. Reverend Dillard attended the barbecue the afternoon of Daisy's death as a community leader, but also to convince Benton to join his wife in counseling.'

'As a counselor, the reverend might have valuable information about the Honeycutts' marriage as well as some insight as to who else might possibly have killed Daisy.'

'Agreed,' Reade said before polishing off his hash browns. 'Then there's Frank and Louella Heritage, close friends of the Honeycutts. Louella was a stay-at-home mom and Frank a commodities trader. Their children played together on a regular basis and they took the Honeycutts into their home following the murder. Just a few months later, though, Louella and Frank penned an open letter to the local paper claiming that Senator Honeycutt was using his political influence to thwart the investigation.'

'That's quite a dramatic U-turn, isn't it? If the Heritages had a hunch that something wasn't right, I could see them distancing themselves from the Honeycutts, but to go public with their doubts . . . I wonder what made them change their minds like that?'

'Don't know, but it sounds as if we're going to find out.' He took the last sip of coffee from his cup, prompting Tish to get up and pour him a refill.

'Thanks. Next is Officer Gus Aldrich,' Reade went on, 'fellow investigator on the Honeycutt case, who backed the Heritages' claims that the senator was purposely trying to sow confusion and obstruct the investigation into his daughter's death. Aldrich resigned just three weeks before Delilah confessed to the crime.'

'Obstruction from the senator. That points to Delilah being the guilty party, though, doesn't it?' Tish freshened her cup and sat back down beside Reade.

'Not necessarily. The senator could simply have been covering up his affair with Priscilla or anything else he didn't want the voting public to know about. He was up for re-election that November.'

'Re-election,' she scoffed. 'His daughter had just been murdered.'

'I know. Re-election would have been the farthest thing from my mind, too, but some politicians are a breed unto themselves.'

Tish reflected briefly upon how Schuyler's mayoral bid had been a divisive factor in their relationship. 'Yes. Yes, they are.'

The meaning of Tish's words was not lost upon Reade. 'Sorry. I didn't mean to—'

'No, it's OK. Election or not, my relationship with Schuyler wouldn't have lasted anyway. It's good that I found that out as quickly as I did.' She took a final bite of toast and pushed her plate aside. 'Anyone else on the list?'

'Just a few more. John and Lucille McIlveen, the groundskeeper and housekeeper I mentioned earlier. Their only son, Russell, was brought up on drug charges just a few days before Daisy's murder. The McIlveens asked the Honeycutts for a loan so they could post Russell's bail. The Honeycutts refused.'

'That's harsh. Does it say in your files why they refused?'

'Probably, but I haven't gotten that far yet. I'll need to do some more homework before we speak with them.'

'Well, with a motive like that, they need to be on the suspect list.'

'Agreed. Viola Tilley,' Reade read aloud, 'the Honeycutts' nanny. She was at the house the morning of the barbecue to help the kids get ready, but she left before the first guest showed up.'

'So, not a suspect,' Tish assumed.

'Since she's now in her eighties, probably not, but Gadsden Carney called her three times in the past six months.'

'Really?'

'Before taking care of Daisy and Walker, Viola Tilley was Delilah and Dixie's nanny when they were growing up.'

'She must have had a lot of information about the family. No doubt that's why Gadsden was in touch with her so often. Maybe we should talk to her before we speak with anyone else so we can get an overview of the case.'

'Maybe . . .' Reade nearly sang. 'There's one more person in this case I think we should contact sooner rather than later. Someone Gadsden was in touch with more often than either Viola Tilley or Walker James Honeycutt.'

'Who?' She finished the last drop of her coffee.

'Leah Harmon, a psychic from Richmond. She first approached the sheriff's office one month after Daisy's murder, but Gadsden refused her services. Recently, however, Gadsden appears to have kept a regular weekly phone appointment with her.'

'Every week? For how long?'

'Six months. The last call Carney received before he was killed was also from her number.'

'You're right. We should definitely talk to her first. Find out what she and Carney discussed during all those phone calls.'

'Leah's address is less than two miles from the senior apartment complex where Viola lives. We can talk to both of them later today and then grab some dinner if you're free then.'

'Before dinner? Yeah, I should be free.'

'Your café closes at . . .?'

'Three thirty,' Tish answered as she rose from her stool. It was opening time.

'I'll swing by and pick you up at four thirty,' Reade suggested. 'If that works for you.'

'Yeah, that's perfect. That gives me plenty of time to tidy up and prep for tomorrow.'

'Cool. There's a sweet little place on the river that has a great outdoor patio. It's nothing fancy, but they serve up Rappahannock oysters and some of the best crabcakes you'll ever taste. That is, if you like seafood.'

'Letitia loves seafood,' said a man's voice from somewhere behind Tish. 'Always has. When she was little, we'd spend a week every July down on Long Island where she'd eat her fill of soft-shell crabs.'

Tish whirled around to find herself face to face with a tall, thin man with graying sandy-colored hair and a heavily lined countenance. 'Dad, what are you doing here?'

'Is that any way to greet your old man?' he said with a laugh.

'Sorry, I'm just surprised to see you.' She leaned forward and gave him a hug and a kiss on the cheek. 'Had I known you were coming to visit, I'd have taken the day off.'

'This isn't really a visit. Thought I'd stop by on my way down to Hilton Head. A friend of mine has a beach house and invited me to stay for the week.'

'Nice friend,' Reade, who had since risen from his seat, remarked.

'Hey, sorry I didn't address you earlier.' Tish's dad extended a hand to Reade. 'It's nice to finally meet you, Schuyler.'

'Dad,' Tish said urgently as she felt her face blush bright

scarlet. 'This isn't Schuyler. This is Clemson Reade, our local sheriff.'

'Sheriff? Sorry, but the way you two were discussing dinner, I thought you had a special evening planned. My mistake.'

'Schuyler and I broke up, Dad. Months ago.'

Her father squinted. 'Did I know this?'

'Yes, I told you in a voicemail message when you didn't answer your phone and again in a text message when you told me to say "hi" to Schuyler for you.'

'Oh.' He shrugged. 'I can't keep track of these things. It's nice to meet you, Sheriff.'

Reade took the man's hand in his and gave it a sturdy shake. 'It's nice to meet you, too, Mr Tarragon.'

'Tarragon? Oh, no, my name's Lynch. Mike Lynch. Mr Tarragon is her' – he pointed to Tish with his left index finger – 'ex-husband. I'm not sure why she didn't get rid of the name when she got rid of him, or why the name Lynch suddenly wasn't good enough for her, but there ya have it. From Letitia Elizabeth Lynch, the namesake of both her grandmothers, to Tish Tarragon.'

'My friends have always called me Tish, Dad. Only you and Mom ever called me Letitia.' She rolled her eyes in disbelief that she was having the same argument at age forty-two that she had at age sixteen. 'As for keeping the name Tarragon, it fits a caterer and café owner.'

'It does,' Reade agreed in an obvious bid to maintain peace. 'I actually wondered if it was her real last name at first, it fits so well.'

'I'm surprised you didn't run my name through the system,' Tish joked.

'I was tempted,' Reade confessed. 'Look, Tish, since your dad is in town, maybe we should postpone our dinner.'

'Nonsense,' Mike Lynch dismissed with a wave of his hand. 'You two kids keep your plans. I have a friend in Richmond I'm staying with so I won't be in town anyway.'

'We're going to be in Richmond, too. We have to take care of some business, then we're having dinner down by the Canal Walk. Why don't you join us? We can meet you at the restaurant,' Reade offered.

'No, no. That friend I'm staying with is going to want to catch up,' Mike declined. 'We can get together tomorrow morning, Letitia. I'll come by for breakfast.'

Tish nodded. 'I'll have Celestine cover for me.'

'This business of yours in Richmond,' Lynch segued. 'Sounds like you're still playing the flatfoot.'

'Tish's contributions to the sheriff's office have been immeasurable,' Reade stated.

'Well, just so long as Letitia doesn't go off getting herself shot again.'

That her father could make the drive south to stay at a friend's beach house, but couldn't make the trip while she was in the hospital convalescing nettled Tish greatly, but this was neither the time nor the place. 'Getting myself shot? Odd. I don't recall that last gunshot wound being self-inflicted.'

'Very funny, smarty pants,' Lynch smiled.

'If you won't join us for dinner tonight, can I at least get you some breakfast right now?' she asked.

'Nah, I've got to go see a man about a horse.'

Reade chuckled, but Tish knew better. Given her father's penchant for the track and betting, he was most likely telling the truth. 'I'll, um, I'll see you in the morning, then.'

'Yep, see ya in the morning.' Lynch gave his daughter a kiss on the cheek and made his way to the door.

When he was out of earshot, Reade said to Tish, 'Are you still up to working on the case? I mean, what with your father here for such a short time . . .'

'I'm totally fine with our original plans. This is a typical Dad visit – he'll stay in town for twenty-four to forty-eight hours and spend most of them doing what he'd do at home, just doing them here instead. In the end, we'll probably have breakfast together, talk a bit, and he'll hit the road, so you and I are good with our arrangements.'

'So long as you're comfortable, that's all that matters. If anything changes – like if your father decides to join us for dinner or he invites you to join him – give me a call.'

'Thanks, Clemson.' Tish smiled. 'That's very kind of you, but I wouldn't wait for the phone to ring.'

'Gotcha,' he said with a nod. 'Then I'll see you at four thirty.'

'Yes, I—' She caught herself about to say she was looking forward to it, but then realized that wasn't quite the appropriate reaction to a murder investigation. 'I'll see you then.'

# FIVE

The remainder of the day passed quickly and Tish soon found herself in the passenger seat of Reade's black SUV, driving to the funky working-class neighborhood of Oregon Hill in Richmond. They came to a stop in front of a two-story, pink-clapboard row house with green trim and an inviting, plant-filled front porch.

Reade swung open the white picket gate and held it open for Tish before following her on to the front porch. In a large picture window, a sign advertised psychic readings by appointment only.

Reade reached up and rang the buzzer that had been installed in the doorframe. Within seconds, a petite woman – scarcely five feet tall – with short-cropped blonde hair and wide, expressive blue eyes appeared in the doorway.

Tish felt her breath catch. It was the so-called 'gypsy' who had been staring at Tish at the Junior League dinner.

Tish didn't believe in psychics, but being the subject of Leah Harmon's constant scrutiny had been unnerving. Had the woman recognized Tish from the local news? Or was there some other, more sinister, reason behind the medium's unflinching gaze?

'Good afternoon. Ms Harmon?' Reade asked.

'Look, I don't accept walk-ins. If y'all want a reading, you need to make an appointment. I can book one while you're here, if you'd like, but I can't do an on-the-spot reading.'

'We're not here for a reading.' Reade held his badge aloft. 'Clemson Reade, Henrico County Sheriff, and this is my associate, Ms Tarragon. We need to ask you some questions.'

Leah Harmon's eyes darted toward Tish and immediately looked away. She said nothing about recognizing the caterer, but her reaction was all the confirmation Tish needed.

Harmon opened the door wide and invited Tish and Reade

inside. 'I should have guessed the police would be in touch. Didn't need to be a psychic to have seen this coming.'

The front door opened into a ten-foot-square room with a fireplace, hardwood floors, and uneven plaster walls painted a soft shade of lavender. In the center of the room stood an oblong dining table covered in an indigo-and-white woven astrological chart.

Leah sat down at the far end of the table, a tarot deck spread before her, and gestured to the couple to join her.

Reade and Tish complied, taking a pair of chairs on one of the table's longer sides.

'What do you want to know?' Leah asked, her hands poised on either end of the deck as if about to give a reading.

'I'm sure you're well aware that Gadsden Carney has been murdered,' Reade started.

'Yes, I read it in the paper this morning. Shame. Real shame. He wasn't a well man, you know. It makes you wonder why . . .' She finished the statement with a click of her tongue.

'Why someone would bump off a dying man? That's what we'd like to know, too. Can you shed any light on the situation?'

She shrugged. 'Only that it's linked to the Honeycutt murder.'

'What makes you think that?'

'I visualized the murder scene while I was reading the article in the paper. I saw Gadsden Carney's photo and the image of his death flashed in my mind. He was at Daisy's grave, wasn't he?'

Reade and Tish exchanged glances. The location of Gadsden's body had not been disclosed to the press.

'Don't bother answering,' Leah said. 'I can tell from your reactions that I'm right.'

Tish could stand it no longer. She needed to inform Reade of Ms Harmon's whereabouts the previous evening. 'Or perhaps you know where Carney was killed, because you were at the Junior League dinner in Ashton Courthouse last night.'

Reade's jaw dropped. 'Is this true, Ms Harmon?'

'It is,' the psychic confirmed. 'I went there to drop off a gift certificate for a free reading for the League to auction off later that evening. I left before the actual dinner started and came back here to meet a client. You can ask the ladies who ran the dinner. They saw me leave.'

'So if you didn't kill Carney, did you happen to "envision" who did?'

'No, it doesn't work like that. I wish it did, but it's not that simple. If I look at a photo, I sometimes see a flash of an image – a very detailed image – in my mind. Other times, it's a gut feeling, like intuition, and at other times, I may hear someone speaking to me. I can never predict when I might receive a message or an image, but I've found that focusing on the cards helps to harness whatever it is that's reaching out to me.' Leah waved her hands over the tarot deck. 'They help to clear my mind of the chatter.'

'Gadsden Carney's murder scene,' Reade segued. 'Can you tell us anything else about it?'

'Yes. He was lying at the foot of the Honeycutt family plot. There was blood coming from the back of his head – lots of it. And there was a woman who had stumbled over his body.' Leah looked up at Tish. 'That woman was you, wasn't it?'

Tish nodded. 'Is that why you were staring at me last night? Did you know what was about to happen?'

'I'm sorry, Ms Tarragon. I didn't mean to stare. I get swept away at times by the images, the feelings. When I saw you, I became overwhelmed by the sense that you and I would be seeing each other again and that we'd be meeting over a matter of the utmost urgency.'

'Well, here we are.'

'Y–yes,' Harmon reluctantly agreed. 'Here we are.'

'Ms Harmon, phone records indicate that Carney called you once a week for the past six months. Why?' Reade questioned.

'For guidance. Although no one was more surprised by his phone calls than I was. I'd first met Mr Carney – then Sheriff Carney – shortly after Daisy Honeycutt's murder. I had seen Daisy's photo in the paper and had a flash similar to the one I had today. It was the first time I ever experienced one. I'd always been intuitive, but Daisy's murder was the first time I ever experienced a true visualization.' Leah rose from her chair and retrieved a manila folder from the locked drawer of a small metal file cabinet in the far corner of the room. 'I was so struck by what I saw in that vision that I sketched it. I work part-time as an artist,' Leah explained as she removed the sketch from the folder and passed it to Reade before returning to her seat.

Reade passed the sketch to Tish and grabbed his tablet. After touching the screen several times, a photograph taken of the Honeycutt murder scene appeared on the tablet's display. From the perspective to the position of Daisy's body to the placement of a bag of children's golf clubs, the elements of the crime scene photo and Leah's sketch were practically identical.

'And you'd never seen a photo of the crime scene when you drew this?' Reade challenged.

'I was a single mother working as a tour guide for the Virginia Museum of Fine Arts at the time. I had no access to police photos and no access to the internet. What you see there I drew from what had flashed before my eyes,' Leah maintained.

'So you brought this sketch to Carney,' Tish surmised.

'Not right away. I was certain he'd think I was crazy. Hell, even I thought I was crazy. Instead, I confided in a friend and showed her the sketch. She thought I should go to the police, but then we both reasoned that if my sketch was of the crime scene – and it certainly looked as if it was – then the police didn't really need it. They knew where Daisy had been found. They didn't need my vision to help them.

'A few days later, however, I heard Daisy's voice,' Leah continued. 'The police were investigating a local guy for Daisy's murder. He lived in the vicinity of the ranch and had a history of abusing children. His picture was splashed all over the news. I stared at it for a good long time, hoping to get a flash or some vibe, but nothing came. That night, however, I heard a child's voice. It was late and I thought at first that my son was playing a trick on me since he was the same age as Daisy, but I checked in his room to find him asleep. Then I heard the voice again. It was Daisy. She told me that she had been killed by someone she knew, someone she trusted. She hadn't been killed by a stranger. First thing the next morning, I called my friend to babysit my son and drove to the Henrico County Sheriff's Office.'

'Did Sheriff Carney see you?' Reade asked.

'Oh, he saw me all right. He saw me and immediately placed me under investigation. According to him, the only way I could have drawn that sketch was if I'd gotten hold of police photos or if I was at the crime scene myself.' Leah drew a deep breath. 'Carney and his men questioned my family, my friends, and my employers, looking for any connection I might have with their current suspect – anything that might explain why I was declaring him innocent of murdering Daisy Honeycutt. Weeks later, I received a phone call from the sheriff's office informing me that I was no longer a "person of interest" in the case, but by then I'd already lost my job at the museum.'

'I'm sorry, Ms Harmon.'

'Thanks, but it's OK, Sheriff. It felt like a catastrophe at the time, but I wound up doing this for a living. Now people come to me to find missing pets and communicate with lost loved ones. Richmond Police have gotten me involved in a few missing person cases and, of course, I do the odd bachelorette party, but I've also made some time for my art and managed to put my son through school, so it all turned out OK. Still, given that history, you can see why Mr Carney's phone call six months ago came as such a shock.'

'What did he say to you?' Tish inquired.

'He apologized, mostly. Said he'd learned that I'd become a professional psychic and that I'd successfully helped the police. Said he was sorry he didn't listen to me that day I went to see him. Then he told me that he was reopening the Honeycutt case – not officially, of course, because he was retired, but unofficially, because there were some elements of the case that didn't sit right with him.'

'Are those the exact words he used? Elements that didn't sit right?' Reade asked.

'Those are precisely the words he used.'

'And how did you respond?'

'I told him I was pleased he was looking into it, because I'd never believed that Delilah Dupree Honeycutt was guilty.'

'Even with her confession?' Tish questioned.

'Even with her confession,' Leah confirmed.

'Why do you believe she was innocent?'

'Because, the day Delilah died, I had a flash. It was an image of Delilah and Daisy together. They were entwined in each other's arms and crying. Those tears were tears of happiness. I could feel how much they had missed each other since Daisy's passing and I could also feel how very happy they were to be reunited. Although they would have liked to have spent more time together here on this plane of existence, they were content to be together in the hereafter as mother and child, forever. I never received another message from Daisy after that. It felt to me as if she was finally at peace.'

'I don't understand how that equates to Delilah's innocence,' Tish said.

'Easy. First, Daisy wouldn't be at peace if she had been reunited with the mother who had killed her. I would have sensed fear or anger or other unresolved issues between the two, but I didn't. There was only joy and love. Second, although I haven't received messages from Daisy since Delilah's passing, I have received them from Delilah. She's expressed regret, shame, and guilt to me numerous times – not about having committed a crime, but some-thing else. Something she did or didn't do that caused Daisy's death.'

'That seems reasonable. Any mother of a murdered child is going to feel that she failed in protecting that child, isn't she?' Reade ventured.

'Yes, but this doesn't feel like simple parental guilt to me.'

'What does it feel like?'

'It's not clear. She's never made it clear, but if I had to guess, Delilah's remorse involves a lack of judgment. I feel that either she trusted the wrong person or she unwittingly allowed Daisy to be placed in a dangerous situation.'

'The situation that led to Daisy's death,' Reade presumed.

'Yes. You're welcome to read the notes I've made through the years. They're in that folder I've given you.' She pointed to the file in Tish's hand. 'I made a copy of that same folder for Mr Carney. After reading the messages I've received, he agreed with my assessment.'

'Then why did Delilah confess?' Reade placed his tablet on the table and sat back in his chair.

'I don't know. I've consulted the cards. I've asked Delilah to talk to me and tell me her reasons. I've even consulted with other mediums, but I've never been able to come up with an explanation.'

'Is that why Gadsden Carney called you every week? To see if you'd made progress?'

'That and to see if I could uncover anything else about the case, but he also wanted to know about his own circumstances. He was extremely ill and worried that he might not live long enough to find out the truth about Daisy's death.'

'Did you tell him he wouldn't?' Reade challenged.

'No, because I didn't see him succumbing to his disease – not yet. I was certain he'd survive long enough to solve the case – until yesterday. Yesterday morning, when I consulted the cards, there was a darkness. A darkness I couldn't quite explain.'

'Did you warn Gadsden?'

'I was going to, but he missed our scheduled phone call yesterday afternoon.'

'He was just outside of town, visiting his daughter,' Reade explained. 'Probably got caught up in family activities.'

'Yes, he told me he and his wife were flying up for the week. We were going to arrange a face-to-face meeting so that I could get a better read of him and to see if Delilah or anyone else might have a personal message for him. He was excited to be back in town where he could investigate the case in person. It was all he could talk about for weeks, so I highly doubt he got so distracted that he forgot to call me. Something was definitely wrong because he also didn't answer the few times I tried calling him after he missed our appointment.'

'Any idea why he didn't speak to you?'

'I can only think of two reasons. Either he was chasing an important lead and was too busy to talk or he had a feeling his life was in danger and was afraid I would confirm his suspicions.'

'Did Gadsden have his eye on anyone in particular in the case? Was there a suspect who stood out from the others?'

Leah Harmon shook her head. 'No. Not that I know of. If he had someone in mind for Daisy's murder, he kept it secret from me.'

Tish frowned. There was also a third explanation for Gadsden Carney's failure to call in for their session. 'Was Mr Carney paying you for your consultations?'

'Yes. I told him not to since this wasn't an official case and he would be paying me out of his own pocket, but when he insisted, I gave him a discounted rate.'

Reade looked at Tish and signaled that he understood the

direction of her questioning. 'Out of curiosity, what is your discounted rate?' he asked.

'I typically charge three hundred and fifty dollars for a one-hour session. I charged Mr Carney two hundred and fifty,' Leah revealed.

'One thousand dollars a month for six months. That's a pretty sweet deal.'

'It covered a good chunk of my rent, yes. I also worked hard for that money,' Leah rationalized. 'What I did for Mr Carney went beyond a one-hour-a-week phone call. Every moment I got, I tried to connect with Delilah and Daisy so that I could help move the case forward. It was frustrating when there were no messages to receive. I felt as if I wasn't doing my job.'

'Did Gadsden Carney ever express frustration or disappointment when you didn't receive a message?'

'Yes, he'd be disappointed, but he understood the unpredictable nature of my business. Spirits have little regard for appointments, calendars, and other human time constraints.'

'So there's no reason for us to suspect that Gadsden Carney might have been on the verge of severing your partnership?' Tish inquired.

'None whatsoever. Despite a rough start all those years ago, Mr Carney and I got along well. I may not have been able to connect with Delilah as much as he would have liked, but Mr Carney valued my insight regarding his personal health. He actually contacted me twice before leaving Florida to make sure his flight went smoothly. You can check the phone records,' Leah instructed Reade.

'If you and Carney got along so well, then you should have no trouble telling us where you were after you left the Junior League dinner last night,' he replied.

'Of course not. Like I said, I was here. I had an after-work reading for a regular client. That reading lasted from seven to seven forty-five. After that, I heated up a Lean Cuisine dinner and ate it in front of the tube. I turned in somewhere around ten thirty.'

'Can anyone vouch for you?'

'Only my cat.' Leah's eyes narrowed. 'Listen, I know what you're trying to do here, Sheriff. It's no different from what Gadsden Carney did to me when I first met him. You're just playing another version of "Let's blame the psychic."'

'I'm not trying to blame you for anything, Ms Harmon. This is a murder investigation. Given the location of Carney's body, I need to investigate whether his death is linked to the Honeycutt case. Part of linking the two cases is ensuring that everyone involved in the Honeycutt case has an alibi for the time of Carney's death. Given that you were at the church yesterday evening does cast suspicion in your direction, but I assure you I'm simply looking at possible connections.'

'I do believe that's your primary motivation, Sheriff; however, you can't tell me that there isn't a part of you that's skeptical of my abilities.'

'You're right. I am a bit skeptical,' Reade answered honestly.

'I understand. You were a man of science at one time, your grandma tells me – she's sorry you couldn't afford to finish medical school, by the way, but she wants me to tell you she's very proud of you—'

At the mention of the grandmother who had raised him, Reade's eyes grew wide.

'And although you've grown and opened your mind over the years,' Leah continued, 'you can't quite explain what I do. And so you've deduced that there must be some sort of angle in it all. I must have been pretending to be psychic just so I could string Mr Carney along for the cash. Well, I hope I just proved to you that I wasn't.'

'You put some fears to rest,' he allowed. 'I still need to ask you to stay where you are in case we need to ask you more questions.'

Leah Harmon smiled. 'I'll be here. Nowhere to go. At least nowhere you two wouldn't find me. You make a great team.'

Reade thanked Leah for her time and rose from the dining-room table.

'Oh, Ms Tarragon?' Leah called just as Tish was heading toward the front door.

Tish turned and looked over her shoulder.

'Your mother knows you covered up for your father. She knows why, too,' Leah said with a wan smile. 'She says, "Thank you."'

# SIX

Slightly shaken and not wanting to be seen talking in front of Leah Harmon's house, Tish and Reade drove the eight blocks to Viola Tilley's senior living center before speaking about what had transpired.

'Well, that was creepy,' Tish declared as Reade pulled the SUV to a halt in the apartment complex parking lot. 'Who else knows that you once went to medical school?'

'Classmates – none of whom I've kept in touch with. Apart from them, just you. Of course, a simple background check would have revealed my educational background.'

'True,' Tish agreed. 'But a simple check wouldn't have given Leah Harmon information about your grandmother or why you didn't graduate.'

'You're right. Who else knows about your father and . . .' Reade's voice trailed off in obvious deference.

'And the housekeeper who'd been hired to help out while my mother was dying? Just me, my father, the housekeeper, and you.'

'Not even Mary Jo and Jules?'

Tish shook her head. 'It happened when I was sixteen. I just tried to block it out all these years, until that one day right before Christmas when we were discussing our families. It all came rushing back to me.'

'I'm sorry,' Reade remarked.

'Don't be. I had to confront it eventually.'

Several seconds elapsed before either of them spoke again.

Tish finally broke the silence. 'One thing's for certain. Leah Harmon is either the real thing or she's a bigger fraud than Bernie Madoff.'

'Real psychic or not, Leah still might be a murderer. If she wasn't producing results quickly enough for Carney's liking, he might have threatened to cut her off financially. Even though we're not talking about Bernie Madoff bucks, getting a chunk of your rent paid for just four hours' work each month is a gig some folks would kill for.'

'Yes, it is, but killing Carney would have ended the gravy train,' Tish challenged.

'Not if he'd already ended the arrangement.'

'But Leah claims she and Carney were on good terms. Carney consulted with her several times before making the trip north,' Tish said. 'Just check the phone records.'

'I don't doubt that we'll find a record for those calls, but records don't tell us what was discussed. Carney could just as easily have called to issue Leah an ultimatum – if she didn't improve her performance, she'd no longer be working for him.'

'And the phone calls she made when he didn't keep yesterday's appointment?'

'We only have Leah's word that Carney didn't make that appointment.'

'But the phone records—' Tish began to argue.

'Hear me out. Since Carney was here in town, what if Leah suggested they forgo their usual call and meet in person instead? Only she didn't want them to meet in her home.'

'So Leah suggests they meet at the cemetery,' Tish followed Reade's train of thought. 'Telling Carney that being at the Honeycutt grave might open the channels of otherworldly communication that have been blocked for so long.'

'Also, since Carney was in poor health and surrounded by family members who'd watch him like a hawk, driving the few miles to Ashton Courthouse would be far more feasible than making the trek to downtown Richmond,' Reade added.

'I agree, but why kill Carney in the churchyard? And more importantly, why do it last night? She knew the dinner was going on – she donates a reading for auction every year. Why not plan to meet him earlier in the day when the church hall was empty?'

'I don't know,' Reade admitted. 'She might have been forced to meet Carney when he was away from his family in the evening. Also, maybe she didn't meet him there with the intention of killing him. Maybe she genuinely thought she'd receive a message while at the cemetery, and when she didn't, and Carney threatened to walk, she feared word might get out that she'd "lost her powers." Or maybe she still held a grudge against Carney from all those years ago. She lost her job at the museum because of him. Maybe when he questioned her ability, she lost her temper.'

'But she painted the loss of the museum job as a positive event. The catalyst that gave her more time for her art.'

'If that was her motive for murder, of course she'd paint a rosy picture.'

'Good point,' Tish noted with a chuckle. 'Sorry, I wasn't laughing at your theory. It's just good to have you back. There were so many times during the bake-off case when I wanted to talk to you and ask your opinion. You know, I nearly called you once.'

'You did?'

'Yeah, I was stumped and wanted to toss some ideas around, but I chickened out. I figured you probably wouldn't have answered anyway.' Tish didn't give Reade a chance to respond. She opened the passenger door and added, breezily, 'But that's all in the past now. You're back and we have a killer to catch, so let's go see the nanny.'

The residents of The Steeples retirement complex had just finished dinner in the communal dining room when Tish and Reade followed a uniformed healthcare provider into the visitors' area of the facility. Once the pair were comfortably seated on a jacquard upholstered settee, eighty-six-year-old Viola Tilley was wheeled from the adjacent dining room to greet them.

She was dressed, as befitted her name, in a lavender floral-printed dress, matching cardigan, and a pair of unlaced tennis shoes. Her mouth was open in a broad, welcoming smile and her white hair stood in stark contrast to her dark, line-worn face, but most remarkable about her appearance was the youthful sparkle in her eyes.

Reade rose to his feet as she approached. 'Well, aren't you handsome?' Viola gushed as the healthcare assistant parked her wheelchair opposite the couple. 'I don't get many visitors, let alone good-looking ones.'

Reade blushed slightly and extended his hand to hers. 'Ms Tilley, pleased to meet you. I'm Sheriff Clemson Reade, Henrico County Sheriff's Office, and this is my associate, Ms Tarragon.'

'What a lovely couple! She's as pretty as you are handsome. Y'all look good together.'

'Oh, we're not—' Tish began to argue, but then decided not to disappoint the elderly woman.

Reade sat back down. 'Ms Tilley, I need to ask you some questions, but first I have some news that might be difficult for you to hear.'

'What is it?'

'A man has been killed,' he said, his voice soft and gentle. 'His name was Gadsden Carney. He was the sheriff in charge of Daisy Honeycutt's murder investigation. He was found at the Honeycutt family plot in Ashton Courthouse.'

The sparkle disappeared from Viola's eyes. 'Daisy. That poor child. Mercy, what was done to her and what misery her passing caused.'

'To her family?' Tish asked.

'To her family and everyone at Cypress Hollow. Walker James, Daisy's brother, was bundled off to boarding school quicker than you could say "boo." I didn't even say goodbye to the boy, he was gone so fast. The house was sealed off by the police, and Delilah and the senator left town and told me, the stable hands, and the McIlveens that we were all fired. I had to find a new job, all while still being torn up and missing those babies.' She shook her head and it looked as though she might cry. 'It was a terrible time. A terrible time. No one wants a sixty-year-old nanny, let alone a sixty-year-old nanny who's answering questions about a murder. The senator made sure I was taken care of, though. He gave me some money to live on and then, later, he set me up in this place.'

'That was generous of him,' Tish remarked.

'He said I'd earned it.'

'Earned it how?'

'By staying loyal and keeping my mouth shut. I never talked to reporters or detectives about Daisy's death. So long as I didn't, the senator took care of me. If I talked, then . . .' She opened her eyes wide and tilted her head to one side to indicate that the senator would have cut off her income.

'What was the senator afraid you'd say?' Reade asked.

'I honestly don't know. The senator was a quiet man. Liked to keep his personal life private, but the tabloids had a field day with him and Delilah and even poor little Walker James. I figured he just wanted to keep the family name out of the papers. The senator even hired a public relations firm to handle things for him. That's how plumb crazy it all got. When Delilah confessed, the newspapers . . . Lord, the things they said.'

'You were the nanny to Delilah and her sister when they were young, too, weren't you?'

'I was. I loved those girls. But that's really going back a ways, Sheriff.' She flashed a weak smile.

'Humor me.' He grinned.

'Not much to say except the Duprees were good to me. Very good to me. That was before the days of fancy nanny agencies. Back then, a family hired a nanny based upon word of mouth. My mama had been nanny for the Duprees' neighbor, so when they found out they were expecting Dixie, they asked her to come work for them. By that time, my mama's arthritis had gotten the best of her, so she told the Duprees no, and suggested they hire me instead.'

'I was just twenty-two and had no experience, but the Duprees hired me anyway, just because my mama recommended me,' Viola continued with a chuckle. 'I was so green those first few days, but mama's advice helped me through it. Two years later, Delilah was born, and I thought I had it all figured out, but the two girls were so different. What worked with Dixie didn't work for Delilah. Dixie was a beautiful child. Anyone who saw her couldn't help but comment on her dark hair and her pale blue eyes. But she wasn't a china doll. Dixie played hard – I can't count how many scrapes and cuts and broken bones she had. Delilah was blonde and pretty in her own right, though not as striking as her sister. While Dixie always ran straight for the playground, Delilah was happiest drawing or singing or dancing. When the girls got a little older, they competed with each other all the time – Dixie wanting to be noticed for her looks and Delilah for her talent – but it went even farther than that.'

'Even to their personal relationships?' Reade prompted.

'You know all about that, huh? Dixie dated the senator before Delilah did. Dixie was a wild child and the senator – just plain Benton back then – was a lawyer looking to get into politics. It never would have worked.'

'How did Dixie feel about it?' Tish asked. 'Did she agree it never would have worked?'

'I think, in her heart, she must have known, but she wasn't

about to admit it to anyone. According to Dixie, the senator was her catch and Delilah stole her man.'

'*Did* Delilah steal Dixie's man?'

'I was out of the Dupree household and working for another family at the time, so I couldn't say for certain. The girls kept in touch with me – Delilah more than Dixie. They wrote letters and called me at Christmas. It was during one of those Christmas calls that Delilah told me she was dating Benton. She said they ran into each other while he was entertaining clients at the supper club where she was singing. He remembered Delilah from the Dupree family dinners he attended with Dixie, and as soon as he heard Delilah sing, he fell in love. At least that's what she said.'

'Did you believe her?'

'I did, but . . .'

'But?'

'Delilah was pretty and talented and sweet, and she loved the senator and those babies of hers with her whole heart, but she liked to get her own way. When she wanted something, she got it, and pity the poor person who told her "no." I know, because I once was that person.' Viola gave an uneasy laugh.

'So you're suggesting Delilah set her sights on Benton Honeycutt and went out of her way to . . .' Tish deliberated her next words carefully. She felt uncomfortable using the term "seduce" in front of an eighty-six-year-old former nanny.

'Get her hooks into him?' Viola completed the thought. 'Like I said, I can't say for sure, but she might have. Dixie sure thought she did – she didn't even go to their wedding.'

'Sounds like Dixie could hold on to a grudge,' Reade observed.

'Yeah, especially when it involved Delilah. In the time Delilah and the senator were together, Dixie married and divorced twice. One of those husbands emptied her savings account and left her nowhere to go. That's when Dixie finally made up with Delilah.'

'Were they close again?'

Viola wrinkled her nose. 'Yes and no. They were sisters, so there was always going to be a bond between them, yet Dixie was still jealous of her sister and the life she had as a senator's wife. Dixie wasn't stupid, though. She knew her sister's life as a senator's wife was helping to pay her way, so she did her best to keep quiet and not stir up trouble.'

'But sometimes they'd argue?' Reade ascertained.

'Lordy, yes. Everyone in that house would stay out of their way when that happened. The last fight they ever had was the night before Daisy's passing and it was a doozy.'

'The night before? I didn't see any reference to that in the original case files.'

'That's peculiar,' Viola said. 'I'm positive someone must have said something to Sheriff Carney about it. I may be frail, but my mind is still all there.'

'Don't worry about it, Ms Tilley,' Reade assured her. 'It's been twenty-five years. That section of file must have been misplaced at some point.'

'Or maybe the police back then didn't think it was important. Senator Honeycutt made such a ruckus about the killer being someone outside the house that the sheriff may not have bothered putting it in the file.'

Reade pulled a face. 'Maybe,' he replied reluctantly. 'So, this argument between Dixie and Delilah. What happened?'

'Dixie had come down to Cypress Hollow for the weekend. When she arrived, Delilah was in a right state. She was already worked up on account of the party – she loved to throw parties, but she always fretted if things weren't exactly so – but then there was the trouble with the senator on top of it.'

'The trouble?'

'Marital trouble,' she answered in a near whisper, as if her former employers might overhear her gossiping. 'They were happy for a while. Walker James was born three years after they were married – that's when Delilah begged me to come work for them. I was happy to do it. It was like old times, except Walker was such a quiet child. Reserved, shy. Not at all like his mama or his aunt – more like his father. Then Daisy came along. Well, if Daisy wasn't the spittin' image of her mama. She could sing too, even better than Delilah did when she was Daisy's age. All that girl did was sing. There were times you wondered if she had an "off" button, but Delilah loved it. That's what started the trouble. Delilah had given up singing to be a mother, so she started grooming Daisy to live the life she never got. There were singing lessons, dancing lessons, piano lessons, and all the recitals and shows that went with them. Well, the senator didn't want Daisy to grow up on a stage. He thought it wasn't right for a Honeycutt and the daughter of a potential future president to be put on display – those were his words – "on display." Delilah told him Daisy was her child, too, and that she'd raise her as she saw fit.

'That summer,' Viola continued, 'Delilah packed up the kids and the four of us left Washington and moved to Cypress Hollow permanently. When Congress was in session or the senator had other business that kept him in Washington, Cypress Hollow was filled with laughter and noise. There were dance parties, music recitals, costume calls, and kids' movie nights. When the senator came back for weekends and holidays, the house would get quiet. The kids' parties were replaced with dinners with the senator's donors and other politicians and dignitaries. It was my job to make sure the children weren't seen. The senator must have known what went on when he wasn't home, but so long as Delilah played the hostess when needed, he seemed willing to overlook things. But then, suddenly, the week before the Fourth of July barbecue, something happened.'

'What do you mean "something"?' Tish quizzed.

Viola shrugged. 'Something between Delilah and the senator. I can't say what, but Delilah was in an absolute state. Spent most of those days crying and visiting with Father Dillard over at St Jude's. She was still beside herself when Dixie arrived for the Fourth of July weekend. That's what they argued about. Delilah must have confided in Dixie about her troubles, and Dixie told Delilah that if she hadn't stolen the senator in the first place, she'd have no trouble keeping him.'

'Ouch.'

'Oh, the things they said to each other were just plain awful. Awful,' Viola reiterated with a shudder. 'Delilah got back at Dixie by saying at least she was able to keep a marriage going longer than two years – that was the longest marriage Dixie had. They went back and forth like that for a little while.'

'How did the argument finally end?' Reade inquired.

'I'll never forget it. Dixie said that if there was any justice in this world, Delilah would lose the senator, her house, and her children.' Viola's eyes welled with tears. 'The next day, Dixie got her wish. Not right away. Not all at once. But that Fourth of July was the day Delilah lost everything. From that day on, nothing would ever be the same.'

Reade grabbed a box of tissues from a nearby end table and offered them to a now-weeping Viola, who drew one from the top and blew her nose into it noisily. 'Sorry, but not a day goes by when I don't think about Delilah and those babies.'

'We understand,' Tish sympathized. 'I can't imagine how difficult it must have been for you.'

Reade, meanwhile, went to ask an orderly for a glass of water. He returned several seconds later with a white paper cup, which he handed directly to Viola. 'Here you go. Drink up.'

'Thank you, Sheriff.' She drank the water and handed the empty cup back to Reade.

'Would you like some more?' he asked.

'No, I feel better now.'

Reade sat back down beside Tish. 'Are you OK to continue talking to us, Ms Tilley? Or should we come back at another time?'

'No, it's good. It's been so long since I've talked to anyone about Daisy's passing. Most people here don't remember what happened and those who do only remember the stuff they saw in the magazines. It feels good to let it out and talk with folks who want to know the truth.'

'Well, if it gets too much for you and you need us to stop, just let us know,' Reade instructed.

'I will, Sheriff,' she promised with a slight sniffle.

'Tell me about the Fourth of July – the day Daisy was killed.'

'I got up with the kids, like I usually did, and did some reading with them. It was summer vacation, but Delilah was a stickler for making sure they kept up with their reading. After that, I took them downstairs for breakfast. What with the argument the night before and the trouble between Delilah and the senator, the mood in the house was tense.'

'So Dixie stayed the night?'

'Yes, I was somewhat surprised she didn't head back to Richmond and yet I wasn't. Like I said, she and Delilah still had a bond. Also, Dixie probably had nowhere else to go for the weekend. As I mentioned, her last husband left her pretty much penniless.'

Reade nodded. 'Go on.'

'After breakfast, I made sure Walker James and Daisy got dressed in play clothes. The barbecue didn't start until one, so I'd make sure they put on their good clothes – matching red, white, and blue outfits – later in the day. I took the kids down to the stables where they brushed the horses and then they went back up to the house where they played on the swings and slide for a spell. When they finished, I brought them inside for some juice and a snack while the caterers set up outside. Walker was in a right mood about the barbecue. He didn't want to take part – he wanted to stay in his room and play computer games. Walker was like that. He was always a loner – playing with his sister was fine, but getting him to play with the Heritage children or kids from school was like pulling teeth.'

'And even playing with his sister didn't go well at times, did it?'

'Yeah, they fought some at times. Typical brother-and-sister stuff.' Viola smiled.

'I don't know of many typical brothers who try to hit their sister over the head with a golf club,' Reade noted.

Viola's jaw dropped. 'Oh . . . *that*. You know, I'd plumb forgotten all about it. With everything that happened with Daisy, it's like it got shoved out of my memory.'

'A traumatic event can do that.'

'You must be right. Until Daisy's death, we thought Walker's behavior was shocking, but then . . .'

'Do you remember what prompted Walker to attack his sister?' Tish asked.

'Daisy was singing. She was always singing. She never stopped unless she was eating or sleeping. Most of the time it was fine, but every now and then she'd sing about things she'd seen. On that day, it was Walker sneaking an extra candy bar for his lunch bag. Daisy gave him an awful time about it, and Walker lost his temper and went to hit her with the closest thing he could find: one of his junior golf clubs. Luckily, I caught him in time or he'd have done some mighty bad damage.'

'What happened to Walker afterward?'

'Delilah grounded him and then signed him up for a church counseling program.' Viola scoffed. 'Poor kid couldn't help what he inherited. His daddy was quiet and had a bad temper, too.'

*And yet it wasn't the senator who had allegedly killed Daisy*, Tish mused. *It was Delilah.*

'Was Daisy singing the day of the barbecue?' Reade asked.

'Course she was. She was singing Christmas carols of all things. Don't know how she'd gotten it into her head to sing them.' Viola shrugged. 'All I can tell you is it started the evening before the barbecue. Reverend Dillard came to visit Delilah late that afternoon. Afterwards, when I was getting the children their supper and then getting them ready for bed, Daisy started singing. Maybe the reverend mentioned Christmas in July or told a story about baby Jesus. I have no idea how it got into her head, but it was stuck there.'

Reade nodded. 'Did Walker James seem to mind his sister's singing?'

'No, he tuned her out, like the rest of us – well, the rest of us who weren't the senator. No, Walker was far more concerned with getting to play video games that afternoon. I made a deal with him that if he played with the other kids until the food was served, then he might be able to go to his room for a while, but he'd have to ask his mama for permission. I was going to a family cookout that afternoon. I was supposed to stay at Cypress Hollow long enough to get the kids ready for the barbecue, but Delilah let me leave at twelve. She also arranged for a car to drive me, instead of me taking the bus. My auntie nearly had a heart attack when she saw me ride up to her house in a big ol' black car,' Viola hooted.

'That was nice of Delilah,' Tish commented.

'It was, but I think she did it for herself, too. Getting the kids ready for the barbecue was a distraction for her.'

'A distraction from what? Dixie?'

'That and, well, just before Delilah told me to leave early, the senator arrived at the house. He had Priscilla Maddox with him.'

'The senator arrived only that morning?'

'The holiday was on a Thursday and the senator said he needed to finish some things at his office before he could make the trip to Cypress Hollow.'

'And Priscilla Maddox?'

'She was the senator's aide. He said she had nowhere to go for the holiday, so he invited her along to stay so that they could get some work done over the long weekend,' Viola explained. 'But it was clear to anyone with eyes in their head that there was more going on between the two of them than a working relationship. The McIlveens and I weren't shocked when the senator finally married her – we were surprised it took so long, but we weren't surprised it happened.'

'How did Delilah react to Priscilla's presence?'

'I left Cypress Hollow an hour after Ms Maddox arrived, so I didn't see much, but the tension I told you about before? It was already bad that morning, but when I left, you could cut it with a knife.'

'Did anything else happen before you left?' Reade asked. 'Any arguments between Daisy and Delilah?'

'No, Daisy was pretty well behaved that morning. She was excited to see the fireworks and to play with the Heritage children. If she'd misbehaved later in the day, it was because she was tired. That's when Daisy got ornery – at the end of the day.'

'Did Delilah ever strike or hit the children when they were "ornery"?'

Viola shook her head. 'Never. She'd rather die than harm a hair on their heads.'

Reade flashed a puzzled glance at Tish. 'I have to ask you a question, Ms Tilley, and it's very direct.'

'That's OK. I prefer folks not to beat around the bush.'

'Do you believe Delilah Honeycutt murdered her daughter?'

'Course I do. She confessed, didn't she?'

'Confession aside, do you, in your heart, believe that Delilah Honeycutt actually murdered Daisy?'

Tears once again welled in Viola Tilley's dark eyes. 'I do, Sheriff. As much as it hurts me to say it, I do.'

'Why? You seem to have had a great deal of respect for Mrs Honeycutt.'

'I had more than respect for her. I loved that girl. Still do.'

'And yet you believe she was guilty.'

'Daisy was a beautiful child, but she could be difficult. Delilah was under a great strain that day. A great strain. I think she went to the garage to get Daisy inside for a bath and Daisy, being tired and ornery after playing outside in the heat all day, said "no." Delilah didn't take it well – she never did like the word no. I think Delilah lost her temper and all the frustrations of the past days came pouring out at that poor child. I think she didn't realize what she'd done until it was too late. She lost her head, that's all. With everything Dixie said to her and then the senator bringing that young girl home – not to the townhouse in DC, but to Delilah's house, the one she lived in with their children – I think Delilah snapped. And I can't tell you how much it pains me to think that if I hadn't gone to my aunt's that day – if I'd stayed back and stayed with those babies at the barbecue – both Daisy and Delilah would still be alive today. And maybe, just maybe, Daisy'd be here visiting me with her babies. That's what I think, Sheriff. That's what I think.'

Tish and Reade sat in solemn silence as Viola Tilley wept.

# SEVEN

After consoling Viola Tilley and watching as she was escorted back to her room to rest, Tish and Reade stepped out of the senior housing complex and into the early evening sunshine. The oppressive mugginess of the afternoon had dissipated, allowing Richmond residents to go about their post-work errands, tasks, and assignations in comfort.

'That was heart-wrenching,' Tish remarked as they walked toward the visitor parking area.

'Yeah, making an eighty-six-year-old nanny cry is something to add to my list of things I never want to do again,' Reade lamented. 'Are you still up for dinner? Because if not . . .'

'I am, but I could use a drink first. How about you?'

'Same.' He waved her away from the visitor parking area and toward the exit.

'Aren't we taking the car?'

'The restaurant's only a few blocks away. When I called to make the appointment to see Ms Tilley, I got approval to leave my car here until later this evening.'

'You're a planner, I see.'

'Not usually,' Reade replied with a cryptic grin. 'I wanted this to be a special evening. I just wish it had started out a bit differently.'

'Comes with the territory. At least I have someone I can commiserate with.' She smiled.

'I'm very good at commiserating. I'm a commiserator from way back,' he joked as he led the way down the Canal Walk to an old factory building that had been converted into an eatery called Justine's. There, outside the front door, they were greeted by a tall, dark-skinned black woman in her mid to late forties.

'Reade,' she welcomed before a look of panic spread across her face. 'I didn't mess up and schedule you and the boys to play tonight, did I?'

'No, this is a social call, Shirley. I was in the area on a case and figured I'd introduce Tish here to some legendary Virginia seafood.'

'Well, then, come on in,' Shirley welcomed. 'Pleased to meet you, Tish.'

'Pleased to meet you, too,' Tish replied.

'Tish has her own little place in Hobson Glen,' Reade explained to Shirley. 'She does the best breakfasts and sandwiches.'

'Hobson Glen? I have family up in Staunton. Next time I'm driving through, I'll stop in,' Shirley proposed.

'Please do,' Tish responded. 'We'd love to have you. Though I warn you, my place isn't as big as all this.'

'We've all got to start somewhere. It's the food that matters.' Shirley grabbed some menus from the inside of the podium. 'I've got one canal-side table left if y'all are interested.'

Reade looked at Tish, his face a question.

'Yes,' Tish approved. 'We won't have too many more nights like these.'

'Ain't that the truth,' Shirley declared. 'In another week or so, we'll have to set up the big fans so our customers don't get over-come with the heat. Night's not so bad, but during the day even the umbrellas don't help much.'

Shirley led the way through the restaurant, past the bar, and out of French doors to the patio. From there, she took them to a corner table along the wrought-iron railing that separated the terrace from the canal below. 'Your usual, Reade?'

'Yes, please,' he replied as he pulled Tish's chair away from the table so that she could be seated.

'And you, Tish? What can I get you to drink?' Shirley asked as she passed her a menu.

'A glass of rosé, please.'

'I got a beautiful dry rosé in from Charlottesville this week. How would that work for you?'

'Perfectly,' Tish answered.

Shirley passed Reade his menu. 'Antoine will come by shortly with your drinks and to take your order.'

The couple thanked her.

'Your band plays here?' Tish asked after Shirley had gone.

'One Saturday a month. We do a circuit of small eateries and clubs on the weekends,' Reade explained.

'Really? I never knew Dixieland bands were that popular.'

'Oh no, this isn't the Dixieland band. I was just filling in the night of Binnie Broderick's library fundraiser.'

'Filling in?' Tish repeated. 'You mean there's more than one sousaphone player in Hobson Glen?'

'Afraid so. These small towns always have their dark side.'

'Dark? That's downright sinister.'

'It's probably best you found out now.'

'Probably.' Tish laughed. 'So what type of music does your band play?'

'Covers, mostly. Top forty, classic rock, standards – whatever gets the audience in a good mood – with a couple of our own tunes mixed in.'

'And what instrument do you play? I assume not the sousaphone.'

'No, I play the drums.'

'A beat cop, huh?' She smiled. 'Appropriate.'

Reade groaned.

'I'm sure you've heard that one a million times.'

'Actually, you're the first,' he admitted with a grin. 'And, hopefully, the last.'

'Sorry, I couldn't resist. So, what other instruments do you play?'

'A little guitar. A little piano. Music is a passion of mine, but it's also my way to relax. Kind of like you and cooking.'

Tish nodded. 'Nothing calms me down like working on a new recipe.'

'Nothing helps me like strumming a guitar and writing new music.'

'I'd like to hear some of your stuff someday,' she said.

'Maybe you can join us here one night, while we're playing.'

Before Tish could answer, Antoine arrived with their drinks. He was in his early twenties and bore more than a passing resemblance to Shirley.

'Hey, Reade,' Antoine greeted the sheriff as he placed the chilled glass of wine in front of Tish. 'Strange to see you on a weeknight. How's it going?'

'Good. How are you? How's summer treating you?'

'Aw, you know. Working here. Doing some interning down at the youth center. Getting some reading done for when I go back to school in August.'

'Antoine's going for his master's in social work,' Reade informed Tish.

'You have my respect, Antoine,' Tish responded. 'That's a tough field.'

'No tougher than Sheriff Taylor's job here,' he teased as he presented Reade with a full pint glass.

'Sheriff Taylor? Isn't *The Andy Griffith Show* a little before your time?' Reade fired back.

Antoine laughed. 'You're forgetting my generation grew up watching TV Land. Now, what can I get you folks to eat?'

'I'll have the Creole-crusted grouper, please,' Tish requested.

'Good choice,' Antoine confirmed. 'And, Reade, how about you?'

'I'll have the Bourbon Street pasta,' Reade announced, handing his menu back to Antoine.

'Any starters?' the waiter asked. 'We got a shipment of soft-shell crabs in today.'

'Talk about timing. Just this morning your dad mentioned how you used to eat soft-shell crabs each summer.'

'I still love them!' she replied.

'That's a yes to the soft-shells,' Reade confirmed.

'Cool.' Antoine wrote in his notebook. 'I'll order this up for y'all. Anything else before I go?'

'Nope, just try to enjoy your time off this summer, huh? It all goes by fast.'

Antoine smiled. 'Don't worry. I have some time booked with friends' – he noticed his mother standing within earshot – 'if my taskmaster of a mama lets me go.'

Shirley wasted no time in giving her son a playful swat on the arm. 'Taskmaster? You want to see a taskmaster? Get that butt of yours into the kitchen,' she ordered with a playful wink in Reade and Tish's direction.

When the faux-feuding Antoine and Shirley had departed, Reade raised his glass. 'To your first day as a consultant.'

Tish touched her glass to his and then took a sip. The wine was crisp, light-bodied, and perfectly chilled. She drew a deep breath and leaned back in her seat. The pathways that ran alongside the canal were occupied by businesspeople leaving work for the day, dog-walkers, joggers, and couples strolling along holding hands. In the canal, ducks begged restaurant-goers for crumbs while a green, canopied canal boat puttered by, its captain describing Justine's as a former paper mill.

'This is lovely.' Tish sighed.

'Yes, it is,' Reade seconded, although his eyes were fixed on Tish instead of the surroundings. 'I'm glad you agreed to join me.'

Tish didn't notice the sheriff's appreciative gaze. She was too busy staring out across the canal. 'I'm glad you suggested we come here.' As she smiled, her eyes met his before she self-consciously looked away again.

Tish chastised herself. Not only had she worked on three cases with Reade, but she served him breakfast every morning except Monday. Why she should suddenly feel so flustered sitting across a table from him was beyond all reason.

'I only wish we could have done this sooner,' Reade added.

'Me, too, but my working as a consultant wouldn't have gone over too well. Schuyler was already foaming at the mouth about me getting involved with detective work. If there had been any mention of officially working for the sheriff's office, he'd have gone ballistic. But that's all in the past now.'

'I, um . . . I was talking about having dinner together, but yes, you're probably right about the consulting job.' It was Reade's turn to stare out over the canal.

The late-day sun reflected off the sheriff's face, highlighting its finely chiseled features and illuminating his gray eyes. The effect was rather pleasing.

Tish wondered if she should attempt to break the silence, but she suddenly found herself at a loss for words. Thankfully, Antoine arrived on the scene with their order of soft-shell crabs. 'Oh, wow. Those look great,' she gushed.

'They sure do,' Reade rejoined. Using his fork and a spoon, he placed one of the two golden crabs on to her bread plate.

Tish gave a surprised, 'Thank you.'

'You're always waiting on me at the café. It's high time the shoe was on the other foot.'

Tish assessed the three shot glasses that accompanied the crab. One contained a creamy white tartar sauce, the next a red cocktail sauce, and the third a red-and-green-flecked yellow substance. 'What's that?' Tish gestured to the third glass.

'That's what they call "soul sauce." Justine's has been serving soul sauce since the days when Shirley's mother, Justine, was waiting tables and Shirley's father, Ted, was running the kitchen.'

'I'll try that.' She took the shot glass, poured a considerable pool of it on her plate, and immediately dunked a bit of crab into it.

'Be careful, it's very—'

Before Reade could finish his warning, Tish popped the piece of crab into her mouth. She instantly regretted it. The sauce – at first buttery and savory and brimming with umami – suddenly exploded, coating her tongue with what felt like magma.

Tears welled in her eyes and beads of perspiration formed on her brow. She had eaten fiery curries before and had enjoyed the gentle tingle they left on her tastebuds afterward, but this sauce felt more like a five-alarm blaze. As the heat rose from the back of her throat to her face and then to the very top of her head, Tish frantically reached for her iced water, gulping down the entire glass before coming up for air, reaching into the bread-basket, and cramming an entire slice of sourdough bread into her mouth.

Stopping mid-chew, she looked up to see Reade staring at her with his mouth open. He pushed his water glass toward her. 'You, um, need to wash that down?'

She nodded and brought the glass to her lips, drinking

approximately three-quarters of it before she felt capable of speaking. 'Sorry, but the sauce is . . .'

'Hot?' He completed the sentence with a trace of a smile. 'Yeah, it's pretty lethal. Are you OK? I can ask Antoine to bring more water.'

'No, I'm good, but thank you.' Tish reached into her handbag and surreptitiously checked her appearance in a compact mirror. As suspected, her mascara had run and crumbs of sourdough had adhered to her mauve lipstick. After wiping away the breadcrumbs with her napkin, she wet a corner of the tissue with her own spit and set to work on the trails of mascara that ran down both cheeks, all the while silently thanking God that this wasn't a first date. 'Thank you for not laughing,' she added when she had finished. 'You are much kinder than Jules would have been.'

'Really? What would he have done?' Reade asked as he ate his soft-shell crab with a dollop of cocktail sauce.

She took a sip of wine and drew a deep breath. 'Record me and post the video to Twitter and Facebook so all our friends could see.'

'Now that's cold,' Reade replied with a laugh. 'No, I'd never record you, but I can't promise that if that happened again, I won't laugh . . . like I almost did just a minute or so ago.'

Tish wrinkled her nose in fake annoyance. 'Thanks a lot, Clemson.'

Reade gestured at the shot glasses full of sauce in the center of the table. 'Can I get you a different sauce by means of an apology?'

'No, thanks. I think I'm just going to stick with a squirt of lemon and call it a day.'

Reade nodded. 'The seafood here doesn't need much embellishment, anyway.'

Tish moved her crab away from the offending sauce on the edge of her plate and cut off a piece with her fork. Without the fiery condiment, the crab was crunchy, sweet, and succulent. 'Mmm,' she groaned. 'As delicious as I remember.'

'No surprises this time?'

'No surprises,' she confirmed as she swallowed another bite. 'Speaking of surprises, how about the bomb Viola Tilley dropped?'

'Are you talking about how Ms Tilley seemed convinced that Delilah Honeycutt murdered Daisy?'

'That's exactly what I'm talking about.'

'I gotta admit I was shocked, given how much she claimed to love both Delilah and Dixie.' Reade took a swig of beer.

'Same here. It really speaks to Delilah's emotional state that day if Viola thinks she was capable of such a thing.'

'Especially when police records show there was absolutely no history of abuse in the Honeycutt household.'

Tish sipped her wine pensively. 'Per Viola Tilley?'

'Per Viola Tilley, per the McIlveens, per the stable hands, per the Honeycutts' closest friends, per Daisy's pediatrician, per Daisy's teachers who described her as "happy, outgoing, and well adjusted".'

'And yet we're supposed to believe that a woman who never once even struck her daughter suddenly snapped and violently murdered her?'

'Viola Tilley believes it,' Reade stated before taking another swig of beer.

'Yes, but why?' Tish asked.

'Maybe it has something to do with the gag order the senator placed on her.'

'Viola told us that was all about avoiding the tabloid reporters.'

'What if it wasn't?' Reade challenged. 'What if Viola knew something – something the senator didn't want to get out?'

'His affair with Priscilla?' Tish suggested.

'Maybe, but would he keep the gag order in place even after Delilah was dead and he and Priscilla had married? That's like shutting the barn door after the horse has already left the stable, isn't it? I mean, the senator married his intern – it wouldn't be too difficult for his constituency to guess where their relationship began. Besides, why would the senator pay that much money to keep the affair secret in the first place, when he was boldly trotting Priscilla around the family's Fourth of July barbecue?'

'Then what do you think the gag order was for?'

Reade shrugged. 'Something about the case, most likely. Something about him or Delilah or Daisy or what happened that day – something the senator didn't want to get out to the press and possibly even the police.'

'And yet, when we asked, Viola Tilley said she didn't know anything. Are you implying that she's hiding something?'

'Not necessarily. Ms Tilley might know something, but she might not understand the significance of what she knows.'

'That's very Poirot of you,' Tish teased as she polished off the remainder of her soft-shell crab.

'*Merci*,' Reade responded as he cleaned his plate as well.

'What do you think about the senator hiring a PR firm?' she continued when they had both finished. 'Seems strange, doesn't it?'

'He was a politician. Politicians always have someone to handle their press and publicity.'

'Yes, but that someone typically works in the politician's office. It's traditionally not some outside firm.'

Reade grunted his agreement. 'That's true. What do you think it means?'

'It means that whatever the senator was hiding required both a gag order and a team of PR experts.'

'You think the two are related?'

Tish nodded. 'Think about it. The senator had lost his daughter and his wife had confessed to the crime. That makes the senator a pretty sympathetic character in the whole drama. Why would he need a PR firm to spin things in his favor? Why not just hire more people for his own office to help handle the media fallout?'

'He was an elected official. He wanted to make sure he didn't lose the public's trust.'

'Yes, but again, why would the public lose faith in him when, for all intents and purposes, he would have been seen as a victim?'

'What about the affair with Priscilla?' Reade suggested. 'He might have been preparing in case word of it leaked.'

'We already dismissed the affair as the cause for the gag order. I'm dismissing it as the cause for hiring the PR firm, too, and not just for the reasons stated earlier, but because compared with his wife's crime, Benton Honeycutt's affair would have been trivial. Come on, this case was on the national news for months. You must remember the day Delilah Honeycutt came forward to confess – I remember it vividly. I was in my friend's car on the way home from school.'

Reade nodded. 'I'd just returned home to find my grandmother sobbing in the living room. She couldn't believe a woman could do that to her own child.'

'The moment Delilah Dupree Honeycutt confessed to murder she became the devil incarnate. Newspapers branded her a monster. Women waited outside the courthouse at her sentencing just so they could hurl insults at her. If her husband's affair had come to light at the time, no one would have cared. If anything, the public would have rationalized his behavior.' Tish waved her hands in the air as if revealing the headline: 'Man married to heartless killer finds love with loyal intern.'

Antoine interrupted their conversation to clear the first course and serve their entrées. 'Creole-crusted grouper,' he announced, presenting Tish with a golden, herb-flecked filet of fish nestled in a bed of collard greens, and served with a square of buttery cornbread.

'It looks and smells fabulous,' she enthused.

'And the Bourbon Street pasta for the sheriff.' Antoine placed a bowl of creamy-sauced linguine, crab, shrimp, and Andouille sausage in front of Reade. 'Can I get you anything else?'

'Just some water when you get a chance,' Reade responded. 'Thank you.'

Antoine deposited their dirty dishes at a nearby busboy station and refilled their water glasses before leaving them to their meals. 'Enjoy.'

'I'm sure I will,' Tish answered, even though Antoine was already gone. She sampled the greens before tucking into the grouper. They were perfectly tender and smoky. 'Mmm.'

'Yeah, many's the time I've sat down after playing a set and ordered a bowl of greens and nothing else. They're just that good.'

'They are,' Tish agreed before plunging her fork into the fish. The breadcrumb crust bore notes of cayenne, paprika, and garlic while the grouper itself was moist, sweet, and flaky.

'I've never tried the grouper,' Reade said, plunging his fork into his bowl of pasta. 'But the oysters here are amazing. I should have asked if they had any available – we could have had those instead of the crabs.'

'No, no, the crabs were perfect. We can get oysters again in the fall, but it feels as though soft-shells are gone before you know it.'

'Just like summer,' he noted.

The pair consumed their dinner while chatting about food, music, and past summer memories. It was an easy conversation – as if she and Reade had known each other for years. As they discussed their memories of growing up in New York, Tish's phone chimed.

It was a text message from a Junior League member looking for a quote.

'Everything OK?'

'Yes, it's a lead on a catering job,' she replied.

'That's awesome! Do you need to make a phone call? I don't mind if you do.'

'No, I'm going to reply to the text and arrange a call for another day. I need to give some thought as to how to cater a *Hunger Games* Sweet Sixteen party for thirty teenagers.'

'*The Hunger Games*? Wouldn't that mean you're not serving any food at all?' he questioned.

Tish laughed. 'For the most part, yes. There are some foods described in the books, but I'm not sure how sixteen-year-olds would react to a buffet of burnt bread, fish stew, and basil-wrapped goat cheese.'

It was Reade's turn for his phone to ring.

'Sorry,' he apologized before retrieving it from his pocket and answering. 'Reade here.'

After replying to her text message, Tish sat back and watched appreciatively as the low-hanging sun cast Reade's dark hair with a reddish glow.

'Yes . . . yes, we are . . . um, can you hold a minute?' Reade put his hand over the phone and held it away from his face. 'It's Dixie Dupree. I left a message for her earlier. She wants to know if we can meet her after dinner.'

'Sure. That's why we're in town, isn't it?'

Reade pulled something of a face and drew the phone back to his ear. 'Yes, we can be there . . . Yes, thank you . . . See you then.'

'Where is she?' Tish asked once Reade had disconnected.

'She's singing at a club over at Shockoe Slip. We'll meet her before she takes the stage at nine. I'm sorry, Tish.' He frowned. 'I'd intended this night to be special, and now we're back to work.'

'It has been special, Clemson. Absolutely lovely. You have no reason to apologize. I actually think I was the one who introduced work into the equation with that text message I received. But it's fine. We have to come back to reality at some point. After all, Gadsden Carney's murder isn't going to solve itself.'

'Yeah, I guess not,' he lamented. 'Rain check for another night when we're not on a case?'

'I would like that.' She smiled as she toasted his glass with hers. 'I would like that very much.'

# EIGHT

Tish and Reade collected the SUV from the senior complex parking lot and drove north past the Hippodrome to The Chandelier Bar. Set in a three-story brick building that had served as a tobacco warehouse after the Civil War, The Chandelier Bar was modeled after the supper clubs of the 1940s, with upholstered booths, potted palms, glass-block partitions, dim lighting, a menu offering vintage cocktails, steaks, and seafood, and a nightly floorshow. But the main focus of the club was the massive central crystal chandelier for which the establishment had been named.

'I never knew this place even existed,' Tish said as she and Reade approached the maître d's podium.

'It's been around for ages. It's popular with Richmond's older guard – businessmen, politicians, society movers and shakers.'

Tish's gaze looked beyond the maître d, to the club floor. There wasn't a single patron under the age of fifty.

'We're here to see Ms Dupree. She invited us to meet her in her dressing room,' Reade explained to the tuxedoed man. He promptly summoned a bartender who led the pair away to Dixie's dressing room.

'Sheriff Clemson Reade, Henrico County Sheriff's Office,' Reade introduced himself to the woman seated in front of the lighted mirror. 'And this is my associate, Ms Tarragon.'

The woman spun around in her seat to face them. She was in her mid-sixties and slim, with a fair complexion that contrasted sharply with her Rapunzel-like, waist-long black hair. The fresh-faced bloom of youth was far behind her, but she still cut a stunning figure. 'Dixie Dupree,' she introduced herself with a graceful extension of her hand. 'But you already knew that.'

Reade took the hand in his and gave it a gentle shake. 'Thank you for meeting with us this evening.'

'Of course. I'd say it was my pleasure, but who takes pleasure in meeting with the police?' she observed with a rich, Virginia drawl. 'Please take a seat.'

Reade and Tish followed Dixie's instructions and sat in a pair of leopard-printed occasional chairs on the side of the room opposite the mirror.

'Hank,' Dixie addressed the bartender, 'could you bring me a martini? Sheriff, Ms Tarragon, can I get you anything?'

Reade and Tish declined the offer.

'Suit yourselves.' Dixie shrugged as Hank left the room, shutting the door behind him. 'Now then, you wanted to ask me about Sheriff Carney?'

'That's right. As you know, Carney was the sheriff in charge of your niece's murder case. He was killed last night,' Reade explained.

'That's unfortunate. I'd spoken with Sheriff Carney recently, but I fail to see what his death has to do with me.'

'Carney's body was found at the Honeycutt family plot.'

Dixie was visibly rattled by the news. She retrieved a silver case from the dressing table behind her and selected a cigarette from it. Placing the cigarette in her mouth, she paused before igniting it with a silver lighter. On the wall above her was posted a *No Smoking* sign.

'The manager lets me smoke in here,' Dixie told Reade. 'Unless you want to write me a ticket.'

'Not my jurisdiction,' he replied with a wry smile.

'I do like a man with a sense of humor,' she purred before taking a long drag of her cigarette. 'Now, what were you saying about Mr Carney?'

'His body was discovered at the Honeycutt burial plot in Ashton Courthouse,' Reade repeated.

Dixie shrugged. 'It's a crazy world. There are lots of people out there who'd do anything for notoriety or kicks. There was a nut some years ago who came forward and claimed he'd killed Daisy and not my sister. He was locked up in the loony bin where he belonged, thank goodness.'

'I agree that there's a small chance this might be a copycat murder or a murder for notoriety,' Reade conceded. 'However, as you just acknowledged, Gadsden Carney had recently launched a personal investigation into Daisy's killing.'

'Yes, I know. Mr Carney told me about the investigation when he called me a few weeks back.'

'What else did he say to you?'

'He asked me questions. Questions you're about to ask me again,' Dixie scoffed. 'Can't understand why. My sister confessed, was sentenced, and went to prison where she later died. Seems straightforward to me.'

'Perhaps it is. However, I owe it to Gadsden Carney to follow through with his investigation and see where it leads.'

'In case one of us killed him?' Dixie smirked. 'You're a little transparent, Sheriff.'

'Good. As a law enforcement officer, it's beneficial to have strong, clear communication skills. Now, if you wouldn't mind telling us where you were yesterday evening,' Reade prompted.

'I was at home. This place was booked for a retirement dinner, so there was no floorshow.'

'Were you alone?'

'Why, Sheriff, that's quite a personal question, don't you think?' Dixie smirked.

Reade merely raised his eyebrows in response, spurring Dixie to reply with a sigh, 'Yes, I was alone. I ordered some Chinese for delivery.'

'From which restaurant?'

'Ginger Taste over on Cary Street.'

'At what time?'

'About seven o'clock.'

'And afterwards?'

'I drank wine and watched a *Real Housewives* marathon on TV.'

Reade made notes on a tablet. 'How about the day of Daisy's death? What do you remember from that day?'

'Again?' Dixie took another long drag on her cigarette and exhaled. 'Not sure what else to tell you about that, Sheriff. There was a big barbecue at Delilah and Benton's house – Washington wheelers-and-dealers mostly, plus a few friends of my sister's. I was already living here in Richmond at the time, but I went down to Cypress Hollow for the barbecue and to spend some time with the kids. Daisy was her usual self that day – singing, laughing, running around, talking all the time. As the barbecue was winding down, I walked down to the stables for a cigarette – my sister didn't permit smoking around the children or the house. When I got back, I heard the sound of sobbing and followed it to the garage. Benton, John McIlveen, and Frank Heritage were all there, watching Delilah as she sobbed and cradled a child in her arms. It was Daisy. She was dead. That's all that kept going through my head until the police came: *Daisy's dead. Daisy's dead. Daisy's dead.* I simply couldn't believe it. None of us could.'

'And what about prior to the discovery of Daisy's body? Did anything unusual occur?'

'No. It was like all the other Fourth of July barbecues Delilah and Benton held. Boring, boring, and more boring,' she sang before taking another puff. 'The food was good, but the company only discussed children, politics, and business.'

'And what about the day before the barbecue?' Tish asked. 'Did anything happen then?'

'No,' Dixie answered, her voice resolute, even though Tish and Reade both knew she was lying. 'Nothing apart from my sister's usual pre-party hysteria.'

'Hysteria?' Reade repeated, clearly saving the revelation of the sisters' argument until later in the conversation.

'Hysteria might be an exaggeration, but not by much. Delilah always needed things to be just so. She put a good deal of stock in other people's opinions, and if things weren't perfect, she'd lose it. When we were kids, she'd fret over getting less than an A on a test. If her hair didn't fall exactly into place, she'd refuse to go to school. When she got married to Benton and was in the eye of the Washington elite, her need for perfection intensified. She wanted to be the best wife and mother in the capital. She gave up her singing and dedicated herself to Benton's senatorial campaign, she sent the kids to private accredited nursery schools, she joined the PTA, and she hosted the best parties. And if you stood in the way of Delilah being the best, she'd tear your head off.'

'She ever try to tear your head off?' Tish asked.

'We're sisters. What do you think?' Dixie replied and took

another puff on the cigarette. 'We were also polar opposites. Whereas Delilah worried about her reputation, I had no reputation to protect.'

'Is that why the senator broke up with you and married Delilah?'

'Been doing your homework, I see,' she noted with a gleam in her eye. 'You need to understand that Benton was first and foremost a politician. His career meant everything to him. He wouldn't let anything stand in his way of being a success and, yes, that included me. I was a wild child back then and Benton loved it – he was reserved and staid, although there was something wild in him, too – but he knew he'd never make it very far in Washington with me by his side, so he broke things off with the promise that we might rekindle things once we'd sown our oats. We'd only been apart three weeks when Delilah made her move. Benton was exactly the kind of man she'd been looking for – someone with ambition and lofty goals. Someone who wanted to project a certain image.'

'Viola Tilley said Delilah and Benton's meeting was a coincidence,' Tish stated.

Dixie smiled. 'Viola's a sweet woman. She'd never say a bad word about anyone if she could help it, least of all Delilah.'

That sixty-four-year-old Dixie was still accusing their eighty-six-year-old nanny of favoring Delilah was a testament to the depths of the sisters' rivalry.

'Then how *did* the senator and Delilah meet?' Reade asked.

'Delilah flashed Benton a sweet smile and invited him to watch her sing, of course. She was singing at a club in DC. The same club where she and I used to perform together until Delilah broke up our act because she disapproved of me drinking and smoking with club patrons after our gigs. Delilah could be very persuasive when she wanted something. Benton didn't stand a chance. But neither did Delilah – Benton wasn't at all ready to settle down.'

Hank the bartender had returned with Dixie's requested martini. She stubbed out her cigarette in an adjacent ashtray, accepted the drink, and immediately took a sip. 'Are you two sure you wouldn't like a drink? Or a cigarette?'

Again, Tish and Reade declined and Hank returned to his duties.

'If Benton wasn't ready to settle down, then why did he marry Delilah?' Tish asked once Hank had left the room.

'Simple. Delilah promised to dedicate herself to Benton and his career. With her, she said, he might even become president.'

'Quite the promise.'

'Yes, but Benton was extremely bright and talented. And Delilah was devoted to promoting him – for a time.'

'What happened?'

Dixie took another sip of martini and smacked her lips together. 'The children happened. Nothing much changed after Walker James was born. Benton was happy to have an heir – someone to carry on the Honeycutt name – but he wasn't very hands-on as a father. Delilah loved being a mother, but she was still dedicated to the campaign. When Daisy was born, however, everything stopped.

'Daisy was Delilah's mini-me – blonde, blue-eyed, beautiful,' Dixie continued. 'Walker James was loved by his parents, but Daisy was the favorite child – there's no other way to say it. Benton loved to trot her out on stage after speeches and Delilah would dress her up for photo ops. The crowd always loved Daisy. When Delilah discovered that Daisy could also sing, well, that completely changed everything. Delilah's focus shifted from Benton's career to Daisy's almost overnight. Having given up on performing herself, Delilah was determined that her daughter would have the singing career she never had.'

'How did that go over?' Tish asked.

'About as well as you'd expect. Not only was Benton angry that Delilah had stepped back from his publicity machine, but he made it clear, in no uncertain terms, that no Honeycutt would make their living by performing music for the great unwashed masses.'

Reade lifted a dubious eyebrow.

'Not his exact words, of course, Sheriff. But definitely his attitude.' Dixie extracted the olive from her Martini and munched on it.

'So it's safe to say that the senator and Delilah's marriage was in trouble,' Reade asserted.

'Very much so,' Dixie confirmed. 'When I arrived at Cypress Hollow for the Fourth of July weekend, Delilah was distraught because she had reason to believe that Benton was having an affair. It shouldn't have come as much of a surprise to her, what with Benton living in DC during the week and only coming home to

her and the kids on weekends, but it did. Add her marital strain
to her usual pre-party hysteria and she was in a real state.'

'Is that when the two of you argued – when you arrived at
Cypress Hollow the day before the party?'

'Yes, I'd only been at the house twenty minutes when Delilah
whisked me off to her bedroom so we could talk. She was frantic.
Earlier that week, she'd been worried and couldn't sleep, so she
got out of bed and called Benton at the Georgetown brownstone.
While they were on the phone, Delilah heard a woman's voice in
the background.'

'Could it have been the television?' Tish suggested.

'That's what I thought, but no. Delilah was positive there was
someone in the room with Benton.'

'Did she ask him who it was?'

'No.' Dixie shook her head and belted back the rest of her drink.
'She just leaped to the worst possible conclusion. Although, to be
fair, one o'clock in the morning was a little late in the evening
for Benton to have company.'

'Senators can work through the night at times.'

'True, but Congress had already adjourned for the summer, so
that wasn't very likely. The morning after the phone call, Delilah
went to the head of her church in search of spiritual advice on the
matter and he suggested that she and Benton attend couples'
therapy.'

'Did they attend?'

'No, that's why she was so crazed that afternoon. She had called
Benton the night before to discuss the possibility of attending a
therapy session over the weekend, but he flat-out refused. Of
course, my sister didn't tell him why she wanted to go to therapy.
I told Delilah that she needed to tell Benton what she'd overheard.
They needed to get it all out in the open, so that they could either
work past it or decide to move on. Well, at the mention of moving
on, Delilah really lost it. She kept saying that she wasn't going to
lose everything because of one stupid mistake.'

'A stupid mistake? That's an odd way to categorize your
husband's affair.'

'Yeah, well, I don't think she was half as concerned about losing
her husband as she was about her family's reputation. If Benton
was having an affair and word got out about it, she could no longer

pretend they were a perfect family. Delilah simply couldn't bear the thought of that happening.'

'Is that when the argument started?'

'Yes, Delilah let me have it with both barrels. She called me insensitive and uncaring and told me I didn't understand her situation – how lonely she was at Cypress Hollow – and the pressure she was under. Well' – Dixie gave a sharp laugh – 'I didn't hold my tongue as well as I probably should have. I'd spent that morning with my attorney filing bankruptcy papers because my second husband had run off with my entire inheritance, so I wasn't much in the mood for hearing about the burdens of being a wealthy senator's wife.'

'What did you say to her?'

'I, um . . .' Dixie drew a deep breath and wiped the tears from her eyes. 'I was horrible to her. There's no other way to put it. We'd argued all our lives, Delilah and me, but that argument was exceptionally brutal. I don't remember every single word I said. I was so full of hurt and anger over my own situation that it all came pouring out, but I remember telling Delilah that her problems were payback for stealing Benton away from me and then . . . then I told her that I hoped she lost everything. I told her that I hoped she lost her marriage, her kids, and her home.

'Those were some of the last words I ever said to her,' Dixie went on, her voice cracking. 'She and I didn't speak to each other at all on the day of the party and then that evening – well, Daisy was gone.'

'You didn't speak to her during the investigation or during her sentencing?' Reade asked.

Dixie shook her head. 'Police cordoned off the house as a crime scene. The McIlveens went home and I went to stay at a nearby B and B while Delilah, Benton, and Walker James stayed with their friends, the Heritages. I was going to drive over to the Heritages' the next morning to check in, but before I was even dressed, I got a call from one of the attorneys Benton had hired. I was ordered to drive straight home to Richmond and not speak to anyone. If the police had questions for me, they had been instructed to go through the attorney. If reporters had questions for me, they were to go through the PR firm Benton had hired to represent the family.'

'So you were represented by the PR firm, too?'

'That's right.'

'Do you know why?'

'Well, back then I thought it was because Benton wanted to cover up the fact that he was having an affair. Priscilla was at the barbecue the day Daisy died. Seeing the two of them together removed any doubts I might have had about Delilah's accusations.'

'And now?' Reade prompted.

'It's obvious they were desperate to conceal the fact that Delilah was the killer.'

'So you believe your sister was guilty,' Tish presumed.

'Doesn't everyone?' Dixie shrugged.

'We thought you might have a different perspective on the matter.'

'Because I knew her so well?' Dixie gave a sardonic laugh. 'I did know her. I knew her probably better than anyone. I knew that Delilah's life was falling apart. I knew her marriage to Benton was on the skids. I knew that the two of them had been living apart both physically and emotionally for years. I know that less than six hours after Daisy's death, the two of them hired lawyers and a public relations firm to handle requests from the police and the press. I also know that less than twelve hours after Daisy's death, they left the Heritages' home and locked themselves up in their Sullivan's Island vacation home. I know that two weeks after Daisy's death, Delilah and Benton bundled Walker James off to a boarding school in Europe. I know that I was ordered to never call or speak to them and to never mention the murder case again. But what I know most of all is that Delilah confessed. That confession destroyed everything she had worked so hard to build – the image of the perfect mother, the perfect wife, the perfect family. From that moment on, she was a child killer and no one would ever think of her as anything else. Delilah would never have put herself in that position if she hadn't been guilty. It was, I can only imagine, a fate worse than prison.'

The trio fell silent. After several seconds had elapsed, Reade spoke up. 'Prior to Delilah's confession, who did you think murdered Daisy?'

The question took Dixie by surprise. 'What do you mean?'

'Police had been investigating Daisy's death for months when Delilah confessed. During that time, you must have had some theory as to who did it.'

'I did,' she admitted.

'And?'

Dixie exhaled noisily. 'It's ridiculous to say anything knowing what we know now. I mean, what's the point?'

'The point is that Gadsden Carney has been found murdered at the Honeycutt family plot weeks after he began re-examining the case.'

'OK,' she capitulated. 'When Daisy was found dead, my mind went immediately to Priscilla.'

'Priscilla?' Tish repeated. 'Why?'

'The way she behaved that day at the barbecue. It was clear she'd set her sights on Benton, but it was also abundantly clear that she had zero intention of sharing him with the children. It wasn't so obvious with Walker James – but then again, he was introverted and shy and didn't hang around the party very much – but it was quite plain to see whenever Daisy was around.'

'What did Priscilla do?'

'It wasn't so much what Priscilla did. It was her attitude toward Daisy. She looked at her with such contempt. It actually reached a point where I felt the need to intervene, so I shooed Daisy away and told her not to go near Priscilla again.'

'What were you afraid Priscilla might do if you hadn't intervened?'

'I don't know.' Dixie shook her head. 'I just didn't like the way she looked at Daisy. It was obvious she hated the girl.'

'Hated her enough to kill her?' Reade prompted.

'Yes, I thought so at the time. When I finally gave a statement – through Benton's attorney – I told the police about it.'

'Yes, I saw that you mentioned Priscilla. It doesn't appear that anyone acted on that information.'

'Of course not,' she scoffed. 'I'm sure they thought I was just lashing out because Priscilla was a home wrecker.'

'What about now? If Delilah hadn't confessed – if the case were still open – would you still consider Priscilla a suspect?' Reade posed.

'Yes, I would,' Dixie answered without hesitation. 'Priscilla wanted Benton all to herself. No wife, no kids. And she got him.'

'Benton still had a son. What about Walker James?' Tish questioned.

'Like I said earlier, Benton and Delilah sent him off to Europe shortly after Daisy's death. I don't know all the details of the years in between, but when I heard that Delilah had died, I called Benton and he spoke to me for a brief time. It was the first time we'd spoken since the barbecue. I asked about my sister's funeral and whether or not Walker James had attended. Benton told me that Walker James was still overseas and that he only came home for two weeks at Christmas. Even his summers were spent at that school, taking part in some special accelerated program. So, you see, Priscilla got precisely what she wanted: Benton Honeycutt on a platter, with no strings attached.'

'And you? Did you get what you wanted?' Reade asked.

'No, I did not, Sheriff,' Dixie replied as she polished off her martini and blinked back tears. 'I fully understand what's implied by your question, but I most definitely did not get what I wanted. When I said what I did to Delilah that day, I was coming from an angry, bitter place. I wanted Delilah to suffer the way I had suffered. I wanted her to know the pain of a difficult marriage because I had known two of them, but I never once wished harm on her or the children. I loved Daisy and Walker James as if they were my own – clichéd perhaps, but true. I was thirty-nine and life hadn't afforded me much opportunity to raise a child, so I lavished attention and affection on those two. Birthdays, Christmas, and summer breaks – even Halloween – always found me at Cypress Hollow with Delilah and the kids. Sometimes Benton was there, sometimes not. Sometimes Delilah and I would bicker – mostly over petty nonsense – but most of the time we laughed and enjoyed the kids, and sang, and had fun. I didn't realize it then, but those days spent at Cypress Hollow would be some of the happiest days of my life.

'When Daisy was murdered,' Dixie continued, her voice trembling, 'that all disappeared. I lost the only family I'd ever had. I was suddenly and terribly alone.'

'What about Walker James?' Tish asked. 'Have you ever tried contacting him?'

'No.' Dixie frowned. 'When Walker James was young, Benton forbade me from contacting him. Now that Walker James is a grown man . . . well, aside from the fact that I don't know how to reach him, I also wouldn't know what to say. The last time I saw him was at the barbecue; he was just ten years old. I was tempted to track Walker James down after Benton's death – just to reach out and let him know he wasn't entirely alone in the world – but, once again, I couldn't figure out what to say. Does he remember me? Does he remember what happened at the barbecue? Or has he managed to put the past behind him and move on? If he has moved on, I have no place reminding him of the terrible events of that day. Walker James has the right to forget and be happy. He shouldn't be haunted – haunted like the rest of us.'

# NINE

Reade steered the black SUV along the winding, wooded highway that led back to Hobson Glen. After spending over thirty minutes in Dixie's smoke-filled nightclub dressing room, they'd opted to drive home with the windows open, allowing the fresh, warm air to dispel the scent of cigarettes from their clothing and nostrils.

Tish leaned back against the headrest and watched out of the passenger window as the setting sun slowly dipped below the treetops, drenching the world in a splash of golden light as it began its final descent. The feeling of the wind in her hair combined with the oncoming twilight reminded her of the drives she and her parents would take on hot summer evenings when she was young. With only a pair of box fans to cool their bedrooms, the Lynch family would pile into their brown Ford LTD and zip along the local roads, counting the roadside rabbits who would leave their brush homes at sunset to graze.

Her thoughts traveled to the Honeycutt children. Had Daisy, in her six short years, known such simple pleasures? What about Walker James? Being shipped off to boarding school a couple of weeks after his baby sister was killed – just when he needed his family the most – must have been a traumatic upheaval for the ten-year-old.

'You're quiet,' Reade noted.

'I'm thinking how Daisy's death impacted so many lives. Viola and the McIlveens lost their jobs, Walker James was sent away from everything and everyone he loved, and Dixie Dupree lost her entire family.'

'It's incredibly sad,' he agreed. 'But I'm not quite ready to strike Dixie from our suspect list.'

'You don't believe her story?'

'I'm not sure. Her grief seems genuine, but I can't overlook the fact that she threatened Delilah – and, indirectly, Daisy – the day before Daisy was murdered. I also can't overlook the fact that when asked about that argument, her initial reaction was to downplay the whole event.'

'And yet Dixie's on stage singing the songs she and Delilah sang when they were younger. That's awfully nostalgic.'

'One could also view it as an admission of guilt,' Reade contended. 'The same could be said about her reluctance to reach out to Walker James. It's difficult to look your nephew in the eye when you know you're responsible for destroying his family.'

'Wishing that your sister loses her family doesn't make it so,' Tish said.

'What if Dixie did more than just wish?'

'You think she killed Daisy?'

Reade shrugged. 'It's a possibility. And then she murdered Carney when he got too close to the truth.'

'But what about Delilah? Why would she confess to a crime she didn't commit?'

'Guilt. Delilah took Benton away from Dixie, leaving her to fumble through two failed marriages, one of which left her financially ruined.'

'So Dixie killed Daisy, Delilah took the blame to make up for what she did to Dixie, and now Dixie killed Carney because he was getting too close to the truth?' Tish bit her lip. 'I suppose it's possible. Having met with her lawyer that morning, Dixie must have been in a terrible emotional state when she arrived at Cypress Hollow for the holiday weekend. The argument with Delilah might have sent her over the edge. The question is why would Benton allow Delilah to confess?'

'Who said he did? Delilah might not have told him. Remember, she was furious with him for bringing Priscilla to the barbecue and refusing to attend therapy sessions.'

'That's true. Delilah's marriage was falling apart. Her daughter was dead. Going to prison probably paled in comparison with the losses she'd endured. The only thing I don't get is why the senator would take Delilah's confession at face value. Delilah had no history of violence toward either of the children. Benton obviously felt safe leaving them alone with her and Viola while he lived and worked in Washington. Why would he believe her capable of such a thing?'

'According to both Dixie and Viola, Delilah was in quite a state that day,' Reade pointed out. 'The senator must have noticed that his wife wasn't herself.'

'Not necessarily. The day of Daisy's murder, the senator and Priscilla arrived at Cypress Hollow just before Viola left and just as the caterers were setting up for the barbecue,' Tish reminded. 'I highly doubt that image-conscious Delilah would have made a scene with the house full of strangers.'

'Especially the caterers,' Reade smirked. 'Those people can be real troublemakers.'

Tish shot him a nasty look. 'Cute,' she remarked, prompting Reade to burst into laughter.

'Seriously, though,' Reade said when he'd regained his composure. 'You're right. Delilah wouldn't have wanted anyone who wasn't family to overhear her meltdown. It would have tarnished her Hostess-with-the-Mostest-Number-One-Mom reputation.'

'I doubt the senator would have liked the gossip, either.'

'If you don't like gossip, don't bring your mistress to the family barbecue,' Reade stated.

'Yes, about that,' Tish started. 'Don't you find it strange that Benton would bring Priscilla to Cypress Hollow? If they were having an affair, why would he parade her in front of his family and colleagues like that? Wouldn't they try to keep the affair hidden?'

'Maybe the senator didn't think anyone would suspect what was going on.'

'Maybe, but why even take the chance of someone catching on? If the senator really wanted to see Priscilla over the weekend, the smart thing would have been for Priscilla to stay in Washington while Benton made some excuse to get back to town early. Taking her to the family home so she can be scrutinized by your wife, sister-in-law, and household staff isn't exactly smart.'

'Some men are too arrogant to care. They flaunt their actions and don't give a damn who knows.'

Tish thought back to her father. 'Yes, I've known men like that. I'm not sure Senator Honeycutt was one of them. If he felt that having a daughter on the stage was a dishonor to the family name, I can't imagine he'd think that flaunting an extramarital affair would be beneficial. Also, we have no actual proof that Benton Honeycutt was having an affair with Priscilla Maddox. All we have is Delilah overhearing a female voice during a late-night phone call and the assertion put forth by both Viola Tilley and Dixie Dupree that Priscilla was up to no good.'

'Are you discounting female intuition?'

'Not at all. Just recognizing that there might have been a bit of jealousy or bias behind that intuition. Benton was living the bachelor life in DC when he suddenly brings a much younger woman to Cypress Hollow for the long holiday weekend – a weekend traditionally reserved for summer family fun. Even the most trusting of eyebrows would have been raised in response.'

'Viola Tilley's certainly were,' Reade commented. 'Are you saying Priscilla didn't have her eye on Benton?'

'No, I'm saying that even if Priscilla Maddox did have designs on Benton, that doesn't mean there was necessarily anything going on between them. At least not at that particular point in time.'

'Yet years later they got married,' Reade argued.

'Yes, but they might have grown closer after Daisy's death. They spent, what, forty, fifty, sixty hours a week together? When Delilah was put in jail, Priscilla probably comforted him. When did Benton divorce Delilah anyway?'

'He didn't.'

Tish was incredulous. 'Wait. You mean the senator remained married to Delilah even after she confessed to killing their child?'

'Yep, until the day she died.'

'Really? I'd have thought the senator would have distanced himself from his wife after she confessed. I don't know how he could have stayed married to the person who killed his daughter. Was his decision a religious one?'

'No idea. It's not in the files I found back at headquarters. Maybe Gadsden turned up something on it, but I won't have his personal paperwork until tomorrow. Might be a question for Priscilla, though. She has a condo on the James River. I've arranged for us to meet with her tomorrow after the café closes and you've prepared the next day's bake, if you're free.'

'Absolutely. In light of Dixie's account of the barbecue, I'm eager to hear Priscilla's thoughts on Daisy.'

'Even if Dixie's right, I doubt Priscilla will admit to hating the girl,' Reade said.

'I don't know. It's been twenty-five years. How old is Priscilla now? Fifty?'

'About that.'

'That's a lot of water under the bridge. The perspective of a passionate twenty-five-year-old is far different from that of a mature, worldly woman. Priscilla might not admit to hating Daisy, but she might admit to being jealous of her. Daisy wasn't just Delilah's favorite; she was Benton's, too. After not seeing him all week, Daisy might have commanded quite a bit of her father's time and attention.'

'Well, we'll find out tomorrow. I also scheduled some time with Frank and Louella Heritage. They're – and I quote – "summering" at their residence overlooking the pro golf course at Coleton Creek.'

'Summering? And where do they winter? Florida?'

'Palm Beach.'

'Of course. Well, I won't hold my breath waiting for those two to come to the café for breakfast,' Tish wisecracked.

'Hey, you never know. Your breakfast burritos are legendary in these parts.'

'Do people who use the word "summer" as a verb even eat breakfast burritos?'

'Sure. They just eat them with a knife and fork.'

Tish laughed. 'Silver or goldplate?'

'I don't know. Which works best in a summer home set by a golf course?'

'Hmm, I'm thinking McMansion, so probably gold,' she guessed.

'Sounds about right. When we finish with the Heritages, we'll travel to the other side of the tracks,' Reade continued. 'John and Lucille McIlveen still live in Ashton Courthouse, but they lost their home back in 2008 due to the housing market crash and now live in a trailer near a business park.'

'Interesting,' Tish mused aloud.

'What is?'

'Benton Honeycutt ensured that Viola Tilley was taken care of in her old age; meanwhile, it would appear that he did nothing to help the McIlveens. Strange, don't you think?'

'Now that you mention it, yeah. We'll see what we can find out from them.'

'And if you're not satisfied with their answer, we can always pay Viola Tilley another visit and see what she has to say. She wouldn't at all mind seeing *you* again,' Tish added with a grin.

Reade leveled her a look. 'She wouldn't mind seeing you, either. Ms Tilley was simply happy to have company. She doesn't get many visitors.'

'Uh-huh. I'm sure that was it,' she wisecracked.

'Come on now,' Reade urged. 'She's a nice lady.'

'She is,' Tish agreed, deciding not to tease Reade any further. 'She's also the only person we've met so far who has a concrete alibi for Gadsden Carney's murder.'

'It doesn't bode well for a case when the only person with an alibi is in assisted living, does it?'

'I wouldn't go that far. We haven't spoken to everyone yet.'

Reade nodded. 'I'm lining up interviews with the rest of our cast of characters. Retired Officer Aldrich is on tap for the day after tomorrow. So is Bishop Dillard – yep, Reverend Dillard is now a bishop. I have a call in to Walker James Honeycutt, to try to fit him in the same day, but I haven't received a reply. Walker owns a tremendously successful software development company. Remember a couple years back when Historic Jamestown brought all their archives online to create a virtual museum? It was Walker James's company that created the site. His company now uses that same technology to create a line of hugely popular video games, which Walker played a role in designing – even though Walker himself is allegedly a bit of a recluse.'

'Considering the trauma Walker experienced during childhood,

can you blame him for wanting to hide away from the world?'
Tish observed.

'I know. Part of me hates to have to tell him about Carney.
Another death associated with his sister's murder is probably the
last thing he needs in his life.'

'He must have heard the news by now. Maybe that's why he
hasn't replied to your call.'

'Could be,' Reade allowed. 'Although I think it's more likely
that he's just incredibly busy.'

'I'm sure you're right. He's probably on a ridiculously tight
schedule. If Walker James does call you and says he can meet
with you during a time when I'm unavailable, just go on without
me,' she instructed.

'Not going to happen. I'm going to aim for whenever you're free.
I didn't ask you to be a consultant just to leave you at the café. Nor
did I ask you to be a consultant to take you away from your business. I'm going to do my best to schedule important interviews for
when you can attend them. If Carney's murder is, in fact, linked to
Daisy's, then Walker James could be our most important witness.
He was in the house when Daisy's body was found in the garage
and he was privy to his parents' actions those days immediately
following her death. Even though he was just a kid when everything
transpired, he might be able to give us some insight into his mother's
guilt or innocence. Insight he might not have had as a child.'

'Insight he couldn't possibly share until now because his father
had the entire household sworn to secrecy,' Tish added.

'Of course, like Dixie said, we have no idea what, if anything,
Walker James remembers. He might have purged the whole thing
from his memory.'

'Or it might have been purged for him,' she suggested. 'What
better way to ensure your son doesn't talk about a painful event
than to erase his memories of it?'

'There's certainly that chance, and yet, with Delilah and
the senator dead, Walker James is the closest we'll ever get to
interviewing his parents,' Reade said.

'True, unless . . .'

Reade's eyes narrowed. 'You're not going to arrange a séance
with Leah Harmon, are you?'

'That might be interesting,' she said brightly. 'But no, I was thinking that Channel Ten is the largest local news station in our area. I could ask Jules if they have some archived interviews with the Honeycutts. It's not the same as you and I asking the questions but watching some footage of them might give us a better picture of Delilah and Benton than relying strictly upon police files and other people's memories.'

'That's a brilliant idea. I have transcripts of police interviews with the Honeycutts, but they don't take note of their reactions or their tone of voice. Also, Officer Clayton just completed a five-day course in reading micro-expressions. We'll have him watch the footage with us and see if he picks up on anything.'

'I'll text Jules tonight,' she promised as the SUV pulled to a halt in the café parking lot.

'Great,' Reade approved. 'And, uh, thanks.'

'No problem. It *is* my job now, isn't it?'

'I wasn't just thanking you for that. I was thanking you for everything you did this evening. It was nice' – he paused as if struggling to find the right words – 'having you as a partner.'

'Yeah, it was nice.' She sighed. Fearing Reade might find her callous, she hastily added, 'I mean to be working with you, not to be investigating your friend's murder.'

He smiled. 'I understood what you meant.'

'Good. I didn't want you to think I was a ghoul or something.' She punctuated the statement with an awkward chuckle.

'That was the furthest thing from my mind,' he assured her.

'Oh.' As she stared into Reade's eyes, she felt her face grow warmer and wondered if she should kiss him, if only on the cheek and if only to thank him for a wonderful dinner. Oddly enough, the expression on his face indicated that he probably wouldn't mind if she did. Still, remembering their business arrangement, Tish thought better of it. 'I'll, um, I'll see you tomorrow.'

'Same time as today?'

Tish thought about the next day's tasks – the Hunger Games party quote and a menu for a wedding at the end of August. Fortunately, Thursdays were quiet enough to allow her to get paperwork done during regular business hours. 'Yes, four thirty works really well. But I'll see you at breakfast first. My dad will be here, but I'll still pop by and say "hello," just in case you have some news.'

'Cool. Until then, sleep well.' Reade bid Tish goodnight and, as had become his custom, watched until she was safely behind the locked door of the café before driving out of the parking lot.

Tish waved out the window and moved to the industrial-grade kitchen, where a pajama-clad Mary Jo stood behind the stove with pancake turner in hand. 'Hey,' she greeted. 'How was your night?'

Tish grabbed a drinking glass from the shelf over the sink and poured herself a glass of water from the tap. 'Off to a slow start. We interviewed three people associated with the Honeycutt case, but none of them moved us any closer to finding Gadsden Carney's killer. How are things here?'

'Good. Just making the kids some grilled cheese as a study snack. Want me to fix you one?'

Tish drank a few sips of water. 'No, thanks. I'm still full from dinner.'

'Oh? Did you stop for something quick on the way home?'

'No, Clemson took me to a seafood restaurant called Justine's. It's on the Canal Walk.'

Mary Jo looked up from the skillet of grilled cheese sandwiches. 'Dinner on the Canal Walk? Nice. How was it?'

'It was wonderful. The food and service were excellent and our table was right on the canal.'

'Ooh,' Mary Jo cooed. 'Sounds like someone was trying to impress you.'

'Hmm? No, it wasn't like that at all,' Tish scoffed. 'Clemson thought we should celebrate my new consultant's position, so he took me to one of his favorite spots. He and his band play there once a month. I told him maybe I'd drive over and give them a listen next time they play.'

'You should. Sounds like fun.' Mary Jo returned her attention to the cast-iron skillet. 'Sheriff Reade is rather good-looking, don't you think?'

'I suppose, if you like that type.' Tish sidestepped the question. She wasn't about to tell Mary Jo that she had been gazing admiringly at him during dinner and the ride home.

'And you're single,' Mary Jo added.

'Newly single,' Tish corrected.

'Oh, come on. It's been three months since you broke up with Schuyler.'

'Which isn't a lot of time, MJ. Rushing into another relationship isn't exactly smart, especially considering that rushing is what broke Schuyler and me up in the first place.'

'What do you mean rushing broke you up? When you met Schuyler, you hadn't dated anyone in years,' Mary Jo argued.

'Yes, but then after a few months of dating, Schuyler rushed me into moving in with him. I should never have let that happen,' Tish lamented.

'You didn't let it happen – you had no choice. You'd been shot and needed a ground-floor living space in which to recover. But that doesn't matter. I'm not suggesting you move in with Reade. I'm just saying that he's nice.'

'He is nice,' Tish agreed. 'Very nice. That's why I enjoy working with him and why I want to continue working with him. What if we were to date and it didn't work out? It could ruin everything.'

'Aha,' Mary Jo exclaimed as she flipped the sandwiches in the skillet. 'So you don't actually object to the idea of dating Reade; you're just afraid of the outcome.'

Tish exhaled noisily. 'No, I don't object—'

Mary Jo emitted a squeal and clapped her hands together.

'But it's not entirely up to me, is it?' Tish went on before her friend could interrupt. 'Clemson has a say in the matter, too, you know. He might not think of me that way. Or he might feel the same way I do – that it's not worth jeopardizing a great working relationship for the uncertainty of romance. Reade trusts me enough to have hired me as a consultant. I don't want things becoming weird and awkward between us. More importantly, I'm not sure I want to date anyone right now. During the last few weeks of our relationship, Schuyler pushed me to limit the amount of time I spent here at the café. Now that he's gone, I'm enjoying being back at work and making plans for the future of my business. This café has been my dream for years and it's the reason I moved to Hobson Glen in the first place, remember?'

'There's more to life than work, Tish.'

'I'm well aware of that. And when the time is right, I'll take action. I promise. Until then, you and Jules will just have to enjoy having me all to yourselves again.'

It was Mary Jo's turn to sigh. 'Well, if we must,' she teased with a roll of her eyes. 'Oh, hey, before I forget, your dad stopped by earlier.'

'Here? At the café?'

'Yes, he came by this evening just before suppertime. He said to tell you something came up and he can't make it to breakfast tomorrow.'

Tish quietly sipped her water, but she was full of questions.

'You OK?' Mary Jo asked after several seconds of silence had elapsed.

'Yeah,' she replied although the tone of her voice implied otherwise.

Mary Jo placed the grilled cheese sandwiches on to two plates, moved the skillet from the burner, and switched off the heat. 'Come with me. We'll talk more upstairs.'

Tish followed her friend through the kitchen and up the back staircase to the two-bedroom apartment above. Gregory was seated cross-legged on the living-room carpet, his back against the pull-out sofa that served as his bed, his books and laptop sprawled across the top of the rectangular oak coffee table before him.

Mary Jo cleared a spot on the table and deposited one of the two plates on to it. 'Grilled cheese. Eat it while it's hot.'

Gregory murmured a thank you and looked up, briefly, from his studies. 'Hey, Aunt Tish.'

'Hi, sweetie,' Tish answered. 'Don't let me interrupt you. Just go on studying so you can pass that exam. I have two trays of ziti and five dozen meatballs in the freezer waiting for your graduation party.'

'Don't worry. I'm not going to miss it.'

'Good,' Tish replied with a nod of her head.

Meanwhile, Mary Jo had gone to deliver the second snack to Kayla's bedroom, where the fifteen-year-old was seated at her desk, her back to the door and her dark hair pinned into a bun similar to the type her mother often sported. Mary Jo placed the grilled cheese sandwich on the corner of the desk and, giving her daughter a peck on the cheek, led Tish to her own bedroom. 'Now then, what's going on?'

Tish threw her arms in the air. 'Nothing. Just the usual visit from Dad.'

'What do you mean?'

'I mean that I should know what to expect from my father by now.' Tish flopped backward on to the bed, her feet dangling off one side. 'He comes here, unannounced, for a so-called visit, yet he's too busy to chat when he arrives, too busy to meet me for lunch, and when Clemson suggests he join us for dinner, my father says he has plans in Richmond.'

Mary Jo perched on the edge of the bed alongside Tish's knees. 'And yet he was here in Hobson Glen at dinner time.'

'Cancelling tomorrow's breakfast plans,' Tish completed the statement.

'Your dad's getting older. Maybe he got his times and dates confused.'

'I'd give that theory some credence if this wasn't the way it's always been. My father has never been present in my life, MJ. Even the times he was physically present, his mind and heart were elsewhere.'

'I have to admit thinking to myself that his visit this evening was the longest he and I have ever spoken to each other,' Mary Jo admitted. 'Even though he was only here for ten minutes.'

'Ten minutes in the twenty-plus years we've been friends,' Tish noted.

'I'm sorry, honey.'

'It's OK. I just need to stop expecting things to be different. Remember how he didn't attend the commencement exercises when we graduated from UVM because he had "car trouble"?'

'I do. I also remember him leaving your wedding immediately after the ceremony. What was the reason he couldn't make the reception?'

'He needed to get back to New York because he was having his driveway sealed the next morning,' Tish recalled. 'Because doesn't everyone schedule blacktop repair for the day after their only child gets married?'

Mary Jo shook her head. 'I just don't get how parents can be like that. Those two out there are my life.'

'Yeah, well, as I said, my father has never been very present.'

'I know he and your mom split up for a while when you were very young.'

'They did. He came back when my mother became ill, but his heart was elsewhere. The rest of him, too. We, um, we had a

housekeeper to help out a few hours a week. I came early from
school one afternoon and caught them together.'

Mary Jo gasped. 'In your house? Was your mother there?'

Tish nodded. 'She was bedridden at that point. They were in
the living room. I saw them from the front porch and then turned
right around and ran off. I couldn't say for sure if they saw me,
but my father's behavior changed after that day. He'd smile more
often when I was around, slip me money to spend on myself – as
if he was trying to purchase my silence or something. Or at least
that's how it felt. I might have been imagining his motivation. My
attitude toward him wasn't exactly objective at that point.'

'My God, you poor thing! Why didn't you ever tell me about
this?'

'Because by the time I met you and Jules, I'd kept it secret for
so long, there didn't seem a point in telling anyone.'

'So you never told your mother.'

'No, she was so happy to have my father back. Had she learned
the truth, it would have killed her. Part of me was also afraid
she wouldn't believe me. I harbored some resentment toward my
father for leaving and she might have thought my accusation was
retaliatory, so I kept it to myself.'

'All this time you never told a soul?'

'No . . . well, not until recently. Clemson and I were discussing
why we weren't visiting with family last Christmas and it just
slipped out. I'm not sure why.'

'You commiserated over not seeing your families?'

'Yes, I suppose that's what it was.' She recalled how Clemson
jokingly called himself a commiserator.

Mary Jo sighed and fell back on the bed. 'Do you think that
might be the problem between you and your father? Do you think
maybe he's been keeping his distance from you because he feels
guilty?'

'I couldn't honestly say. I've never confronted him about it. I'm
not even sure that he knows that I know.' Tish gave a sardonic
laugh. 'However, my dead mother apparently does.'

'What?'

Tish told Mary Jo about Leah Harmon's parting words.

'Spooky,' Mary Jo said when Tish had finished.

'Yeah. So since you asked me what was wrong, now you know.'

'Are you going to talk to your dad?'

'I don't know. I don't know what good it would do. As I said, he's always been somewhat absent in my life. I'm not sure if telling him what I saw all those years ago will change that.'

'Well, fortunately, you don't have to make a decision by tomorrow morning. You can take some time and think it over.'

'Thank goodness, because it's been a long day.'

'And while you decide, if you need to talk again, just know I'm here.'

Tish reached over and took Mary Jo's hand in hers. 'Thank you. That means a lot to me. You really helped tonight.'

'I'm glad. By the way, there's a silver lining to your dad's cancellation tomorrow morning. Now you can spend the whole day sleuthing with Reade.'

Tish propped herself up on her elbows and looked at Mary Jo askance. 'What about the café?'

'I put in some extra time with Augusta May last week and my work for the bake-off committee is all caught up,' Mary Jo said, referring to her other part-time jobs. 'So I'm here all day. And Celestine is booked to work from opening until two o'clock. That leaves me alone for just the last little while, which is fine. It's Thursday. It will be quiet except for a few stragglers coming in for an afternoon pick-me-up of coffee or cake. I can prep for the next day's bake while they linger.'

'That doesn't work, MJ. I have a party quote and a wedding menu to prepare tomorrow. Oh, and I need to defrost some brioche to bake as hamburger buns – I'm donating them to the Rotary Club barbecue on Saturday.'

'So, take care of what you need to do first thing in the morning and then meet Reade.'

'Well, if you're sure you'll be OK with everything . . .'

'Absolutely. Tomorrow's also Gregory's and Kayla's last day of finals, so once we close for the day, I can rest and relax.'

'Oh, that's right. Why don't I pick up some dinner on the way home tomorrow? It will be a nice break from cooking for the two of us and an end-of-year treat for the kids.'

Mary Jo sat up. 'That would be fabulous. What are you thinking?'

'The Thai place offers mid-week discounts on takeout orders. How does that sound?'

'Perfect.'

'Cool.' Tish rose from the bed and smoothed her dress over her hips. 'I'll ask Jules if he'd like to join us. I have to text him about something anyway.'

'Work-related?'

'Yeah, I need him to look into some old footage.'

'The Honeycutt case?'

Tish nodded.

'How brutal,' Mary Jo bemoaned. 'I don't envy you this one. That case even made the headlines in California.'

'Yeah, New York, too.'

'How's Reade doing?'

'He's hanging in there. He'll feel a lot better when we solve this thing. That's for sure.'

'And you?'

'I'm OK. I was better before we met that psychic and my father canceled our breakfast, but you're right. I should make the best of tomorrow.'

'Atta girl. By the way, Celestine told me you showered at her place this morning.'

'I did. I was trying to avoid getting involved in the morning melee.'

'Sorry about that. It's been a hectic week, but one that's soon going to end. Until it does, why don't you use this quiet time to take a shower? Even better, take a bath.'

Tish tilted her head backward and felt a pang of tension pain between her shoulder blades. 'You know, a bath sounds really good right about now.'

'There you go. Might as well use tonight to relax and recharge, so tomorrow you'll be feeling and looking your best for your first full day as a consultant. You want me to run the water for you?'

'No, I'm going to text Jules and give Clemson a call first,' Tish replied.

'You're right. Reade probably needs to adjust his plans for tomorrow now that you're available. Oh, I almost forgot to tell you, I got a new bottle of that pale pink nail polish you like so much. After your bath, why don't you give yourself a manicure?' Mary Jo pasted on an innocent smile.

'Thanks, but it's some paperwork, a bath, and then bed for me.'

'Of course. You have a long day ahead.'

'I do,' Tish agreed. Mary Jo's sudden concern regarding her appearance hadn't gone unnoticed 'You know, Jules and I had a secret nickname for you back in college.'

'You did?'

'Yes, "Cellophane" because you can be extremely transparent.'

Mary Jo's jaw dropped open in mock horror as she drew a hand to her chest. 'Me? I'm just looking out for my best friend.'

'I know and I love you for it, but your best friend is fine, so go back to mothering your own little chicks.' With that, Tish turned on one heel and went downstairs to her bedroom to retrieve her nightclothes and tend to the necessary communications.

# TEN

Having decided that Clemson's workplace would afford more quiet and privacy than a table at the café, Tish arrived at the sheriff's office at nine in the morning, bearing two cups of coffee and a *Portrait of the Artist as a Young Ham* breakfast sandwich. With her café duties off the docket, she was free to deviate from her traditional baking and cooking garb of black T-shirt, black pants, and leopard-print loafers. This time, she chose a short-sleeved wrap dress in an alluring shade of peacock blue and a pair of mustard slingbacks. Bogged down by menu planning and estimates, she'd only had time for a quick shower the previous evening but, unbeknownst to Mary Jo, she had polished her nails a pale mauve hue – not because she was seeking to impress Clemson Reade, but because doing so made her feel more confident and put-together.

'Good morning,' she sang as she waltzed into his office. 'I've brought some coffee and your favorite break—'

Tish's voice broke off as she noticed a tall man with dark-blonde hair standing in the corner, his arms crossed tightly in front of his chest. He was dressed in a well-tailored dark-blue suit, white button-down shirt, red tie, and a pair of brown wingtip shoes, and the expression on his face was one of extreme displeasure.

'Hello, Schuyler,' Tish greeted icily. 'Or shall I call you Mayor Thompson?'

'Seeing as you're still renting the café building from me, Schuyler is just fine.'

'I'm sorry to have interrupted the two of you,' she apologized to Reade, who was seated behind his desk, his arms stretched behind his head in apparent frustration. 'The sergeant on duty waved me through.'

'It's fine,' Reade said.

'This actually involves you, too, Tish,' Schuyler stated.

'Me?' a surprised Tish asked.

'Yes, you are a paid consultant for the sheriff's department, are you not?'

'I am,' she confirmed.

'And you are working with Sheriff Reade on the Gadsden Carney murder case, aren't you?'

'Yes.' She flashed a puzzled look at Reade, who shook his head slowly to indicate he had heard about all he wished to hear from Schuyler for one morning.

'There have been grumblings from the Hobson Glen Town Board and the Henrico County Council about the two of you poking your noses into the old Honeycutt case.'

'The Honeycutt case relates directly to Gadsden Carney's murder,' Tish asserted.

'The Honeycutt case is closed and certain, er, concerned parties would like to make sure it remains that way. Since your office, Sheriff Reade, is located here in Hobson Glen, I volunteered to speak to you both on the board and council's behalf.'

*Volunteered? I'm sure you were chomping at the bit*, Tish thought to herself.

'So these "concerned parties" you mention are asking me to overlook the fact that Gadsden Carney's body was found at the Honeycutt family plot,' Reade assumed.

'Not necessarily *overlook*,' Schuyler quibbled, 'but possibly downplay the connection.'

'I haven't even spoken to the media about the connection between the two cases, so I'm not exactly sure how I could downplay it any further, other than to deny there's any connection at all.'

'That's the thing, Sheriff. Apart from the location of Carney's body, there is no actual connection to the Honeycutt case, is there?'

'That's what we're investigating . . . Mr Mayor.' Reade leaned back in his chair and folded his hands on his chest.

'Please, I know I'm here on official business, but let's keep this informal. Call me Schuyler.'

'OK, Schuyler. What, precisely, are you and those concerned parties suggesting?'

'We're not suggesting anything,' Schuyler again equivocated.

Tish, with a roll of her eyes, plopped the cardboard tray of coffee on Reade's desk and served the beverages while they were still hot before taking a seat in an adjacent chair.

'OK, then, what are you and those interested parties inferring, implying, proposing, evoking, or however else you'd care to phrase it?' Reade asked before taking a sip of coffee.

'We're saying that there's absolutely no reason to re-examine the Honeycutt case. Daisy Honeycutt's murderer has been dead for over twenty years and is buried in the cemetery at St Jude's Episcopal Church. This is obviously the work of a sick individual celebrating a twisted anniversary.'

'I disagree with you. The evidence overwhelmingly suggests that Sheriff Gadsden Carney's murder was, in fact, linked to the Honeycutt case, which he had been re-examining, in great detail, in the months prior to his death.'

'*Former* Sheriff Gadsden Carney,' Schuyler corrected, 'was re-examining the case in an unofficial capacity. Neither you nor your office or any other government agency had given him permission to do so.'

'That's correct. According to Carney's files – which arrived yesterday – he was waiting until he'd unearthed enough new evidence before approaching this office to make his request to reopen the case.'

'You are, of course, aware that former Sheriff Carney was suffering from a malignant brain tumor. Given the symptoms associated with his illness, I would think that any of his files, statements, or investigations would be viewed as utterly worthless in the eyes of the law.'

'Perhaps by an attorney,' Reade allowed, 'but not an investigator. I also have it on good authority that Gadsden Carney never suffered from delusions, hallucinations, or any of the myriad of other mind-altering symptoms you're suggesting he experienced.'

'Perhaps not, but a man facing final judgment is going to measure his past actions by a far higher bar than a man with twenty, thirty, even forty years ahead of him. He's going to second-guess things of which he was once certain and see shadows where there are none.'

'So Carney imagined that there was a reason to re-examine the case?' Reade scoffed. 'Sorry, but he was the most leveled-headed man I knew.'

'And yet he was obsessed with the Honeycutt case,' Schuyler was quick to note.

'A case like that will haunt a man. A man with a soul, anyways,' Reade said with a smirk.

At Reade's insult, Tish's eyes grew large, but she sipped her coffee in silence.

Schuyler scowled. 'Let me make it clearer for you, then. The Honeycutt case brought much pain and suffering to the Ashton Courthouse community. These people have since moved on with life and would prefer not to revisit the tragedy that occurred so many years ago.'

'Tell those people not to worry. I understand how painful it might be to relive the events of that fateful day and I promise to be the soul of both sensitivity and discretion.'

'But you're still investigating?'

'Absolutely. Gadsden Carney might have been retired, but he was still a lawman. His murderer needs to be brought to justice. I would think you'd back that position as a government official.'

'I do. However, pursuing the Honeycutt case isn't going to bring justice to anyone. It's a dead-end for everyone involved, including you.'

'Oh?' Reade prompted.

'There are several people in this area – including people who serve on the town board and the council – who think you're no longer the right man for your position. First, there's the matter of a civilian being shot while on your watch.'

Tish leaped from her chair. 'How dare you, Schuyler! How dare you use my injury to intimidate Clemson into dropping this investigation. How dare you even—'

Reade had risen from his spot behind the desk and placed a hand on her shoulder. 'It's OK, Tish. It's OK. Let him say what he has to say so he can leave.'

Schuyler held his hands up in mock surrender. 'Sorry, Tish. I didn't mean to upset you.'

Tish sat back down and drank back a mouthful of coffee. She was so angry her hands were shaking, but Reade stood behind her, one hand on her shoulder, silently assuring her that all would be well.

'Out of deference to Tish, I'll drop that particular topic of conversation,' Schuyler continued. 'Suffice to say your behavior after said incident is even more questionable. Leaving your post for a sabbatical was interpreted by many as an admission of wrongdoing and by others as evidence that you were psychologically unsound – that the event had shaken you.'

Reade returned to his desk. 'It did shake me. If I had lost . . .' he started, then corrected course. Tish had already imagined how the sentence would end, and it sounded strangely and vaguely familiar. 'It would have shaken any law enforcement officer. And any law enforcement officer who'd experienced what I had would have been placed on mandatory leave.'

'That might be true, but you left town without a word to anyone.'

'I wrote a letter to the county council and discussed the situation with my deputies to ensure they were prepared to take my place until an interim sheriff could be secured,' Reade explained. 'I may not have issued personal "goodbyes" but I followed protocol to the letter.'

'Hmph,' Schuyler grunted skeptically. 'Then there's the matter of you taking a knee at last month's Black Lives Matter protest.'

'What's wrong with that?' Reade challenged.

'Nothing, except certain people viewed the act as being inappropriate for someone in your position. What if the protest had ended violently? You would have been seen as endorsing it.'

'Oh, come on! It's inappropriate for a policeman to take a knee in solidarity? Those were mothers, fathers, students, and families gathered for social justice. There was no risk of violence. When you report back to your buddies, tell them that next week I'll be marching in the local gay pride parade as well. Why? Because I want everyone who lives within my jurisdiction to know that I am here to serve and protect them. Each and every one of them, not just "concerned parties" like the ones who have your ear.'

'So that's your answer, huh? You're going to ignore our warnings and pursue the Honeycutt case no matter what?' Schuyler asked with a vague grin.

'I'm going to ignore your warnings and follow the evidence wherever it leads me,' Reade stated. 'As sheriff, I am sworn to faithfully and impartially discharge my duties to the best of my abilities. You might want to reiterate the word "impartially" to the folks at the board and council.'

'I will,' Schuyler affirmed as he moved towards the office door. 'This probably won't be the last you hear from us.'

'I'm sure it won't be.'

Schuyler nodded his farewell to the sheriff and then turned toward Tish. 'Bye, Tish. That's quite the dress you're wearing. I don't recall you wearing dresses like that when we were together.'

Tish folded her arms across her chest and gave him a stern look. 'When we were together, the atmosphere was always far too chilly.'

'Hmph, yeah, I suppose it was. Talk to you soon, Sheriff,' he warned before finally departing through the office door and down the hallway that led to the building's entrance.

'Grrrrrr,' Tish growled as soon as Schuyler was out of sight. 'What an insufferable, arrogant . . . ugh! I don't know how I was ever in a relationship with him.'

'Sounds as if he's still not over that relationship,' Reade suggested.

'Schuyler was over our relationship while we were still in it. What he's not over is me breaking up with him before he could break up with me.' She shook her head. 'But enough of that – what about you? What was all that about concerned parties and you taking a knee? It sounded to me as if he was threatening you. Like if you didn't stop looking into the Honeycutt case, you'd lose your job or worse. That's a threat. Don't you think that's a threat?'

'I do,' Reade affirmed as he rose from his chair.

'Well, it's illegal to threaten a law enforcement officer, isn't it?'

'It is.'

'So what are you going to do?'

Reade calmly picked up the wax-paper-wrapped parcel from his desk. 'First, I'm going to microwave this breakfast sandwich.

Then I'm going to make us more coffee. And then you and I – with some help from Clayton and Jules – are going to solve this case.'

'But what Schuyler did was unethical and illegal. Aren't you going to file a complaint?'

'No, because we have better things to do today than to be on hold with the governor's office. Also, Schuyler was prompted to come here by more than just the town board and the county council. All that talk of concerned parties who don't wish to relive the tragedy?'

'Someone in the Honeycutt case,' Tish grasped.

Reade nodded and led Tish out of his office and to the break room.

'Walker James Honeycutt, Priscilla Maddox Honeycutt, and the Heritages all have the cash and clout required to apply that kind of pressure,' he reasoned.

'Don't forget Dixie Dupree. She may have lost her inheritance, but we don't know what kind of connections she's made while singing at The Chandelier Bar. You did say it was a gathering spot for Richmond's high-rollers.'

'Excellent point. I'll have someone check into her list of friends.' Reade opened the door of the microwave, placed his sandwich inside, and, after turning the unit on, moved to the stove. 'Coffee?'

Anticipating the stale automatic drip coffee that was usually hanging around the sheriff's office, Tish was about to decline when she saw Reade extract a glass cylinder from the cupboard above the cooktop. 'Wait one minute. Is that a French press?'

'Everyone here is accustomed to drinking your coffee, but your café closes early, so we invested in two French presses for the off hours. We got two so that we have one to use while the other is in the dishwasher.'

Tish laughed. 'I've ruined you all for life, haven't I?'

'Ruined isn't the word that comes to mind,' Reade answered with a broad smile.

Tish wondered which word Reade would use to describe her impact on him and his team, but she didn't say anything; instead, she opted to watch in awkward silence as he measured coffee into the press and then set the teakettle on to a burner to boil. 'So, you said you received Carney's files?' she prompted.

'Uh-huh.' Reade beckoned with his index finger and led Tish to a conference room two doors down from the break room. There, upon the long rectangular tables typically reserved for meetings, stood stack upon stack of white bankers' file boxes, each labeled with a specific number in a series of thirty-two. In the corner, two uniformed officers fed documents into a high-volume scanner while, in the center of the room, like Gaia rising from the chaos, stood Officer Clayton arranging items on a rolling whiteboard.

'Good thing Carney wasn't obsessed,' Tish said with a hint of sarcasm.

'I know, but I wasn't about to give our lord mayor more ammunition,' Reade laughed. 'He was practically punch-drunk with power as it was.'

Clayton, out of uniform and dressed in a casual ensemble of blue chambray shirt and jeans, looked up from his work. 'Mornin' Sheriff, Tish. You're right on time. I just got this evidence board together. Carney had it posted on the wall above his desk back in his home in Florida. Looks like it's a floor plan of the Honeycutt mansion, with some notes and photos added to it. Mrs Carney said that in the weeks before his death, her husband would stare at it for several hours each day.'

'Thanks, Clayton. Good work,' Reade commended. 'Wheel it into my office so we can get a better look at it.'

Clayton did as he was instructed. Meanwhile, Reade and Tish collected the breakfast sandwich from the microwave, prepared three mugs of coffee, and then met Clayton in the sheriff's office, shutting the door behind them.

'So, what do we have?' Reade asked before taking a bite of breakfast sandwich.

The trio stood before the whiteboard upon which had been taped a twenty-four-by-thirty-six-inch floor plan of Cypress Hollow. Various colored arrows pointed to locations on the floor plan and were labeled with the names of those affiliated with the case.

'I positioned the arrows to match the photos the Florida police sent us of Carney's office, but I had no idea what they signified until I unpacked this journal,' Clayton explained, holding a brown spiral-bound notebook in his hand. 'They're the locations of everyone at Cypress Hollow at the time Daisy was killed.'

Reade and Tish stepped closer to the board and examined both the plans and the attached house photos carefully. Cypress Hollow was a sprawling, south-facing center-hall Colonial erected in the early 1920s by Benton's grandfather, Mitchell Honeycutt. Early in their marriage, Benton and Delilah decided to remodel Cypress Hollow into a country house befitting the family of an up-and-coming senator. Electricity and plumbing were updated to current building codes, windows replaced with panes of energy-saving glass, vintage lighting fixtures rewired, and walls covered in designer wallpaper with coordinating drapes and upholstery. However, the biggest changes to the house came via the additions of a state-of-the-art kitchen, a rear conservatory, a bright turquoise front door and shutters, and a massive family room and play area that linked the east wing of the house to the freestanding barn, which had been converted to a four-car garage.

'The "X" in the garage is where Daisy's body was found,' Clayton explained. 'The arrows are pretty much self-explanatory.'

Tish scanned the arrows to determine how they correlated to the list of witnesses she and Reade were going to interview. The majority of arrows pointed to locations outdoors on the Cypress Hollow compound: Priscilla Maddox was on the west side patio just outside the conservatory, Louella Heritage was poolside, Dixie Dupree was visiting the stables, Frank Heritage was on the miniature putting green just north of the playground, John and Lucille McIlveen were in the center of the backyard area, just north of the pool, Benton Honeycutt was by the creek that ran along the property's eastern edge, and Delilah Honeycutt, her arrow bearing a question mark, had been placed just outside the garage. The Reverend Dillard's arrow was positioned in the front driveway with a note that he had left the barbecue before the time of the murder.

Inside the house, just two arrows pointed to areas of importance. A blue one indicated the second-story east-wing bedroom where Walker James Honeycutt was listed as playing video games. And, in the bedroom beside Walker's, an orange arrow identified the presence of Viola Tilley.

'This plan isn't quite right,' Tish announced. 'Viola Tilley shouldn't be on it.'

Clayton opened the photo of the floor plan as it hung on Carney's office wall and showed it to Reade and Tish. 'That's exactly where

Sheriff Carney had the orange arrow. According to his journal, Viola Tilley had the bedroom between Walker James and Daisy Honeycutt.'

'I'm not disputing the location of her bedroom,' Tish clarified. 'I'm disputing that she was in that bedroom at the time Daisy was killed. She told us she was at her aunt's house for a Fourth of July party that day.'

'Which has been her story from day one,' Reade added. 'And in the files I found here at the station, it's the story corroborated by Viola's family, the Honeycutts themselves, and the Honeycutts' driver.'

'Hmm,' Clayton mused. 'I'll keep digging through Sheriff Carney's files to see if there's a reason he might have placed her there.'

Reade nodded his approval. 'I think we need to keep on searching, but we also need to keep in mind that this floor plan might not be one-hundred-percent accurate. Carney may have used it as a visual tool to help him test different scenarios, but let me know what you find.'

'Yes, sir. I'll keep you posted,' Clayton promised before turning on one heel to commence his journey back to the document-filled conference room.

'Clayton, wait,' Reade called after him. 'One more thing. We need your help this afternoon. Mr Davis at Channel Ten News has pulled some archive footage of the Honeycutts from the vault and has arranged for us to view it at one o'clock. I thought you could sit in and put your newfound micro-expression analysis skills to use.'

'Sure. It would be great to use what I learned. I'm also not going to lie – a break from all those files would be sweet, too.'

'No doubt. Tish and I will meet you there later. In the meantime, she and I have a date.'

'A date?' Tish and Clayton repeated in unison.

'With Walker James Honeycutt. We're meeting him at his house over on Three Chopt Road in Richmond at ten.'

'Three Chopt?' Clayton questioned. 'That's an old-money neighborhood.'

'Well, the Honeycutts are old money,' Tish remarked.

'Yeah, but Walker James isn't old and I'm sure he's made enough money of his own that he could live anywhere he wanted. It's weird that he chooses to live in an old house in an old neighborhood filled with – sorry, guys – old people.'

'Why is he apologizing to us?' Reade asked Tish.

'Why do you think?' she retorted.

'OK, first off, we're not old. Second, you've heard about Walker James outside this case?' Reade asked the officer.

'Yeah, he's the hottest games developer in the industry,' Clayton replied. 'He supposedly never leaves his house, but his games are total fire. Like, so dope. I'm surprised he agreed to meet with you. Gaming conferences have been after him for years.'

'He didn't agree to meet with me. His lawyer did.'

'He's already lawyered up? I guess when you're worth millions, that's the smart thing to do.'

'Yes. There's also a saying about apples and trees,' Tish quipped, referring to the game guru's parents' haste in retaining legal representation. 'So, are we speaking with Walker James or his attorney?'

'Both,' Reade replied before thanking Clayton and instructing him to return to his duties. 'We've been given a thirty-minute window during which the attorney assures me, and I quote, "All the questions that can be answered will be answered."'

'If Walker James already has his lawyer in on this, it seems doubtful he's the one putting the screws to the council and board to get us to stop the investigation,' Tish said.

'I'm not sure I agree with that assessment. His attorney knows that there's only so long her client can avoid me before I go to a judge for a court order, so she emails me first thing this morning and agrees to a last-minute meeting. Meanwhile, the lawyer or Walker James calls some people in local government and asks them to apply pressure so that I'll either cancel the meeting or at least throw them some softball questions.'

'The timing of Schuyler's visit this morning was awfully strange,' she acknowledged. 'Not only did he come here just before our meeting with Walker James, but he showed up at a time in the morning when he'd normally be meeting with his own staff to prepare for the day. The Schuyler I knew would never have scheduled a visit with us until at least nine thirty.'

'He's that much of a slave to his schedule?'

'You have no idea.' Tish held a hand aloft as if to signal that she had no more to say about the subject.

Reade grabbed a set of keys from his desk drawer and escorted Tish out of his office. 'Well, either Schuyler's new gig as mayor has greatly altered his daily calendar or someone told him that meeting with us was an urgent matter.'

# ELEVEN

Tish and Reade drove up to the ivy-covered wall surrounding 6319 Three Chopt Road at five minutes before ten. Leaning out the driver's side window, Reade spoke their names into the front gate intercom and presented his badge to the webcam. Within moments, the gate panels swung inward, granting them access to the circular driveway, the Charles Gillette-designed front gardens, and the stately, white-shingled Colonial Revival structure beyond.

As they drew closer to the house, Tish felt her jaw drop. 'Am I imagining things or does this house look like . . .?'

'Cypress Hollow.' Reade filled in the blank, his voice a near whisper. 'My God. It even has the same slate roof and turquoise front door.'

'Creepy,' she declared as Reade pulled the SUV to a halt before the front walkway.

'Yeah, just a little.'

The pair stepped from the SUV and proceeded up the impeccably maintained stone-and-brick walkway to the front door, where they were met by an extremely attractive blonde in her early thirties. 'Sheriff Reade. Ms Tarragon.' She shook their hands. 'I'm Milla Lebrecht, Mr Honeycutt's personal attorney. He's waiting for you upstairs in his office.'

She led them through a well-appointed foyer with hand-painted wallpaper and high, paneled ceilings and up the sweeping curved staircase to the second floor. Turning right at the top of the landing, they were led into a darkened corner room that had been painted a deep shade of gunmetal gray.

'Good morning,' welcomed Walker James Honeycutt in a soft-spoken voice. Seated behind a glass-top adjustable-height desk upon which rested a laptop, a cell phone, and a stand that supported five separate computer monitors, he had glasses, light-brown hair cut in a trendy low fade, and a line-free face that appeared much younger than his thirty-five years.

Milla directed them to the two chairs opposite the desk and then stood behind her client in a move that befitted a bodyguard more than it did an attorney.

'What can I do for you today?' Honeycutt asked.

Reade introduced himself and Tish. 'We're here to investigate the murder of former Sheriff Gadsden Carney. His body was found at your family plot over at Ashton Courthouse.'

Honeycutt expressed little emotion. 'Apart from the sad coincidence of the poor man dying at my family's gravesite, I'm not sure what his death has to do with me. I never even met him.'

'But you have spoken to him on the phone.'

'Yes, a couple of times.'

'Our records indicate that he called you on five occasions.'

'Was it that many? It didn't seem like it.'

'What did you and Carney discuss?' Tish asked.

'My sister's murder. For some ungodly reason, Carney felt the need to review the case again.'

'Where were you the day before yesterday between eight-thirty and eleven at night?'

'Where I always am. Here at the house with Milla. I'm sure you've heard that I don't go out much,' he said with a sniff.

'What did you tell Gadsden Carney about the day your sister died?' Reade quizzed.

Honeycutt shrugged. 'Same as I'll tell you, which isn't much. I remember being upstairs in my room, playing *Rayman*. I'd gotten it for my birthday that March and was obsessed. Then I remember my mother in the garage. She was kneeling over Daisy and screaming and crying. I had no idea what was going on at the time. I couldn't tell if Daisy was alive or dead. I couldn't even remember walking down the stairs to the garage, to be honest. I just stood there in confusion until my father came and brought me back to my room. He locked the door and told me to stay there until he came and got me.'

'Then what?' Tish prompted.

'I did as I was told. I stayed in my room – I don't know how long. I might have fallen asleep – I don't know. My father eventually came back and got me, and we drove to the Heritages' house. No one said anything. No one even told me that Daisy was dead. We rode to their house in silence and I was sent to bed. Early the next morning, we left for our house on Sullivan's Island. Two weeks later, I was sent to a French boarding school. I never saw my mother again.'

'Do you remember anything else from that day? Anything unusual at the barbecue? Any arguments?' Reade prodded.

Honeycutt shook his head. 'No, I just remember hating the fact that we were having a barbecue. My mother loved parties. She would always dress Daisy and me in matching outfits and parade us for everyone to see. I preferred the weekends when Dad would come home and the four of us would do things together without a whole bunch of people around. That barbecue could have taken place two weeks or two years before my sister's death for all I remember of it.'

'What about Daisy? Was there anything different about her or her behavior that day?'

'Not that I remember, no. But as I said, I could be confusing that day with any number of other parties my mother held. Daisy was singing, probably. She was always singing. She never stopped.'

'Did her singing ever bother you?' Tish inquired.

Milla charged forward. 'I object to that question. Walker James was all but ten years of age. How he felt about his younger sister when they were both children has no bearing whatsoever on your investigation.'

Walker James reached up and patted her arm. 'It's OK, honey. I don't mind.'

'You may not mind, but I still advise you not to answer,' Milla persisted.

'This is what happens when your personal attorney also happens to be your girlfriend.' Walker James smiled at Reade and Tish. 'Daisy's singing didn't usually bother me. I'd learned to tune it out most of the time, but there were days when I wished our house were quieter. There were also days when I wished I could sing, too.'

'So that you could join Daisy in a song?' Tish ventured.

He shook his head somberly. 'So that my mother would pay as much attention to me as she did to her.'

Several seconds of silence elapsed before Reade spoke again. 'Just a couple more questions before we go. Do you recall there being anyone else in the house with you at the time your sister was killed?'

'No, but I was pretty focused on my game.'

'You didn't hear anyone in the room next to you or downstairs?' Reade continued, clearly thinking of the floorplan they had seen earlier that morning.

'No, I don't remember hearing anything.' Honeycutt's mood grew tense. 'Like I've been telling you, I don't remember very much at all from that day. I remember Cypress Hollow vividly. Some of my best memories took place in that house. I could walk you through every square inch of the place, describing how it looked – the furniture, the wallpaper, the way the light poured into our playroom in the evenings. How it sounded – the squeaky floorboard in the hallway outside my room, the peepers outside my bedroom window in the spring, the murmur of the TV at night after Daisy and I had gone to bed. And the smells – Mrs McIlveen's citrus floor cleaner, Nanny Viola's oatmeal on winter mornings, Christmas cookies in December. I go there often in my dreams. Sometimes I feel like part of me will always be trapped there, doomed to rattle around the hallways and the grounds like the ghost in some Gothic novel.'

'Is that why you've modeled this house after Cypress Hollow?' Tish asked.

'Partially. The house was designed this way when I bought it, but I did add the turquoise door and other design elements. I figured everyone thinks of me as "that poor little boy whose sister was murdered," so I might as well play along. It's funny. When people hear you're a video game designer, they assume you're a guy who's never grown up. What they don't understand is that when Daisy died, my childhood died with her. That might sound selfish, but it's true. Nothing was ever the same again.'

'It must have been difficult to be sent away from your family and friends,' Tish sympathized. 'Did you contact any of them when you returned to the States?'

'After college, I stayed with my father and Priscilla until I got on my feet and found my own place, but I never reached out to anyone else. All through school, my father had banned me from speaking to anyone I'd known back then, so it had become second nature to go about my business and ignore their existence. After my father died, I started to think about all the people who'd once been in my life, but especially Nanny Viola. She had always been so kind to me. I knew my father had helped to place her in an assisted living facility here in town, so one Saturday afternoon I decided to pay her a visit.'

'I'm sure she was thrilled to see you,' Tish said.

'Not really. My sudden appearance gave her a shock – a bad one. In my eagerness to see her, I hadn't called ahead of my visit. The nurses chased me away so they could attend to her. I haven't gone back to see her since, nor have I attempted to contact anyone else from my past. None of them has seen me since that day. I realize that to see me now only reminds them of Daisy . . . and my mother.'

Reade gave Honeycutt a chance to drink some water before presenting him with the next question. 'Two weeks before your sister's murder, you threatened your sister with a golf club. Do you remember that incident?'

Milla, again, leaped forward. 'That's out of line. My client was ten—'

Walker James held a hand aloft in a bid for silence. 'I don't remember it at all. The first I even heard about it was when I first came back to the States and watched one of those gruesome anniversary news specials.'

'Do you believe your mother murdered your sister?' Reade posed.

'I do,' he answered without hesitation. 'My mother wouldn't have confessed and let the real killer go free. My father wouldn't either. Had he any doubt that my mother had committed the crime, he would never have allowed her to confess. They would have wanted the person who killed Daisy to face the full wrath of the law.'

'And you? What did you want for Daisy's killer?'

After a long pause, Honeycutt said, 'Forgiveness.'

'I don't mean your mother. I'm talking about before your mother confessed. What did you want for your sister's killer?'

'Forgiveness,' came the answer again.

Reade was incredulous. 'This person brutally murdered your sister and, in your words, stole your childhood.'

Silence ensued, then Walker James repeated, 'Forgiveness.'

Milla Lebrecht escorted Tish and Reade to the front door of the house. 'I trust you got all the information you needed.'

'For now, yes,' Reade answered, 'but we may need to speak with Mr Honeycutt again.'

'You won't get a second meeting, Sheriff,' she threatened. 'We cooperated with your investigation because we want justice for Mr Carney, but I will block any attempt you make to contact Walker James again. He's told you everything that he remembers from that day. If what he's told you isn't enough to help your case, then you'll have to go somewhere else for information.'

'Are you speaking as his attorney or his significant other?'

'Both. Walker James has spent the past twenty-five years trying to build a new life and you people keep coming in and dragging him back to the past. You and Sheriff Carney are just the latest in the ongoing parade of characters that won't let him move forward with his life. Reporters who claim to want to ask him questions about his business, video game fans at conferences, even his neighbors – each and every one of them only wants to ask him about that day, about his sister, about his mother. When he and I first started dating, a so-called friend of mine told him that the ability to commit murder was an inherited trait and that we should think twice before settling down and having children. That was five years ago, and although we're still together, part of Walker James believes that nonsense. You want to know why he lives here shut away from the outside world? That's why. Because the world won't let him let go of that. I can't stop reporters from calling, but I can stop you and I'll do so by any legal means necessary. I won't see Walker James hurt any longer. I just won't. Now, if you'd please leave.'

Reade and Tish accommodated her request and stepped out on to the wide, brick front stoop, leaving her to slam the door loudly behind them.

# TWELVE

Louella Heritage, clad in an all-white golfing ensemble of polo shirt, visor, and short skirt, offered her condolences as she poured four glasses of lemonade from a crystal pitcher. 'We're terribly sorry to hear about Mr Carney, Sheriff.'

'Thank you,' Reade replied. 'And thank you for being gracious enough to allow us to move our interview to earlier in the day.'

'It was no trouble. Now that Frank's retired, our schedule is wide open except for the occasional board meeting. And golf, naturally.' She sat down at the end of the rectangular patio table, the verdant, rolling landscape of the Hermitage Golf Course stretched out behind her.

'We're happy to help the police in whatever way we can,' Frank Heritage added from the other end of the table. His golfing attire consisted of a pink polo shirt, dark plaid shorts, and a white ball cap. 'I do, however, ask that you keep this conversation private and not involve the press in any way. When Louella and I first spoke out about Benton and Delilah, we received a very large, very vocal backlash from the public for what they perceived as us betraying our friends. We don't want to travel down that road again.'

'We assure you this meeting will remain confidential.'

Frank gave a single nod. 'Now, you said on the phone that you folks believe Mr Carney's death is linked to Daisy Honeycutt's murder?'

'We do,' Tish confirmed. 'Carney's body was found at the Honeycutt family plot in Ashton Courthouse and, as you know, he'd recently begun to re-examine the case.'

'Yes, we spoke to him – what? – three times over the past month?' Frank asked his wife.

'Three times,' Louella verified. 'I can't imagine why anyone would kill Mr Carney over the Honeycutt case. Daisy and Delilah have been gone for nearly a quarter-century now.'

'Twenty-five years,' Frank said somberly. 'We've been contacted by reporters trying to book us for anniversary interviews like it's some sort of damned celebration. I can't stomach folks out there trying to make a buck off a dead little girl. You know, a publisher once asked us if we'd be interested in writing a book about our friendship with the Honeycutts. I told them no and that even if I were down to my last nickel, my answer would still be no. Vultures, the lot of them.'

Reade steered the Heritages back to the matter at hand. 'What did you discuss with Mr Carney during those three phone calls?'

'Everything we knew about the Honeycutt case, of course,' Louella replied. 'We were friends with Delilah and Benton for years. And our kids were friends with each other, too, but you must have that somewhere in your files.'

'We do, but we'd like to hear it directly from you.'

Louella waved a well-tanned, bangled arm in the air. 'Oh, where to start! I first met Delilah while waiting to pick up the kids from school one afternoon. It was a beautiful spring day and we'd both decided to wait outside our cars, so we got to talking and discovered that our girls were in the same pre-school class and that our boys were one year apart. We decided to get the kids together for a playdate that weekend and the friendship grew from there. Before you knew it, we got the guys in on it, too, and our families were getting together all the time.'

'So you were close to each other?' Tish asked.

'Very. At Easter, we'd do a joint egg hunt, and for Mother's Day the guys and kids would cook Delilah and me brunch. We had some good times, didn't we, Frank?'

'We sure did. Walker James could get a little sullen at times,' her husband recalled.

'Yes, he was a moody little boy,' Louella agreed.

'But our son Frankie has always been good-natured. If Walker James wouldn't play with him, he'd go off and join the girls. They were always happy to have his attention.'

'Before Daisy's death, were you aware of any marital problems between Delilah and Benton?' Reade questioned.

'I didn't know for sure,' Frank answered. 'I suspected something was wrong because Benton had started spending more time in Washington and less time at home, but he never said anything to me about it. Whenever I saw him, he seemed like his usual self. Louella, however, talked to Delilah almost every day.'

Louella nodded. 'I asked Delilah about Benton's absences. She assured me that he was simply busy with congressional matters, but I could see that it bothered her. Delilah was like a swan – calm on the surface but paddling like hell under it. With Benton gone so often, she started focusing more of her time on Daisy's singing. Too much time, in my opinion. Daisy was only six, but it had reached the point where she was spending nearly all her non-school hours either taking lessons or rehearsing for a recital. Delilah even canceled several of Daisy's playdates with our daughter. It was all too much – for Daisy *and* Delilah.'

'Did you tell her that?' Tish asked.

'I did. Delilah dismissed my concerns and said she was preparing her daughter for a successful career. She wasn't very happy with me for butting in, so, for the sake of our friendship, I never mentioned it again. It was a matter for she and Benton to discuss anyway.'

'Were you aware of Delilah's suspicions regarding her husband's infidelity?'

'No,' Louella replied after taking a long sip of lemonade, 'but Delilah wouldn't have told me about that. We were good friends and I loved her like a sister, but I was a member of the community. Delilah wanted everyone in the community to think that her life was perfect – she wouldn't have given anyone reason to think otherwise. Including me.'

'Jumping ahead to the day of Daisy's murder, did either of you notice anything odd or unusual? Any tension or strain?'

'Delilah was a stress-bucket,' Louella described. 'That was typical for her when throwing parties, but there was something else in the air. Benton had brought one of his aides – Priscilla, his future wife – from Washington down to Cypress Hollow for the weekend, and it was abundantly clear she wasn't welcome there.'

'Did Delilah tell you that?' Tish asked.

'No, she slapped on her usual smile and went on with things, but you could see from the strain in her face that Priscilla's presence was both unexpected and unwanted.'

'She looked more tired than I'd ever seen her,' Frank added.

'I soon saw why Delilah was so upset. Priscilla was glued to

Benton's side, staring attentively at him, hanging on his every word. She didn't even give him a moment alone to play with his kids. Every time they'd come around, why, the look on her face—' Louella stuck her nose up in the air in imitation of Priscilla. 'I decided to give Priscilla a tour of the house, just as an excuse to get her away from Benton and to keep her out of Delilah's sight for a time. Well, after the tour I asked her what she thought. She said, "There's too much wallpaper. It will take some work to take it all down, but I have a cousin who's a master craftsman. He'll have the place looking less like a funeral home in no time." Can you believe it? She was talking as if she was going to be the next owner of Cypress Hollow!'

'Technically, she was,' Frank reasoned. 'Don't think they ever sold the place.'

Louella's brown eyes peered over the top of her sunglasses. 'That's not the point, Frank. The point is that Priscilla wanted Benton even back then. Remember that afternoon when I told you what she'd said?'

'The way Louella ran up to me, I thought one of the kids was sick. Then she told me about Priscilla. I don't like to get involved in other people's family matters, but I felt I should talk to Benton and ask him what was going on. He told me he was aware that Priscilla had a crush on him, but he knew what he was doing. He claimed that Priscilla had a keen – that was the word he used, *keen* – political mind that could help him with his career. I asked if Delilah was OK with the whole thing. Benton said that he and Delilah had agreed that if it was good for his career, it was good for the whole family.'

'Did you believe him?' Tish asked.

'I believed that *he* believed that to be true, but seeing Delilah's face every time she caught a glimpse of Priscilla said otherwise.'

'Do either of you recall anything else of note from that day? Anything that transpired before the murder?' Reade queried.

'I can't think of anything. How about you?' Frank turned his weathered countenance toward his wife.

'No. Except . . .' She bit her lip and ran a hand through her bleach-blonde hair. 'Lucille McIlveen was not herself that afternoon. Her son, Russell, had been brought in on drug possession the night before. He was only twenty-one at the time, but he'd been in and out of the system for years. He was looking at doing some serious time for his latest offense.'

'Did Lucille talk to you about it?' Reade questioned.

'Only to tell me what I just told you.'

He nodded. 'Moving ahead to the murder. Tell me what happened.'

'I was on the patio, watching our kids take their last laps in the pool. Our kids were always the first ones in and the last ones out. It happened every year and I always felt awful, them out there splashing around while Delilah was trying to get Daisy cleaned up, but she never seemed to mind.' Louella took her sunglasses off and dried her eyes with the back of her hand. 'Daisy was nowhere to be found, so Delilah assumed she'd gone inside to play with Walker James, which she often did. Delilah went into the house to fetch them and get them ready for a bath. A half hour later, maybe more, I heard screams coming from inside the garage. It was the most horrifying sound I've ever heard. I pulled the kids from the water, gave them their towels, and told them to wait by the pool while I investigated. Then I rushed forward to open the rear garage door.'

'The door was unlocked?'

'Yes, it was usually unlocked. The back part of the garage was used to store the children's pool toys, bikes, and other sporting goods. Daisy and the other kids must have been in and out of that garage a dozen times that day.'

Reade jotted notes in his tablet. 'What happened next?'

'Well, I got to the garage, but the McIlveens had beaten me to it. John swung open the door and there was Delilah, knelt over Daisy, sobbing. Daisy looked as though she might have been sleeping, until I saw the blood on the back of her head.'

'You said the McIlveens beat you to the door. Where were they before Delilah screamed?'

'Delilah had rented a tent to provide shelter for guests in the event of rain and to keep buffet items and cold drinks out of the sun. Lucille was in the tent, packing up the leftover food and running it to the kitchen. I could see her from where I was sitting.'

'Were the caterers helping her?'

'No, they'd long since gone. John McIlveen was outside

collecting the trash from the party. He walked past me toward the children's play area shortly before the screaming started.'

'And where were you, Mr Heritage?'

'I was taking a few last swings on the putting green several yards behind the children's play area. I heard the screams and a lot of commotion coming from the direction of the house. Knowing that the kids were still in the pool and fearing the worst, I immediately went to see what had happened. When I got to the garage, I saw Delilah kneeling over the body. Louella and the McIlveens were there, too.'

'When did everyone else arrive on the scene?' Tish posed.

'It's difficult to say in all the confusion,' Louella hedged. 'I was so focused on Delilah and comforting her that I didn't watch the door, but I'm pretty sure Frank was next after the McIlveens. Then Benton arrived. He couldn't bear to look at Daisy, so he draped a blanket over her. It was a blanket the kids used for backyard picnics and tea parties. Once Benton was there to tend to Delilah, I ran back to the pool to check on our kids. On my way out, I bumped into Priscilla. She asked what had happened. I told her Daisy was dead.'

'How did she react?'

'I didn't stick around long enough to find out. I didn't want the kids wandering into the garage and seeing their friend like that.'

'I was there,' Frank spoke up. 'Priscilla was quite possibly the least helpful person I've ever witnessed in a crisis. She went into high-drama mode. She began crying and shouting and carrying on and wanting to know what had happened. You'd have thought she was Daisy's mother instead of a guest who'd given Daisy the stink eye all afternoon. I tried to calm her, but to no avail. Finally, Benton asked Lucille McIlveen to get Priscilla out of the garage and take her to the kitchen to make some tea and to call the police. None of us had cell phones back then.'

'Which way did they go to get to the kitchen?' Reade asked. 'Around the outside of the house or through the garage?'

'It's funny you ask that. Lucille started for the back door of the garage, but Benton called her back and told her to take Priscilla through the garage instead. I didn't think much of it at the time, probably because I wasn't thinking it was a murder case – I thought it was a scooter accident or something – but later on, it struck me as odd. Mighty odd.'

Reade nodded. 'What happened next?'

'Dixie arrived. She'd been down by the stables – that's where she'd always go for a smoke. She demanded to know what was going on. Benton told her Daisy was dead. Delilah couldn't manage a word through her tears. Dixie rushed to her sister's side, sobbing, and the two of them cradled Daisy's body until Dixie had the good sense to suggest they put Daisy's body back where Delilah had discovered it.'

'Delilah had been holding Daisy's body that entire time?'

'Yes. Benton also gave Daisy a kiss on the forehead before covering her. You should have all this in your files,' Frank stated. 'I told the police everything.'

'I do have it. However, given former Sheriff Carney was reinvestigating the case when he was killed, I thought it best that we do so as well,' Reade explained. 'Where was Walker James during all this?'

'He was upstairs in his bedroom,' Louella stated.

'The entire time?'

'Yes, thank goodness. I can't imagine how he would have reacted if he had come downstairs and seen his sister like that.'

Reade and Tish exchanged shocked glances.

'You're positive he never stepped foot in the garage?' Tish quizzed.

'Positive. After I gave my statement, the police let me take the kids home. Benton went upstairs and got Walker James so he could come home with us.'

'So the police didn't speak to Walker James that evening?'

'The police didn't speak to any of Daisy's family members that evening. Benton called their attorney who, in turn, told the police that Benton, Delilah, Dixie, and Walker James were in absolutely no condition to give statements. I had been back at home with the kids less than five minutes when Delilah and Benton pulled into our driveway. Frank spent more time with the police than all of them combined.'

'It's true,' Frank confirmed, pulling his cap over his silver head. 'The moment the police ruled Daisy's death a homicide, Benton called his attorney and handed the receiver to Sheriff Carney. I don't know precisely what was said, but the police didn't try to ask any more questions. Dixie appeared genuinely confused by the situation. She had just started talking to the police when Benton swooped in and dragged her away, telling her to stay at a nearby inn. Delilah and Benton, however, weren't confused at all. They knew exactly what they were doing. They were eager to leave. They didn't want to stay in that house one second longer.'

'One could put that down to the trauma they had just endured,' Reade ventured. 'The urge to run away and escape your surroundings can be a fight or flight response.'

'I agree, but when taken in conjunction with all the other strange behavior Benton and Delilah exhibited in those early days, Louella and I don't think that's the case.'

'Go on,' Reade urged.

It was Louella's turn to tell the story. 'I understand the concept of shock, Sheriff. I also understand that not everyone grieves the same way, but when Benton and Delilah arrived at our home that evening, I would never have guessed that their daughter had just died. Benton stepped through the door and immediately asked to use the phone in Frank's office. Delilah took Walker James by the arm and led him upstairs to the guest bedroom, despite my suggestion that he'd be better off playing with his friends than lying, sleeplessly, in bed. While Benton was on the phone, I admit I listened outside the door. He made calls to two different attorneys – one for himself and one for Delilah. Then he called another firm whom he asked to help speak with the press. He called another number after that, but I stopped listening. My head was spinning and I wanted to get back to the kids. When he'd finished with his calls, Benton said goodnight to me and joined Delilah and Walker James upstairs.

'As you can imagine, Frank and I didn't sleep very well that night,' she continued. 'Not only were we grieving the loss of a little girl who'd spent many a happy day at our home, but we were fearful for the safety of our own children. Worrying that someone might break in and do to them what was done to Daisy, we took shifts checking in on them. It was during one of the last shifts of the night that Frank caught them.'

'Benton had the family suitcases in hand, Delilah had Walker James's hand in hers, and they were sneaking down the back staircase,' Frank described. 'I asked where they were going, and Benton said that he'd reserved a plane to take them to their home on Sullivan's Island. I explained to Benton that it would look bad for him and Delilah if they left town without speaking to the police, but Benton didn't care. He was dead set on leaving, so they left. Later that day, I received a call from Benton's attorney – the one he called immediately after finding Daisy. He asked me and Louella for statements about what we saw and did the day of the murder and what we told the police.'

'What do you think Benton and his attorney were trying to achieve?' Tish asked.

'I'm no legal expert,' Frank demurred, 'but it felt to me like Benton and his lawyers were already trying to build a case for the defense.'

'Do you both believe that Delilah Honeycutt murdered her daughter?'

Louella and Frank Heritage looked across the table at each other and nodded somberly before stating in unison, 'We do.'

'From letting people walk through the garage to covering his daughter with a blanket, and from flying off to South Carolina to using his attorneys to do his talking, Benton did his best to undermine this investigation,' Frank opined. 'It's obvious he was covering for his wife.'

Louella concurred. 'All I have to say is that if it were my daughter lying dead in that garage, I'd have commandeered the entire goddamn US military to hunt down who did it. I wouldn't have avoided speaking to the police. I would have worked with them. I wouldn't have skipped town. I would have knocked on every door in the neighborhood to see if anyone had any information. And I certainly wouldn't have shipped my surviving child off to boarding school two weeks later. I would have held my baby close. If you'd seen Delilah's face that day, you'd agree with me. Her perfect life was slipping through her fingers and she was desperate. Poor little Daisy was caught in the crossfire of her parents' marriage. She'd been pushed so hard it's no wonder she rebelled that day. Just like it's no wonder Delilah snapped. No wonder at all.'

# THIRTEEN

'Well,' Tish said with a sigh as Reade drove to the last interview of the morning.

'Well, indeed,' he commiserated.

'Two more witnesses in the case who believe Delilah Honeycutt was guilty.'

'Witnesses who also have indirect evidence that Benton knew his wife committed the murder and did his best to undermine the investigation.'

'Which doesn't bode well for our current investigation. If Delilah actually did murder Daisy, then there's not much chance the two cases are related, is there?'

'I wouldn't go there yet. We just made a crack in the case. A small one, but a crack nonetheless.'

'Walker James,' Tish exclaimed.

'Yep,' Reade acknowledged. 'He claims he was in the garage and then Benton took him upstairs and locked the door. The Heritages claim he was in his room the entire time.'

'Dixie also didn't list Walker James as being present in the garage when she arrived, remember? She said she saw Benton, Delilah, Frank Heritage, and John McIlveen. That corroborates the Heritages' account.'

'If Benton had arrived at the garage first, he might have seen Walker James standing there and escorted him upstairs, but according to the Heritages, Benton arrived on the scene a few seconds after they did. So why does Walker James claim he was there?'

The pair fell silent for several moments before Tish spoke again. 'When I was two years old, my grandparents took me to Disney World,' she recounted. 'I was far too young for any of my experiences there to register in my memory. However, after years of hearing my grandparents tell stories about that trip, I eventually began to "remember" following Minnie Mouse into the employee break room and being frightened of the fake crocodiles on the Jungle Cruise.'

'So you internalized your grandparents' stories of the trip and adopted them as your own memories,' Reade paraphrased.

'Exactly. I don't care how hard the Honeycutts worked to shield Walker James from the maelstrom of police and paparazzi, at some point he must have learned about the gruesome details surrounding his sister's death. Daisy Honeycutt was a blonde little rich girl and Benton Honeycutt a United States senator – the story must have been covered overseas. Walker James lived in that house. He could easily visualize where and how Daisy's body was discovered just as well as he could imagine his mother crying over the body.'

'There's a psychologist in the metro DC area who we've worked with on a few domestic disturbance cases. I'll give her a call.' Reade turned the SUV off the main road and into the Colonial Estates Mobile Home Park and followed the signs to section twenty-one. The McIlveens lived in number 219, a tidy unit clad with tan vinyl siding, forest-green shutters and trim, a carport, and, in place of a lawn, a well-tended garden of hostas, yellow roses, purple bee balm, white hydrangea, and fiery foxtail lilies.

Reade pulled the SUV into the blacktop driveway and stopped behind the 2010 silver Honda Accord that was parked there. He and Tish then walked up the drive to the carport, mounted a set of whitewashed plywood steps, and tapped on the frame of the metal screen door. 'Mr and Mrs McIlveen? Sheriff Clemson Reade and Ms Tish Tarragon. Henrico County Sheriff's Department.'

Lucille McIlveen was a tall, formidable-looking woman with dark, gray-tinged bobbed hair and piercing eyes. She was dressed in a rust-and-navy patterned cotton-knit A-line dress and a pair of house slippers. She propped open the door. 'Come in.'

The door opened directly into the McIlveen's yellow-hued living room. Containing a set of circa-1980 floral-print sofas, white Swiss-dot tie-back curtains, and lots of bric-a-brac, the room was dated, but clean and cozy. In a brown recliner set in front of a box fan sat a man with a gardening magazine sprawled across his lap. He was in his mid to late seventies, balding, and dressed in a pair of khaki shorts and a short-sleeved plaid button-down shirt.

'John, the police are here,' Lucille McIlveen announced, placing the accent on the first syllable of the word 'police.' 'Put that magazine away.'

While Lucille gestured to her guests to sit on the sofa, John closed his magazine, but kept it in the same location.

'What can we do for you folks?' she asked, sitting on the sofa across from them.

Reade leaned forward and folded his hands on his lap. 'We're here to ask you about Gadsden Carney. I believe he's been in touch with you recently.'

'You mean that police fella who was in charge of finding Daisy's killer?'

'Yes, that's the man.'

'Yeah, he called us up about a month or so back. Said he was dissatisfied with the outcome of the case, whatever that meant. Bit late in the game to be dissatisfied about anything regarding that little girl. Still, we answered his questions best we could.'

'Mr Carney was murdered two nights ago,' Reade informed them. 'His body was found at the Honeycutt family plot.'

Lucille leaned back and fingered the gold crucifix around her neck. 'Well, that is too bad, but I suppose that's what happens when you don't allow the dead to rest in peace.'

'We believe that his death is linked to Daisy's murder.'

John McIlveen laughed. 'How is that possible? Daisy and her mama have been moldering in their graves these last twenty-odd years.'

'I understand it seems impossible. In many ways, it seems that way to me, too,' Reade confessed. 'However, if you could tell me what you told former Sheriff Carney, I'd appreciate it.'

John's laughter abruptly died down. 'All right, Sheriff, what do you need to know?'

'I need you to tell me exactly what you told Carney.'

'OK, though I'm sure he wrote down what we said . . .'

'He did, but Ms Tarragon and I would like to hear from you and your wife directly.'

John moved the gardening magazine on to an adjacent end table. 'Well, for a start, we'd been working and living up at Cypress Hollow for nearly ten years before the senator took over the place. Old Man Honeycutt couldn't travel down as much as he'd like, so he hired Lucille and me to look after the place for him. Let us live in a little house on the grounds. Lucille took care of the Cypress Hollow house, I took care of the grounds, and we'd tackle the bigger projects together. I got to love gardening while working for Old Man Honeycutt. He let me do whatever I wanted to keep the grounds looking good and he footed the bill. Those were some happy years – just Lucille, our boy, and me.'

'I've only seen Cypress Hollow in photos, but your garden here is lovely,' Tish complimented him.

'Bought those plants bit by bit these past years. It ain't like Cypress Hollow back in the day, but it's mine. With these knees, I couldn't manage another Cypress Hollow anyway,' he said with a chuckle.

'When did Benton Honeycutt take over ownership of Cypress Hollow?'

'After Old Man Honeycutt died. Oh, maybe 1979 . . . 1980. Nothing changed much until he got married, then *everything* changed. Mrs Honeycutt redid the whole house, added on more space than a family could ever use, and she uprooted the whole garden – my garden – so she could build a bigger swimming pool. It was an awful mess.'

'I take it you didn't see eye to eye with Mrs Honeycutt,' Reade presumed.

'Very few people saw eye to eye with Mrs Honeycutt,' Lucille interjected. 'Letting that boy sit in his room to play video games for hours while teaching Daisy all that show business stuff, but never teaching either of them a word of scripture. Senator Honeycutt didn't approve of it, either – her putting Daisy up on a stage for everyone to gawk at.'

'Did you ever hear the Honeycutts argue about Daisy's music and dance lessons?' Reade asked.

'No,' John McIlveen said decisively. 'Lucille and I aren't the types to listen at doors. We've always kept ourselves to ourselves.'

Lucille nodded. 'Unless there was a party going on, John and I would be back in our cottage right after I served the family supper. Nanny Viola insisted that the children clear the table and load the dishwasher. In my opinion, those kids could have done with a few more chores, but at least she tried.'

'If you didn't hear the Honeycutts argue, then how do you know the senator objected to Daisy's training?' Reade persisted.

'Because Mrs Honeycutt scheduled all of Daisy's lessons, rehearsals, and recitals for days when the senator wasn't at Cypress

Hollow. If the senator was in favor of Daisy's performing, I figure Mrs Honeycutt would have scheduled those things so that he'd be able to see them,' Lucille correctly reasoned.

'Was there any tension between them the day Daisy was killed?'

'I'd say. The senator had brought some young Washington chippy with him for the long weekend. He claimed she was an aide. John and me, we wondered what, precisely, she was aiding.'

'So you thought they were having an affair,' Tish surmised.

'Sure did. I'm sure everyone at the barbecue did, too. The way she hung on every word he said and swanned about the place like she owned it. Anyone who happened into that yard might have thought *she* was Mrs Honeycutt. I don't abide by the senator bringing a woman like that 'round his children, but I don't blame him for looking for affection elsewhere. It's not right for a husband and wife to live apart the way they did. It's not good for the children, either.'

'Tell us about the hours leading up to Daisy's death,' Tish urged.

'It was a beautiful, sunny day – Mrs Honeycutt was always lucky with the weather. Ms Dixie had arrived the night before and, given the mood in the kitchen that morning, she and Mrs Honeycutt had had another one of their fights, which didn't help Mrs Honeycutt's state of mind none. She always got into a tizzy the day of a party, but everything was going smoothly, considering. The caterers were on time and the children were in good spirits – even Walker James, who could be a fussy so-and-so. It was just going on noon when the senator came in the door with that woman with him. The mood in that house, and especially that of Mrs Honeycutt, got worse.

'Despite all of that,' she went on, 'all the guests seemed to have a good time. Most everyone was gone by six thirty. Only the Heritages, close friends of the Honeycutts, stuck around. The Heritages were always the last family to leave. Their kids swam like fishes and never wanted to leave the pool. No one minded, though. They were nice folks, the Heritages. In fact, Mrs Heritage once told Mrs Honeycutt that she was pushing Daisy too hard. Her words fell on deaf ears, but I admired her for saying them just the same.'

'What were the two of you doing when Mrs Honeycutt discovered Daisy's body?'

John was the first to answer. 'I was emptying the garbage cans from the party. There were about a dozen of them on the grounds. I was emptying the one by the children's play area when I heard the screaming. I couldn't tell at first where it was coming from, so I looked around. The only person I could see was Senator Honeycutt. He was about one hundred yards away by the creek that ran behind the house down to the stables. He was crouched down over the creek and it looked like he was praying.'

'Was that usual for him?' Reade questioned.

'Oh, yeah, he loved that spot. It was the lowest point in the hollow and, standing there, you could see the house to the south and the hills to the north. He'd sit there for hours some days, if he had a problem he had to think about. I ain't never seen him pray like that before, but with two women in the house that weekend, it seemed as good a time as any for him to take up the habit.'

'What did you do next?'

'When I figured out the screams were coming from the house, I legged it there as fast as I could. I bumped into Lucille on the way and we both opened the garage door to find Mrs Honeycutt . . . and Daisy. Mrs Heritage was right behind us.'

Reade turned his attention to Mrs McIlveen. 'And you?'

'I was in the tent, tearing down the chairs and tables, putting the silverware in the dishwasher, packing away the leftovers, and washing the chafing dishes so everything could be collected by the rental company the next day,' Lucille explained.

'So you were traveling between the house and the tent in the backyard?'

'That's right. Spent most of the time from dessert onward cleaning up.'

'Did you hear or see anyone or anything while you were in the house?'

'I didn't see anyone, but I did hear Mrs Honeycutt's voice once. She was shouting at Daisy, saying she didn't like her behavior.'

'Were those the exact words she used?'

'No, not exactly. She said, "Your behavior today has been intolerable."'

'Did you hear Daisy's reply?'

'No, John and I made a point of not interfering with the children.

That was Nanny Viola's job. I also never heard Mrs Honeycutt so angry before. I wasn't about to get in the middle of that, so I dumped whatever dishes I was carrying into the sink and went back out to the tent to finish packing leftovers and the like.'

'Is that when you heard the screams?'

'Oh, no. Not yet. I heard Mrs Honeycutt shouting at Daisy around six thirty or so. She always liked Daisy to say goodbye to their guests – part of the entertaining thing, I guess – but Daisy had skipped off somewhere. I didn't hear the screams from the garage until just about seven.'

'And when you heard the screams, you ran directly to the garage.'

'That's right, like John told you. Mrs Heritage was right there with us. Mr Heritage and Senator Honeycutt joined us a little while after that and then, later, that hussy, Priscilla. She just added to the drama with her crying and carrying-on. The senator had me take her into the house. I didn't like being stuck with her, but it just wasn't fitting, her going on like that in front of him the way she did. Daisy wasn't her child.'

'What happened next?' Reade urged.

'Ms Dixie arrived,' John answered. 'She did her best to console Mrs Honeycutt, but she couldn't help but fall apart herself.'

'Meanwhile, I called nine-one-one from the kitchen. Police and an ambulance got to the house a few minutes later. John and I gave our stories to some deputy . . .'

'Deputy Gus Aldrich?'

'That's it. That's the man.'

'The Honeycutts didn't give statements,' John interrupted. 'They were too high-and-mighty to talk to anyone. The minute it was mentioned that Daisy was murdered, they skedaddled, taking Walker James with them. Because of the barbecue, the entire property was treated like a crime scene, and we were forced to leave our home. Mr Heritage was kind enough to pay for us to stay at the inn in town – Ms Dixie stayed there, too, that night – and then, later, at a motel near the interstate, but the Honeycutts left us high and dry. Those weeks were downright awful. We'd lost our home, our jobs, and then, all of a sudden, our faces were on the front of the supermarket tabloids as possible suspects.'

'Why were you considered suspects?' Tish asked.

'On July third, our boy, Russell,' Lucille answered, 'was arrested on drug possession. It was his second offense, which meant jail time. We couldn't afford a lawyer, so we were going to let the public defender handle Russell's case, but I couldn't – we couldn't – let him sit in prison until the trial came up. Russell needed help, so that afternoon John and I went to Mrs Honeycutt. The first time Russell was arrested, she gave us money to pay all his fines and to enroll him in the government-run drug program the court requires, so we asked if she and the senator would help us again. Mrs Honeycutt flat-out refused.'

'How much did you ask for?'

'Five thousand for bail and another eight thousand to send him to a Christian rehab center to help get the poison out of him,' John replied, while Lucille, reaching into the pocket of her dress, retrieved a tissue and blew her nose. 'We gave the Honeycutt family the best years of our lives and it wasn't like they didn't have the money.'

'Mrs Honeycutt wondered whether we should be bailing Russell out so quick. She thought it best he spend some time in jail so he could start to detox. Detox,' Lucille scoffed. 'This from a woman with enough prescription bottles in her medicine cabinet to put a pharmacy out of business. She also didn't like the idea of a Christian rehab center. She said she had a friend who'd been hooked on diet pills and had success with a rehab center in Baltimore. I told her that we wanted our son somewhere where people would pray over him and with him – according to James chapter four, verse seven, "Submit yourselves therefore to God. Resist the devil, and he will flee from you." Our boy needed a place where he could submit himself to God and be redeemed through the love of Jesus Christ.'

Reade gave a brief pause. 'How did Mrs Honeycutt respond to your argument?'

'She said she didn't feel comfortable giving us the money until she spoke with her husband. Well, the senator wasn't coming home till the next day and, what with the barbecue, who knew when she'd get around to discussing it with him. In the meantime, our son was sitting in a jail cell,' Lucille explained, her voice growing frantic. 'It wasn't her boy, all alone, wondering if and when his mama and daddy were coming to get him.'

John rose from his spot in the recliner and sat beside his wife. 'Now, now,' he consoled, patting her hands. 'This is a difficult subject, Sheriff. To find ourselves as suspects in a murder when all we wanted to do was save our boy . . .'

'I do understand,' Reade said. 'Where's your son now?'

'Dead,' Lucille answered through her sobs.

'We never were able to get Russell out on bail,' John explained. 'He spent the next eighteen months in jail. When he finally got out, we rejoiced and thanked Jesus, but the power of the poison was too strong for him. Less than a week after getting out, he met up with some of his old gang and that was that. He overdosed in a friend's back bedroom. The people in the house were so high they didn't notice he was dead until a day later. "Do not be deceived: Bad company ruins good morals." The first letter to the Corinthians, chapter fifteen, verse thirty-three.'

Reade and Tish conveyed their condolences.

Lucille sniffed and dried her eyes. 'You can be as sorry as you like, but it won't bring him back. No, there's only one person responsible for Russell's being gone and that's Delilah Honeycutt. If she'd just given us the money when we asked for it, we could have gotten him out of jail, and his lawyer could have delayed his sentence until after he got through the Bible program, but she was more concerned about where her money was going than my son's wellbeing. It ain't Christian, but I'll never forgive her. My child was worth no less than either of hers. "Rich and poor have this in common: The Lord is the Maker of them all." Proverbs chapter twenty-two, verse two.'

'Do you believe Delilah Honeycutt murdered her daughter?' Reade asked.

Lucille folded her arms across her chest defiantly. 'There's not a doubt in my mind. That bathroom full of pills to make her happy one minute and sleepy the next – there's only so long a person can live like that before they snap. But, on top of that, there was no God in that house. Had Mrs Honeycutt welcomed Jesus into her home, none of it would have happened.'

'But Mrs Honeycutt was consulting with a member of the church, Reverend Ambrose Dillard,' Reade pointed out.

'She may have been consulting with Reverend Dillard, but there was no piety in her heart.'

'One last question for you both, and then we'll be on our way. Where were you two evenings ago between eight thirty and eleven?'

'We were at our church from six until nine, preparing for this week's prayer weekend. Then we came home, watched the news, and went to bed,' John said.

'Are you and the press going to try to blame this murder on us, too?' Lucille retorted.

'No, ma'am,' Reade replied. 'Not unless the evidence proves that's where the blame belongs.'

'I'll tell you where the blame belongs, Sheriff. Mr Carney brought this all on himself. That poor girl had found peace until he came around digging up the past, bringing up things that were better off buried. Carney went out of his way to change what we all know is the truth and God struck him down. So shall it always be with sinners. Romans chapter one, verse eighteen – "For the wrath of God is revealed from heaven against all ungodliness and unrighteousness of men, who by their unrighteousness suppress the truth."'

# FOURTEEN

'That was . . .' Tish struggled to articulate her reaction to their interview with the McIlveens.

'Interesting?' Reade suggested as they drove back toward the Hobson Glen town limits.

'I was going to say "fire and brimstone," but "interesting" fits the bill, too,' she said with a grin. 'What was your take on the McIlveens?'

'I don't think I've met two people who spoke so much about God and yet showed such obvious contempt for another human being.'

'Same here. I feel terrible about what happened to their son, but I must admit if I were Delilah Honeycutt, I'd have been reluctant to drop eight grand into a Bible-based rehab center, too. At least, not without more information, such as whether it was registered with the American Medical Association.'

'I totally agree with you. Eight thousand in 1996 dollars was a hefty price tag for a rehab clinic that may or may not be accredited.'

'I also think Delilah wanting to discuss a thirteen-thousand-dollar expenditure with her husband before writing a check was valid, too.'

'Specially since they'd already bailed Russell out of trouble once and the McIlveens clearly expected a hand-out again and not a loan.'

Tish shook her head. 'You don't think they took revenge by killing Daisy and then murdered Carney to cover up their guilt, do you?'

'I admit the thought crossed my mind. The only problem is, if they did, why would Delilah confess?'

Tish threw her hands up in the air. 'I don't know. I don't know what to make of anything. Perhaps watching some old footage will help. It would be nice to hear the Honeycutts give their version of events and maybe get a glimpse of what was going through their minds at the time.'

Reade pulled into the Channel Ten News parking lot and accompanied Tish into the lobby of the building where Jules was waiting. 'Hey, y'all,' Jules greeted them. 'I have lunch and the TV set up in my boss's office – he's on vacation this week. Clayton's already here.'

'Wait, you bought us lunch?' Reade questioned as they followed Jules across the busy newsroom floor.

'Of course not.' The journalist laughed. 'Tish did. She dropped it by before meeting you this morning. You didn't really think she'd let a lunchtime meeting go un-catered, did you?'

Reade glanced at Tish, who merely smiled. 'It's a disease,' she explained.

Reade laughed. 'You're amazing. You know that?'

Tish shrugged as she stepped into the office where Clayton was waiting. 'Not really. You guys are actually doing me a favor. Our lunch is a new menu item I've been experimenting with and I thought I'd test it out on some of my best customers.'

While the three men expressed their delight at being nominated as guinea pigs, Tish extracted four six-inch-long, wax-paper-wrapped parcels and placed them on the coffee table where Jules had arranged napkins, soft drinks, bags of chips, and paper plates. Unwrapping the bundles, she explained, 'These are Spanish boca-dillo. There's the traditional version with marinated pork loin, Manchego cheese, pickled piquillo peppers, sliced tomatoes, and a red mojo sauce on a baguette, and there's a vegetarian version that swaps marinated Portobello mushroom for the pork. If you guys give them the thumbs-up, I'll put them on my menu as *Fromage to Catalonia.*'

'I'm a Southern boy,' Jules exclaimed, snatching a half-baguette of the traditional sandwich and a can of Dr Pepper. 'I've never met a pig product I didn't like.'

'May I try one of each?' asked Clayton, ever polite.

'Of course,' Tish replied. 'They both need to be tested.'

Clayton plated a half of each sandwich, grabbed a bag of salt and vinegar chips and a bottle of water, and plopped on to the adjacent loveseat, only to be met with a slap on the arm from Jules. 'Not there,' he ordered with a side-glance toward Tish and Reade.

Clayton followed Jules's gaze. 'Oh,' he muttered and, rising from his spot, sat down in the high-backed tufted office chair that had been wheeled to one end of the coffee table.

'Not there, either. That's the lumbar-support chair from my cubicle. You sit over there.' Jules directed the young officer to the tubular steel chair at the other end of the coffee table.

'Wow, I've never seen Jules in the office before,' Reade whispered to Tish as he stole the other half of Clayton's veggie bocadillo and put it on his plate. 'He's awfully particular.'

'And obvious. Very, very obvious,' Tish quipped before serving herself half a veggie bocadillo and a bottle of water and joining Reade on the loveseat.

'There. Isn't this cozy?' Jules stated with a broad grin.

Tish glared at him from over the top of her bottle of water.

Jules's smile quickly disappeared. 'Oh, Tish.' He cleared his throat. 'This sandwich is an absolute keeper. Your customers will love it.'

Tish swallowed her gulp of water. 'You really think so?'

'Mmm,' Clayton agreed, his mouth full of sandwich. 'They're both terrific. I don't miss the meat in the veggie one at all. In fact, in some ways I like it better than the traditional.'

'Bite your tongue,' Jules teased.

'Clayton's right,' Reade agreed. 'The mushrooms are hearty but have a great flavor. What's in the mojo sauce?'

'Dried chili, red wine vinegar, and olive oil,' Tish described.

'It's terrific. I might go in for another half when I've finished this one.'

'Same here,' Jules concurred. 'That pork is so tender, it's hard to believe you're a Yankee.'

'You're playing the I-Can't-Believe-You're-A-Yankee card? Now I know it's a successful sandwich.' Tish laughed.

The foursome consumed their lunch with gusto, punctuating the silence only to groan in delight or to compliment Tish on the food. Although the mood was relatively light, it was obvious that their minds were all focused on the task at hand.

When they'd finished eating, Jules placed the empty wrappers and dirty napkins and plates in the office wastepaper basket and moved to the television that had been placed on the opposite side of the room. Picking up a remote, he switched the television on and slid a DVD into the side of the unit. 'This interview aired on our affiliate station on July eleventh, 1996. One week after Daisy's murder.'

'And nearly three months before the Honeycutts finally sat down – with their attorneys in tow – to talk about the events of that day,' Reade clarified.

'Yes, that's actually the first question in the interview. But I'm not going to say any more. I'm going to hand over the remote to Officer Clayton so he can pause as and when needed.' Jules pressed the DVD function on the remote, prompting a sharp intake of air from the room's occupants as the blue screen was replaced by the image of Benton and Delilah Honeycutt.

They were both dressed in well-tailored suits – Benton's in navy with a gray tie and a white, button-down dress shirt, and Delilah's in black with a simple gold chain, small gold hoop earrings, and understated makeup. Benton's graying brown hair was trimmed short on the sides and slightly longer at the crown in an attempt to draw attention away from his receding hairline, while Delilah's long blonde hair had been trimmed into several then-trendy long layers which had been professionally blown dry for maximum volume.

Clayton stood up and took the remote from Jules. 'Thanks. Before we start this video, I'm going to point out the Honeycutts' appearance. The dark clothes, the tasteful jewelry – they've all been carefully chosen to convey the message that these people are grieving. They look as if they literally just attended a funeral, even though their daughter's body still had not been released for burial. Whether they did this themselves, or if they were prompted by their PR firm, I can't say, but given they'd received a lot of negative press for not speaking with the authorities, I would say someone, somewhere, recognized that the Honeycutts needed to manage public perception.'

Clayton pressed play and the video snapped to life. Off camera, a male interviewer introduced the senator and his wife and thanked them for speaking with him. The couple nodded and quietly thanked him for granting them time on his show; in reply, the interviewer expressed his condolences.

The interviewer then launched into the interview. 'The first question on my mind – and probably on the mind of everyone in America – is do you have immediate plans to return to Virginia and speak with the police about your daughter's murder?'

'Oh, absolutely,' Benton Honeycutt assured the interviewer as his head moved repeatedly from right to left. 'We want them to know everything there is to know about what happened that day.'

Clayton paused the video. 'The senator's gestures here indicate that he's lying.'

'Well, we know he's lying,' Jules interjected. 'Like Reade said, it was three months before they consented to police interviews.'

'I understand,' Clayton acknowledged, 'but in the files, the Honeycutts claimed that their delay in speaking with the police was due to Benton's congressional duties and Delilah's fragile emotional state. This interview shows that Benton had absolutely no intention of speaking with the police.'

Clayton rewound to the beginning of the interviewer's question and pressed play. 'Watch. Benton's mouth is saying yes, but his body is saying otherwise. His chin is down in a protective position a boxer might take and he's clearly shaking his head to indicate no.'

Clayton let the DVD play to reveal Delilah mimicking her

husband's head gesture and saying quite slowly, quite deliberately, 'Everything. We want to tell them everything.'

'Delilah is also shaking her head no when she's saying yes, although her head movement is slightly less emphatic than her husband's,' Clayton analyzed upon pausing the DVD. 'However, her slower movement might be due to the fact that she's obviously been sedated either via alcohol or drugs.'

'The Honeycutts' housekeeper said Delilah had a medicine cabinet full of prescription bottles,' Tish revealed.

'There you go. The Honeycutts' words are interesting, too,' Clayton continued. 'The interviewer asks if they're *going to* speak with the police, but both Benton and Delilah state that they *want to* speak to the police while simultaneously sending signals that indicate that their statements are untrue.'

'So they're not just saying that they're not going to speak with the police,' Jules extrapolated. 'They're also saying they don't want to speak with the police.'

'That's correct. I can only read what I see, so I can't determine why they don't want to speak with them, but it's quite clear that was the reason for their reticence.' Clayton pressed play again and the quartet watched the television with rapt attention.

'What about the rumors that you and your wife called your attorney just hours after Daisy was discovered dead?' the interviewer challenged.

'The rumors are true. We did make that phone call,' Benton replied, his head held high.

Clayton paused the video. 'The senator is telling the truth here, but he's presenting it as a challenge. His chin is up and no longer protecting his neck – that vulnerable part of the body that we instinctively try to protect from predators. This is a fight response rather than a flight response. It's basically the nonverbal equivalent of "Come at me, bro," which is a strange position to take in this situation. The purpose of this interview was to manage the public and the media's perception of the Honeycutts, and yet here's the senator literally staring down his nose at his interviewer. He's alienating the audience.'

The video jumped to life again. 'I was told by a close friend who came round and happens to be an attorney that in the majority of child killings the police target the parents,' Benton, his eyes wide, informed the interviewer. 'That friend strongly advised me to get my lawyers in on this before the police decided to focus on my wife and me as the prime suspects.'

'That's a lie,' Reade asserted. 'Frank Heritage was the only friend on the scene that evening and he worked in finance, not law.'

'That's right,' Tish echoed. 'The only lawyer – well, former lawyer – in the Honeycutt household at the time of Daisy's murder was Benton Honeycutt himself.'

Clayton nodded as he paused the DVD. 'The illustrators of a lie are in the footage as well. Benton licks his lips before he speaks and he stares at the interviewer without blinking or moving any other part of his face or upper body. Also interesting, again, is his choice of words. Rather than saying, "in the majority of cases like ours," he says, "in the majority of child killings." This is distancing language which is used to downplay the connection between the person speaking and the actual truth.'

The video resumed. 'Tell us,' the interviewer urged, 'what happened the day Daisy died.'

'It was the Fourth of July and we'd just held our annual barbecue,' Delilah said, as her face grew pinched and tears began to slide down her cheeks. 'Everyone had gone home and it was time to give Daisy and her brother their baths and get them into pajamas before we drove over to see our local fireworks display later that night. We–we put the kids in pajamas because they'd always fall asleep on the drive home. When I couldn't find Daisy outside, I went into the house to look for her. That's when I found her in the garage. I wanted to believe she was OK, but I knew she . . .' Delilah's voice dissolved into sobs.

'The tension beneath the eyes and around the mouth erupts into tears,' Clayton noted. 'I can't read anything there but genuine grief.'

Tish blinked back tears. So much had been said about Dixie's wild, dark good looks, but Delilah's pale, delicate beauty, although less exotic, was just as exquisite. Even in tears, her face red from crying, she was lovely, and behind her sad, downturned eyes there was a sense of quiet strength and resilience.

The interviewer waited until Delilah quieted to speak again. 'Is it of your opinion that someone broke into your home that evening and killed Daisy?'

'Of course it is,' Benton asserted, yet his head moved ever-so-slightly from side to side.

'No one in that house could have committed such a crime,' Delilah maintained. 'We loved that girl. Everyone at the barbecue that day loved that girl.'

Clayton pressed pause. 'She's using distancing language again – "that house," "that girl," "such a crime." Normal language would have referred to Daisy by name or as "our daughter" and would have spelled out the crime as murder. There's also exaggeration – although most of the barbecue guests probably *liked* Daisy, it would be inaccurate to state that they all *loved* her. She's overreaching in order to convince us this wasn't an inside job.'

'What will you remember most about Daisy?' the interviewer continued when the video resumed.

'Her spirit, her smile, and the way she always sang. No matter what was going on, she always had a song in her heart.' Once again, Delilah broke down in what appeared to be genuine grief.

Benton looked down and to his left and bit his bottom lip. 'Yes, I'll always remember how she'd greet me with a song when I'd come home for the weekend,' he said emotionally before burying his face in one hand.

'Whoa,' exclaimed Clayton.

'What is it?' Reade prompted.

'Let me watch this again,' Clayton requested. Upon reviewing the clip a third time, he muttered, 'Duper's Delight.'

'What?'

'Duper's Delight. I never expected to spot it in an interview with a dead girl's parents but watch this.' Clayton replayed the clip, pausing to point out the different elements of Benton Honeycutt's reaction. 'First, his eyes are looking downward and to the left, which indicates that he is most likely using the right side of his brain to think of an appropriate answer, rather than actually speaking from memory. The lip-biting – a stress reaction – further corroborates this theory. Benton then covers his face. This is an outright illustrator of a falsehood. This is evidence enough that he's not telling the truth about his feelings for his daughter and her singing, but look what happens immediately after he breaks down. He moves his hand away from his face and looks up at the interviewer as if to verify that his emotional breakdown produced the desired effect, but his face shows absolutely zero emotion until . . .' Clayton froze the screen.

'He's smirking,' Tish noted.

'He's definitely smirking,' agreed Reade, leaning forward in his seat.

Clayton nodded. 'It's only there for a split second, but this is what's known as Duper's Delight. The senator looks up, sees that his emotional display has struck the right chords, and then smiles at his ability to successfully dupe his audience. It's a classic tell that someone is lying.'

'Benton *was* lying,' Tish said. 'According to the Heritages, the McIlveens, and Dixie Dupree, Benton hated Daisy being groomed for show business. It was one of the biggest problems in his and Delilah's marriage.'

Reade nodded. 'The video substantiates what we already know.'

'Yeah, but just *how much* did Benton hate Daisy singing?' Jules asked. 'Did he hate it enough that he might have accidentally killed Daisy while trying to silence her?'

'Daisy *was* singing Christmas carols on the day she was murdered. And he had Priscilla with him – a woman who, by all accounts, didn't want Daisy around.'

'So Benton kills his daughter and Delilah takes the blame?' Tish challenged.

'You heard Louella Heritage this morning. Delilah was constantly pushing Daisy to take more lessons and spend more time rehearsing. If that chronic push to make Daisy sing is what resulted in her death, Delilah could have felt as though she was indirectly responsible.'

Tish pulled a face. She wasn't a mother, but if she were, she was reasonably certain that anyone who harmed, injured, or in any way placed her child in danger would bear the full brunt and fury of her wrath, regardless of matrimonial or familial bonds.

'You're not buying it, are you?' Reade inferred.

'Delilah taking the blame is one thing. Letting Benton get away with murder is another matter entirely.'

'Maybe they had an arrangement. Maybe Benton promised to try to have her pardoned after an appropriate amount of time had passed. He was a US State senator, after all. He had a good deal of power.'

'You mean maybe they struck some sort of deal?'

Reade gave a single nod.

'Hmm,' Tish pondered aloud. 'I suppose it's possible. However, it doesn't help us with the murder of Gadsden Carney. Benton Honeycutt's been dead well over a year.'

'Let's watch the rest of the video and see what else is in it.'

At Reade's suggestion, Clayton pressed play. 'The local Virginia authorities,' the interviewer started, 'have issued a statement to the residents of Henrico County assuring them that there is nothing to worry about. That there is no killer on the loose—'

Delilah interrupted. 'But there is a killer on the loose,' she insisted, a cry in her voice. 'Look at the heinous crime that's been committed. The person who did this broke into our home and he's still out there. This person is out there right now looking for someone else to harm. No one is safe until this person is found. No one.'

Clayton paused. 'Once again, Delilah uses distancing language. A "heinous crime has been committed" – not "our daughter's been killed." She refers to "the person who did this" and not "our daughter's murderer." She does, however, use the phrase "our home." That's the only time so far in this interview that she's verbally claimed ownership of anything. However, there's something else in this clip that's interesting. I'm going to replay this and ask you to watch Benton closely as Delilah issues her final warning.'

'Benton is mouthing the last few words Delilah's speaking,' Tish observed with surprise. 'Her statement was rehearsed.'

'They hired a PR firm. It's not surprising if that firm helped them to prepare some answers before going on their first television interview,' Reade said.

'And yet they made so many other mistakes. It seems doubtful that a PR firm would have let them go on air using distancing language and that they wouldn't have coached them to nod their heads when saying yes.'

Clayton spoke up. 'I'm with Tish on this one. Body language analysis hasn't become a sanctioned police tool until recently, but it's been used in PR and advertising for decades. The Honeycutts weren't trained by a pro – they'd have been far more polished. When they rehearsed that line, they did so on their own.'

'Some interviewers provide their guests with sample questions prior to taping. What we saw might have been a sample question; that's why the Honeycutts seemed more prepared. I'll do my best to find out if that was the case here,' Jules offered. 'But it might be difficult to find those transcripts after all this time.'

'It might also be interesting to find out when the sheriff's office issued the statement telling residents not to worry,' Reade directed. 'This interview was conducted one week after Daisy's murder. That's not a lot of time for Carney to make such a sweeping assessment.'

Clayton aimed the remote at the TV and the clip of Delilah resumed. 'There are two people out there who know the truth about what happened that day . . . the person who did this and someone that person might have told. Those people need to do the right thing. They . . .' She broke down in sobs.

'Two people?' Jules repeated. 'That's oddly specific.'

'Yeah,' Reade agreed. 'Why not say, "someone out there knows something"? That's the phrase we use when asking the public for information.'

'She's also not using any quantifiers,' Tish added. 'Is she trying to say there are *at least* two people out there who know the truth? Or is she saying there are *only* two people out there who know the truth? If it's the latter, how does she know that? How can she be certain that the killer only told one person what he or she had done? The killer could have been seen breaking into their garage or they could have been bragging to friends. To say that just two people know the truth is absolutely bizarre, unless . . .'

'Unless you're one of those two people,' Reade completed the thought.

Meanwhile, on the television screen, Benton Honeycutt reached for his wife's hand and squeezed it tightly. 'What Delilah was beginning to say is that she and I have established a tips hotline and are offering seventy-five thousand dollars for information that leads to the arrest of the person who committed this crime.'

'Can you stop the video for a second?' Reade requested.

Clayton immediately obliged.

'I want everyone to take note that the Honeycutts' tip hotline was established before the pair had even spoken with the police,' Reade stated. 'Think about that for a moment. It's quite common for parents of means to offer a monetary reward for information regarding a missing or murdered child, but those rewards are typically offered in conjunction with the police. Not this one. Likewise, the first few hours in a homicide investigation are critical, and the Honeycutts spent them refusing to be interviewed by police, hiring attorneys and PR people, appearing on television, and then setting up a private investigation to run concurrently with that of the sheriff's office.'

Reade nodded to Clayton and the latter resumed the video.

'Are you confident that you'll find the person who murdered your daughter?' the interviewer asked.

'Absolutely,' Benton answered, his chin once again raised. 'Absolutely. It is my life's mission to find out who did this—'

'Strange phrasing here.' Clayton paused the DVD. 'A life's mission is literally something you've devoted your entire life to, but when this interview took place, Daisy had only been gone one week. The police or the Honeycutts' investigation could have identified the killer the next day or the day after that, so why would he refer to it as his life's mission?' He restarted the video.

'Whoever is guilty will be found and they will be punished.'

While Benton spoke, Delilah nodded her head slowly and then suddenly closed her eyes and turned her head downward. Clayton, for the final time, paused the DVD. 'Guilt. A classic expression of guilt.'

# FIFTEEN

'What if we're wrong, Clemson?' Tish asked Reade after he presented his badge and steered the SUV through the security gates of the Riverview Luxury Condominiums in Richmond. 'What if Gadsden Carney's death has nothing to do with Daisy Honeycutt's murder? Maybe we're looking in the wrong place. Maybe Gadsden's wife killed him – it's a tough job being a caregiver to a dying man.'

'So Mary Lee Carney, under a great deal of pressure, doesn't kill her husband while they're alone in Florida but waits until she and Gadsden are in Virginia visiting their daughter to do the deed?' Reade opposed. 'And then, instead of slipping her husband an extra painkiller or some other drug – which would have been extremely easy for her to do – and watch him drift off peacefully, she instead lures him to the Honeycutt grave in Ashton Courthouse, all while under the watchful gaze of her daughter and son-in-law?'

'OK, you needn't go any further. I realize that theory doesn't make any sense. It just seems like every road we take leads back to Delilah Honeycutt murdering her daughter.'

Reade pulled the SUV to halt in the area marked as visitors' parking. 'I know. It's frustrating, but what does your gut say?'

'That the two cases are somehow linked.'

'Mine says that, too. We need to keep reviewing the evidence and following our guts, Tish. It's the only way we'll get to the bottom of this.'

'Did they teach you that at the police academy?' She smiled.

'No, that was Sheriff Gadsden Carney's advice to me my first week on the job. I figure he was probably following his gut when he reopened his files on the Honeycutt case. We should, too. By the way, after Clayton's presentation, I called Gus Aldrich, the deputy on the case, and asked if we could move up our meeting. He's agreed to meet us this afternoon. Perhaps he can clarify some things.'

Tish and Reade stepped out of the car, entered the main lobby of the building, and took the elevator to the penthouse. After several seconds elapsed, the doors opened on to the only penthouse apartment in the building. Priscilla Maddox Honeycutt, impeccably dressed in a powder-blue suit, ivory blouse, and nude kitten heels, was waiting for them.

'Sheriff Reade. Ms Tarragon.' She greeted them with the friendly handshake and business card palm-slip of a seasoned bureaucrat. 'Please, come in.'

She led them to a traditionally furnished sunken living room with an extensive view of the James River and, beyond, Richmond City Center. Tish and Reade selected a beige sectional sofa and sat down beside each other. Priscilla chose a velvet upholstered tub chair opposite them and crossed her legs at the knee.

The second Mrs Honeycutt expressed her sympathy. 'I was sorry to read about former Sheriff Carney's death. When Daisy was killed, I'd never before experienced death, let alone grief . . . Sheriff Carney was patient and kind while questioning this embarrassingly hysterical young woman. I apologized for my reaction when we met last week, and he was just as gracious as the first time I spoke to him.'

'You met Gadsden Carney last week?' Reade questioned.

'Yes, it was a teleconference, not a physical meeting,' she clarified. 'I'd anticipated a telephone call, but my assistant set it up as a Zoom meeting. It's a generational thing, I think. If it's not a text, then it must be a video call. She doesn't quite understand that I don't necessarily want to see everyone I speak to or that I may not want them to see me.'

Tish glanced at the Honeycutts' wedding photo which hung above a marble encased fireplace. The years had seen the loss of Priscilla's slender, girlish figure – traded for fine lines around her dark brown eyes – but otherwise, she still looked much like the auburn-haired, freckle-faced intern Benton Honeycutt had married.

'What did you and Carney discuss?'

'The case, naturally,' she replied matter-of-factly. 'He told me he'd reopened the investigation because he didn't feel as though the case was well and truly closed.'

'And you? What do you think?'

'Delilah confessed, went to jail, and died in prison more than twenty years ago. I'm not sure how much more closed a case could be. However, I was as gracious to Mr Carney as he had been to me, so I told him everything he wanted to know.'

'Which was?'

'He asked me to recount the events of that fateful day – the day Daisy was murdered.'

'Will you do the same for Ms Tarragon and me?'

'Might I infer from your question that you believe Mr Carney's death might be related to Daisy Honeycutt's?'

'You may,' Reade allowed.

'Ah, interesting,' Priscilla responded. 'I'll start from the beginning, then.'

Where Priscilla might have started had Reade not said that Carney's and Daisy's deaths were connected was anyone's guess.

'I went to Cypress Hollow that long Independence Day weekend to break up Benton and Delilah's marriage,' she said blandly. 'I'd been hired as an aide just before Christmas and I immediately fell in love. Benton was twice my age, but he was strong, intelligent, and powerful, and I knew, as soon as I saw him, that I wanted him for myself.'

'So the two of you started an affair,' Reade presumed.

'No. At least, not a physical one. We'd have lunch together, sometimes dinner, and talk until all hours. I'd just moved to Washington and was lonely, and Benton, although married with a family, was lonely, too. We connected. A few days before the fourth, I mentioned to Benton that I'd be staying in my apartment for the long weekend. It wasn't entirely untrue. My roommate had invited me to some gathering down at the National Harbor with friends of friends, but apart from that, I'd have been at home reading, eating takeout, and watching TV. Benton was shocked that a woman my age didn't have a busy social life and invited me to Cypress Hollow. There were some big names in politics attending and he thought I should meet them to help advance my career. So, after finishing some last-minute business on Thursday morning, off we went.

'When we arrived, I strutted into that house as if I owned the place. I think I even told one of Delilah's friends that when I moved in, I'd change the wallpaper, or something stupid and hurtful like that. The housekeeper and the nanny made it clear via eye contact that they were on to me, but Delilah, if she knew, kept it to herself. She was the epitome of the old-fashioned Southern hostess, even though I was an absolute brat. If I had just one ounce of Delilah's grace under fire . . .' Priscilla said wistfully, tears brimming in her eyes.

'I spent the entire day with Benton, chatting with his connections, meeting his friends,' Priscilla continued. 'It was wonderful. At some point during the day, I met Walker James and Daisy. Walker was as introverted as Daisy was extroverted and didn't take too much interest in me, but Daisy – Daisy was such a strange little girl. She was blonde and lovely, like her mother, but she kept singing the same Christmas carol repeatedly. She was so fixated on that song that I remember wondering if she was developmentally challenged, but then she spoke to me and at once I saw that she was fine. In fact, she was extremely intelligent. She asked me who

I was. I told her I was her daddy's friend. She responded by asking me if I was going to kiss her father. I was so startled that I didn't know how to answer. Thankfully, Daisy's aunt came by and sent her to play with the other children.

'That was my only encounter with Daisy,' Priscilla stated. 'She came back later, to see her father, but before I could speak with the girl, a friend of the Honeycutts decided to take me on a tour of the house, where I made my idiotic comment about redecorating. I would have inserted myself between me, Benton, and Daisy, too, if I'd been in Delilah's friend's shoes.'

'Where were you when Daisy's body was discovered?' Tish asked.

'I was on the patio outside the conservatory on the west side of the house. Most of the guests were leaving and Benton had gone to say his goodbyes. He also went to speak with Delilah. Naive, foolish me hoped he'd gone to tell her that he was in love with me.'

'But he didn't?'

'No. Not until later in our relationship – after Delilah was in prison – did he admit that he'd fallen in love with me as I had fallen in love with him.'

'What did Benton discuss with Delilah?'

'I haven't a clue. I had a headache – a product of drinking a glass of wine in all that sun and heat – and went to the side patio to relax and enjoy some quiet in the shade. I'd brought a book along to read, but I ended up just lying there with my eyes shut until I heard a car door slam. I looked up to see a car pull away from the front gate and speed down the road.'

'You said that guests were leaving the barbecue, so why would the slamming of a car door make you sit up and take notice?' Reade questioned.

'Three reasons. First, it was a single door slam and not the sound of a family getting into a car. Second, unless they were close friends or family members, everyone attending the barbecue was asked to park their car on a section of lawn well past the garage, at the other end of the house. I shouldn't have heard anything from where I was sitting. And, third, the speed limit on that road was twenty-five miles per hour, but the car I saw was traveling much faster than that.'

'Did you take note of the make and model?'

'No, the car was moving too fast and I've never been very good at identifying automobiles. It was a blue sedan – possibly an older one judging by the square and boxy shape of it.'

'And you saw the car immediately before Delilah found Daisy in the garage?'

'No. I wasn't wearing a watch, but I'd estimate it was maybe ten or fifteen minutes earlier. I closed my eyes again and tried to rest, but the car really bothered me. The homes and ranches in that hollow were all fairly exclusive, and I started to wonder if the car I saw might belong to a burglar. Even if it didn't, I was fairly certain Benton wouldn't want drivers speeding down the road like that – not with two young children – so I got up to look for him. As I approached the pool area, I heard crying and saw the garage door was open. I went to see what was going on and bumped into Delilah's friend, the blonde one who'd given me the house tour. She told me Daisy was dead. I just couldn't believe my ears, but when I stepped into the garage, I saw for myself it was true.

'Delilah was kneeling over an old blanket. From beneath the blanket, arms and legs splayed outward. I recognized the tiny floral sandals at the end of those legs from earlier in the day. It was Daisy. Delilah picked her up and cradled her in her arms, sobbing the entire time, and I . . . I lost it. I had treated the entire weekend – the situation with Benton and his family – like a game, and suddenly his daughter was dead. I saw the grief on his face and I felt like the most horrible person on earth. I don't remember exactly what happened next. I think I might have screamed or fainted, and the housekeeper took me into the kitchen and made me tea while she called for help.'

'What then?' Tish prompted.

'I sat there and waited for the police. I can't say how long it took for them to arrive. Time seemed to have stood still.' Priscilla drew a deep breath. 'Sheriff Carney interviewed me and I told him everything I knew. Everything I told him again in our Zoom meeting. Everything I've just told you.'

'Did Benton speak to you again that day?'

'No, he was on the phone with his lawyer and then he took off with Delilah and Walker James. I didn't see him again for weeks. After I gave my statement, I was allowed to go back to my

apartment in DC by train. Sheriff Carney took my contact information and was kind enough to have one of his men give me a
ride to the station. I contemplated resigning from my post, but my
roommate talked me out of it. When Benton finally returned for
the congressional session, I asked him if I should offer my resig-
nation and find a position elsewhere. He told me that under no
circumstances did he want me to leave.' Priscilla's eyes welled
with tears. 'I kept my distance from him at first, but over the
course of the next few months, as the investigation into Daisy's
death ramped up, he and I gradually resumed our schedule of
lunch dates and late-night talks. On the weekends, however, when
there was no work to be done, he'd fly back to South Carolina.'

'Did he talk to you about the murder?' Tish asked.

'Only to vent frustration over how the investigation was going.
He thought the police were wrong to be spending so much time
looking into him and Delilah when there were other suspects to
be found. Of course, then Delilah confessed to the whole thing.'

'Do you believe Delilah was guilty?'

'I do,' Priscilla answered without hesitation.

'Why?'

'Because she confessed. You don't understand – I was standing
in her backyard, eyeing up her husband, talking about moving into
her home, and the woman didn't bat an eye. Those who knew her
well might have noticed a change in her personality, but to everyone
else at that barbecue, she was the life of the party. A woman with
that kind of resolve doesn't confess unless she's guilty.'

'Did Benton believe Delilah was guilty, too?'

'Yes. Yes, he did.'

'And yet he remained married to her,' Reade remarked.

'He also visited her in prison every Sunday. You might be
shocked by that behavior, but my husband was an honorable man.
Benton didn't wish to put Delilah through any more strain than
she'd already experienced. He also recognized the role he'd played
in Daisy's death. He told me that if he hadn't spent so much time
away from home – if he hadn't allowed himself and Delilah to
drift apart to the point where she was alone with the kids all the
time – then maybe Daisy would still be alive. That he didn't notice
the signs and do something to prevent his daughter's murder was
his biggest regret.'

'You and the senator didn't have children of your own, did you?'

'No. Benton had a vasectomy shortly before we were married. He made it clear that he didn't want any more children. It was fine with me. Between our marriage, our careers, and our love of travel, there was always plenty to keep us happily fulfilled.'

Tish wasn't sure if she'd become overly sensitive to people's facial expressions, but she was almost certain that Priscilla had, for the briefest of moments, flinched while assuring them she was 'happily fulfilled.'

'One last question,' Reade prefaced. 'Where were you two evenings ago between eight thirty and eleven p.m.?'

'Here,' Priscilla replied matter-of-factly. 'I left my office and came straight home. I was here all evening.'

'With all due respect, Mrs Honeycutt, you weren't here all evening,' Tish argued.

'Well, how—'

'You were at the Junior League dinner presenting a check at approximately seven that evening. I was there as well.'

'Oh! Oh, yes. Silly me. I was at the dinner presenting a check from our foundation, but I didn't stay. I shook a few hands, had some punch and some pimento cheese canapés and then came straight home.'

'What time did you get here?' Reade asked.

'Eight-ish. I roasted some salmon and vegetables and streamed the London Symphony in concert. You can verify with my internet service provider if you'd like. It cost fifteen dollars.'

'That's OK.' Reade declined. 'I don't need that right now. Thank you for your time.'

As Priscilla escorted them to the elevator, Tish noticed a baby grand piano in the corner of the room. 'Oh, that's lovely! Do you play?'

'No,' Priscilla replied. 'That belonged to Delilah. Benton didn't have the heart to get rid of it.'

# SIXTEEN

'So Delilah killed their daughter, but Benton didn't file for divorce because it would have caused *Delilah* too much pain?' Reade asked in disbelief, as he and Tish walked across the condominium parking lot. 'Then, not only does he remain married, but he visits Delilah in prison because he feels partly responsible for the murder.'

'Don't forget the piano,' Tish reminded. 'Benton kept Delilah's piano, too.'

'I don't get it at all. It's just plain—'

'Love,' Tish interrupted, prompting Reade to stop in his tracks. 'What?'

'Love,' she repeated, as she stopped walking as well.

'Yes,' he agreed as he took a step closer and gazed into her eyes. 'I believe you're right.'

*Was Reade still talking about the case?* Afraid of the answer, Tish cleared her throat and proceeded toward the SUV. 'Despite his emotional affair with Priscilla and the fact that he and Delilah were living separate lives, Senator Honeycutt obviously still loved his wife.'

Reade followed Tish and unlocked the front doors of the SUV by pressing the button on his key fob. 'How could that be? How can you still love the woman who murdered your child?'

'I don't know,' she replied, stepping into the passenger seat. Reade closed the door behind Tish and climbed behind the steering wheel.

'Actually,' she went on after he'd settled into his seat, 'it's the biggest problem I have when I try to imagine Delilah and Benton rehearsing together for a television interview or when I hear that Benton led people through the garage in order to destroy evidence. Why would he act as his wife's accomplice? Why would either of them aid the other in eluding arrest?'

Reade started the engine and pulled out of the parking lot. 'They were both concerned with appearances. The senator didn't want his daughter performing on stage and Delilah needed to be seen as the perfect wife and mother. Having a murder in the family wasn't on either of their agendas.'

'I suppose.' Tish shrugged. 'But that's the sort of thing that one would expect to drive a couple apart over time. Instead, it appears to have brought the Honeycutts together.'

'And left Priscilla out in the cold for a while.'

'Yes, she seemed awfully understanding of Benton's situation, didn't she? And yet did you notice her expression when we asked her if she and Benton had children?'

'I did. I thought for a minute I might have imagined it. I'm glad you noticed it, too,' he said excitedly. 'What did you make of it?'

'Priscilla wasn't even thirty when she and Benton married. Expecting a woman that age to give up on the idea of having children is quite a lot to ask, don't you think?'

'Well, Benton was getting a bit long in the tooth to start another family and he already had an heir,' Reade speculated. 'Delilah also wound up putting the kids first in their marriage. Benton probably wanted to avoid going through all that again.'

'Maybe,' Tish replied tentatively. 'So where next?'

'We're off to meet Deputy Aldrich and then Bishop Dillard. I hope you don't mind the busy schedule. I want to make the most of the time I have with you today.'

'Not at all. I want to help as much as I can, although I have to say it's weird to be mentally busy and not physically busy. Right now, I'd normally be tallying the day's receipts, running the last load of dishes, checking stock, and preparing for the next day's baking.'

'Are you OK?'

'Yeah, I know the café's in good hands with Celestine and Mary Jo. Although I still might call in and see how the day went.'

'Take all the time you need,' Reade urged. 'If I need to reschedule—'

'No, I doubt we'll need to go that far. Just think of me as a new mom leaving her kid with the sitter for the first time. All nerves.'

Reade nodded. 'Then our next stop should make you feel like you're back at home. Just promise me you won't get up and clear tables.'

\*     \*     \*

Retired Deputy Gus Aldrich sat in a red vinyl booth in a back corner of the Westwood Fountain, an old-school lunch counter tucked at the back of an extensive Richmond pharmacy that sold homemade chocolates, local souvenirs, and a wide variety of magazines in addition to prescriptions and over-the-counter remedies.

'This place gives me life goals,' Tish confided to Reade as they entered the space that housed the lunch counter.

'It's great, isn't it?'

'Fantastic. I would love to have my café housed in a historic building like this.'

'You'll get there someday. And probably sooner than you think,' Reade asserted.

'As Celestine would say, "From your mouth to God's ears,"' Tish whispered as they approached the retired deputy's table.

'Sheriff,' Gus greeted Reade as he rose from his spot and shook hands. He was short, stocky, in his mid to late fifties, and dressed in a vibrantly printed Hawaiian shirt and stonewashed denim jeans. 'Ma'am.'

'Ms Tarragon,' Reade introduced Tish as he slid on to the bench seat beside her. 'Thanks for rescheduling our meeting.'

'No problem. I'm doing a little job in this part of town. Your call gave me an excuse to come by this place for a late lunch. Which reminds me, I'd better bring home a slice of their blueberry pie for my wife. She'll kill me if she finds out I was here without her. You been here before?'

'Many times, but not recently. I have a new favorite spot up in Hobson Glen.' He flashed a smile in Tish's direction.

'Really? As good as this place?'

'Better.'

'Smooth,' Tish said beneath her breath, prompting Reade's grin to widen.

'Hmm, you'll have to give me the name of the place before we're done,' Gus advised. 'I'll check it out next time I'm up in those parts.'

'Yeah, give me a call and I'll meet you. So, about Gadsden Carney . . .' Reade started.

'It's a shame. A crying shame. He was a good man and a good sheriff who got into something that was way over his head. I still have friends in law enforcement. They told me he was found by that girl's grave. Is that true?'

'It is.'

'Well, damn . . .' Gus scowled. 'That case did all of us dirty, you know? None of us walked away the same.'

'I don't see how anyone could ever be the same afterward,' Reade sympathized. 'Care to tell me about it?'

'The case? Sure, but you don't really think it has anything to do with Carney's death, do you?'

'I do. You know as well as I do that if this were a copycat killing or some kind of strange tribute, Carney's killer would be crowing about their handiwork. My office hasn't heard a peep from anyone. No one's taken ownership of it.'

'That's highly irregular,' Gus acknowledged.

'Also, Carney had reopened the Honeycutt case – unofficially.'

'Reopened? What the—' Gus slid his eyes toward Tish and softened the tone of his words. 'What was he thinking after all this time?'

'I don't know, but something incited him. Something that may have gotten him killed.'

A waitress approached the table. Tish and Reade ordered two sweet teas. Gus, having already eaten his lunch, ordered two slices of blueberry pie – one to stay and the other to go.

'I gather you believe that Delilah Honeycutt murdered her child,' Tish stated once the waitress had left.

'No, I don't,' Gus said frankly.

Tish and Reade's faces registered surprise.

'The woman I saw that evening was in genuine pain and distress. She was grieving like any mother would. Nah, it was the father who caught my eye. He didn't shed a tear for that little girl the whole time I was there. Colder than a well-digger's backside in January, the man was.' Gus glanced at Tish. 'Sorry for the visual, ma'am.'

Tish wasn't at all bothered by the description. 'Aside from his lack of tears, what else made you suspect Benton Honeycutt?'

'For starters, on a ratio of twelve to one, child murders are committed by parents or a family member. Twelve to one,' he repeated slowly. 'In this case, you also had obstruction and tampering with evidence on a grand scale. All committed by the father.'

'Tell us about what you found that evening,' she urged.

'In a word, a mess. The case was an absolute shambles from the start. The mother was still there at the crime scene – in the garage – kneeling over her daughter's body. The aunt was right beside her, consoling the mother and praying. Meanwhile, the groundskeeper and a family friend were right behind them, trying to get the ladies out of the place so that we could get in. Mind you, the gentlemen persuading them had already walked all over potential evidence. Later on, we found out that the senator had let the housekeeper and a guest tread through the garage and into the kitchen and that the mother had moved the body from its original location. I swear I wouldn't have been surprised if the senator had called down to the stables and asked for the horses to be paraded through. That's how compromised that space was.

'Then there's the matter of the body,' Aldrich went on. 'There had been sixty people at the barbecue that afternoon and, according to personal video recordings from the guests, Daisy had been in contact with all of them in some fashion – hugging and kissing them hello, playing tag, asking them to push her on the swings. It was already a touch DNA nightmare, but then the father put a blanket over her dead body. That blanket was something the children used while playing. It was kept in the garage and hadn't been washed in months. The thing was loaded with unidentifiable DNA, fibers, pollen, and even contained dog hair from a family pet the Honeycutts had put down the previous winter. The moment Benton Honeycutt placed the blanket over his daughter, everything on that blanket transferred to her body. It was impossible to trace anything to a single human being.'

'And you believe Benton Honeycutt did those things deliberately?' Reade quizzed.

'I do. To let people walk into a crime scene or to touch your child's body or to place something over their face so that you don't have to look at them are, taken separately, completely understandable mistakes a parent in that emotional situation might make, but to do all those things and then refuse to answer our questions? Come on,' Gus said with disgust. 'Also, Benton Honeycutt wasn't your typical parent. He started his career in the US Attorney's Office for the Eastern District of Virginia. He was well aware of the proper way to lock down a crime scene. He was also aware of how to clean one . . .'

'Meaning?'

'A set of golf clubs and some croquet mallets were found near the girl's body. They'd been wiped clean, but no rag or cleaning agents were discovered in the garage. According to the house-keeper, the only cleaning paraphernalia in the house was in the kitchen and the upstairs laundry room.'

'Meaning that whoever cleaned the clubs and mallets knew where the cleaning products were kept,' Tish summarized.

'Exactly. The clubs lined up with two of Daisy's head wounds. Comparison to the mallets was inconclusive, but they'd obviously been cleaned because matter from the golf clubs might have been transferred to them.'

'If Benton was Daisy's killer, why would Delilah confess?'

'Easy. She witnessed her husband fly into a rage at their daughter and did nothing about it. Accessory to murder.' He shrugged.

The waitress had returned with their order. When she left, Gus expounded on his theory in between bites of pie. 'Kid was singing all day, wasn't she? That's enough to get on any parent's nerves, but a father who doesn't *want* his daughter to sing? Guy lost his temper, swung at the kid, and accidentally killed her. Mother is terrified, appalled, but doesn't want to lose the big house or her husband's status, so she helps cover up the crime. Bang – the two of them are permanently trapped in a codependent noose. If one of them rats out the other, they both go down.'

'Yet Delilah confessed,' Reade argued before taking a sip of sweet tea.

'Because we were going after the boy. We filed a Hague Evidence request with the French government so we could question Walker James while he was there in boarding school. The government seemed ready to grant our request when Delilah came forward and confessed. The kid was in his room playing video games when the murder occurred. He must have overheard the whole thing. If we had interviewed him, he'd have dropped them both in it. That's why they shipped him off to Europe so quick.' Gus shoveled a forkful of blueberry pie into his mouth.

'Walker James was a minor. The school could have overturned the evidence request on behalf of the parents.'

'They could have, but we would have appealed, which would

have resulted in a lengthy legal battle and Walker James being placed at the center of a media frenzy. Mrs Honeycutt may have covered for her husband, but I think she genuinely loved her children. Seeing her only surviving child hounded by the press was the last thing she would have wanted, so she confessed before the press could even catch wind of our evidence request.'

'What about the sedan Priscilla Maddox saw outside the house?' Tish questioned.

Gus shook his head and washed his pie down with a large gulp of water. 'A bunch of hooey, obviously invented to take the attention off the senator. Priscilla, if you recall, became Mrs Honeycutt a few years later. None of the neighbors we spoke to saw a vehicle of that description on Cypress Hollow Road at that time of day.'

'It was a dry, sunny Fourth of July,' Reade noted. 'At six thirty in the evening, everyone you spoke to was probably in their backyards grilling. They weren't looking out their living-room windows. Also, the security system at Cypress Hollow had been switched off and all three doors in the garage – the back, the front, and the one that led to the kitchen – were unlocked when you and Carney arrived.'

'Yes, but the senator's security detail was at the front gate for the duration of the party. We checked their logbooks and no one was allowed on to the premises who wasn't invited or authorized to be there.'

'And after the party had ended? Where were they?'

'Benton Honeycutt discharged them for the day so they could get home and enjoy some of the holiday with their families. According to them, he gave them a tip for the afternoon and said that he'd set the alarm system after they'd left. Another two security agents were expected at eight.' Gus leaned forward in his seat. 'Look, I know what you're trying to do, Sheriff. The Eastern District DA was breathing down our necks to do the same thing – collar someone from outside the house – but hard as we tried, we couldn't do it. Our database came up with the names of just two men within a twenty-five-mile radius who fit the right profile. The first was in jail awaiting bond for a drug offense on the day of Daisy's murder. The second was up in Ocean City, Maryland, for the holiday with a flock of witnesses to corroborate his alibi. When that well ran dry, we looked at possible enemies of the senator. There was an environmental group that wasn't too keen on his voting record, but they never leveled a threat against the senator or his family. Nor did anyone from that organization try to access Cypress Hollow at any point that day. I don't know what else to tell you. We looked at every angle . . .' Gus shrugged.

'And you came up empty.' Reade completed the sentence.

'Emptier than a divorced man's kitchen cabinets. Didn't stop the DA from pushing the narrative that the killer was from outside, though. The DA was a staunch supporter of the senator. Like back-pocket staunch. He even tried to discredit a member of the senator's security detail because he was caught smoking a joint back when he was a teen.' Gus flashed a look of disgust. 'When Delilah confessed, I expected charges would be filed against the senator for his part in the cover-up, but nothing happened. Nothing at all. The senator wasn't even questioned about what he knew. It was all swept under the carpet. The DA put party politics before finding justice for a dead little girl. I just couldn't stomach it, so I resigned as deputy and became a private investigator. My wife had to go back to work so we could afford insurance, and it's been tough at times, but at least I can sleep at night. I know the work I do – tracking down birth parents, reuniting estranged family members, letting some wife know that yes, she is too good for husband and should move on – is actually helping people.'

'Twenty-five years have passed since Daisy's death. Do you still stand by your belief that Benton Honeycutt was her murderer?' Reade posed.

'Absolutely. There was a moment that evening I'll never forget. I was standing outside the entrance to the kitchen while Sheriff Carney began interviewing Dixie Dupree. The senator came rushing out of his office with a cordless phone in his hand. His attorney was on the line. I told him he couldn't interrupt the sheriff because he was with a witness. The senator looked me straight in the eyes before pushing past me. He had the steeliest, meanest look on his face. I remember it clear as day because I actually placed my hand on my holster in reaction to him. I thought for sure he was going to kill someone if he didn't get in that kitchen and put a stop to the sheriff's questions. Fortunately, Carney saw him and stopped the interview before anything physical happened, but in that moment Benton Honeycutt convinced me he could kill.'

# SEVENTEEN

'Gus Aldrich made a good case for Benton's guilt,' Tish said as Reade drove the SUV from Richmond's West End to the city center. 'Still, I'm not entirely convinced. Once again, why would Delilah confess? Wouldn't it be more likely she'd turn her husband in for the murder than take the blame herself? Why let him get off scot-free? I understand she might have been charged with accessory to murder, but it's better than taking the full rap and never seeing her son again. I'm sure a good attorney could have talked the accessory charges down due to her circumstances.'

'I have the same questions,' Reade admitted. 'Part of me can't believe either of them did it and yet I can't deny the crime scene tampering and the Honeycutts' lack of cooperation. Nor can I deny that the triggers of a child abuse situation were there – marital stress, parental stress, Benton's perspective that Daisy's behavior was problematic, Delilah's potential substance abuse.'

'What I find confusing is the timeline. Benton was the fifth person – after the McIlveens and the Heritages – to arrive in the garage, not the first. If he murdered Daisy, when did he do it? And if he didn't kill Daisy, why did he feel the need to devise such an intricate plan to throw the police off the track? When he arrived in the garage with everyone else that evening, did he see Delilah kneeling over the body, assume she committed the murder, and decide at that moment to try to keep her out of jail? Or did he know of the crime earlier?'

'I foresee us spending some time with Gadsden Carney's map in the near future,' Reade predicted. 'And at Cypress Hollow itself.'

'You've arranged for us to visit the scene?'

'Not yet. I'm awaiting a phone call from the caretaker. The place has been standing dormant all these years. The Honeycutts were never able to sell it. Now with the senator and Delilah both dead, I guess they've given up trying. It was taken off the market shortly after Benton Honeycutt passed away.'

Reade parked the SUV in a municipal lot and placed his emergency service permit in the windshield before accompanying Tish on the two-block walk to the Mayo Memorial Church House, which accommodated the main office for the Episcopal Diocese of Virginia. Located across the street from the historic Jefferson Hotel, the circa-1890 Church House was built in the Greek Temple form. The two-story by five-bay stucco-over-brick façade with a low-hipped roof was dominated by a three-bay, two-story Ionic portico, the symmetry of which was broken by the location of the entrance in the right bay.

Checking in with the cleric at the front desk, Tish and Reade were directed up the main staircase to the second floor where, at the end of a long hallway, a woman – presumably the bishop's assistant – greeted them and, upon opening a set of intricately carved, heavy wooden doors, allowed them admittance to a spacious room with wood paneling, red damask drapes and upholstery, and a marble fireplace. Near the fireplace, in the traditional clerical garb of black suit and white collar, stood Bishop Ambrose Dillard. He was approximately sixty years of age, slightly under six feet tall, and despite his gray hair, stomach paunch, and glasses, it was easy to see that he had been, in his youth, rather handsome.

'Ms Tarragon. Sheriff Reade,' he welcomed them, gesturing toward a pair of Victorian walnut-and-leather chairs. 'May we get you some coffee or tea? Or perhaps some ice water?'

Tish and Reade declined refreshments, prompting Dillard to dismiss his assistant and take a seat behind his antique mahogany pedestal desk. 'What might I do for you?'

'We're here to investigate the death of former Sheriff Gadsden Carney,' Reade informed the bishop.

'Sheriff Carney?' the bishop repeated as he stared at a spot between Tish and Reade. 'Oh, yes. Yes, the law enforcement officer in charge of the Daisy Honeycutt murder investigation. I remember him well from back in those days. He was always on television, giving updates. Tall fellow. No-nonsense type – clean-shaven, receding hairline, plain spoken. Did his best to seek justice for poor little Daisy, but in the end . . . Well, it's just heartbreaking, isn't it?'

'Yes, it is. Had you heard from Mr Carney recently?'

'Yes, as a matter of fact. He called here a few weeks ago – it was a brief call to go over my statement from that dreadful, dreadful day.' Dillard looked Reade squarely in the face as if he suddenly remembered the reason for their visit. 'You said you're investigating his death. What's happened to him?'

'You mean you haven't seen the papers or watched the local news?'

'No, I haven't. We're in the midst of searching for a second suffragan – an assistant bishop – and I've been spending my days sifting through and speaking with potential candidates. I've gone to bed at eight o'clock every night this week.'

'Mr Carney was found murdered at the Honeycutt family plot in Ashton Courthouse.'

'Murdered? How terrible. Have you caught the person?'

'No, that's why we're here. We believe his murder is linked to that of Daisy Honeycutt.'

Dillard removed his glasses and stared, open-mouthed, at Reade. 'It's been nearly twenty-five years. Delilah, the senator, and Daisy are all gone. How is that even possible?'

'That's why we'd like to discuss what happened that day.'

A shaken Dillard placed the glasses back on the bridge of his nose and nodded slowly. 'Of course. Daisy's murder caused great pain and suffering to the Ashton Courthouse community. I'll help you in any way I can to prevent it from doing so again.'

'How did you meet Delilah Honeycutt?'

'Through the church. I was the newly appointed rector of St Jude's in Ashton Courthouse – the youngest rector in the Virginia Diocese. Delilah wandered in one morning after our Friday-morning coffee social. She looked lost – as if she had stumbled into the nearest building she could find. I soon learned that she was, indeed, lost, although not in the geographical sense of the word.

'She'd just dropped her children off at school and was on her way home when she realized that she'd nothing to do,' Dillard continued. 'Daisy's birthday party had taken place that past weekend, the next party to plan was still far on the horizon, and Daisy's next recital was taking place in Ashland, rather than at Cypress Hollow. I immediately saw that she wasn't just lost, but alone. An odd thing to say about a married woman with two children, but that was very much the case. Delilah's husband lived in Washington and came home only for weekends and holidays, so parties and recitals and her children were all she lived for, really. As lovely as those things are, they're poor substitutes for the affection and support of a spouse or significant other.

'After learning of Delilah's background,' the bishop went on, 'I convinced her to use some of her spare time volunteering for the church. I'd expected her to volunteer in a musical capacity, but she explained that her Sundays were frequently spent at Daisy's recitals or entertaining her husband's political allies. Instead, she volunteered for our senior outreach program delivering meals and chatting with the housebound. She was extremely well liked by all the seniors she visited, but it wasn't quite enough for Delilah. She was a performer at heart and she missed entertaining, so, sadly, she lived vicariously through Daisy.'

'Did you ever tell Delilah that you disapproved of her living through Daisy's talents?' Tish asked.

'I did, once. She didn't take it well. Then it occurred to me that Delilah's husband and several friends had already spoken to her about the subject, so, instead of adding to their negativity, I opted to reserve my judgment and be her friend. I knew from speaking with Delilah that she disliked going to Daisy's recitals alone, so I offered to accompany her when my schedule allowed.'

'And she accepted?'

'Yes, happily. I saw Daisy perform many times – usually when Delilah was hosting, as I was typically too busy with parish work to travel any distance. Daisy was quite a gifted singer. I think she enjoyed receiving praise from someone other than her mother.' He smiled. 'In response to my positivity, Delilah brought Daisy to church to sing on the odd free Sunday. Our congregation always enjoyed Daisy's performances.'

'Did the senator join Delilah and Daisy?'

'No. Walker James was always there, albeit reluctantly, but the senator wasn't very . . . spiritual. He was more focused on worldly concerns.' The bishop suddenly sighed. 'Walker James. Poor boy. I haven't thought of him in quite a while. I feel incredibly guilty for not keeping up with that young lad. Lad? He's a grown man by now. Have you spoken with him yet?'

'We have,' Reade confirmed. 'He's made quite a name for himself in the video game industry. Lives in Richmond.'

'Good for him. He always did like his games. I used to counsel him, you know. He had some jealousy issues over his sister. He used to get angry about his father's absences and the amount of time his mother spent with Daisy. I got him involved with the church's youth outreach program. He was just beginning to come out of his shell a bit when . . .' Dillard's voice trailed off. 'I would very much like to contact Walker James, if you wouldn't mind sharing his information with me, Sheriff.'

'From what he told us yesterday, he'd probably like to hear from you, too. I'll give you his business number,' Reade agreed. 'His staff will convey the message to him. It's the protocol I followed when contacting him.'

'Much obliged.' The bishop thanked Reade.

'The day of Daisy's murder, you were at the Honeycutts' barbecue, were you not?'

'I was,' the bishop confirmed.

'Were you there as a friend?'

'I attended in multiple capacities. First, of course, was as a friend to the family. Second was as a community leader – the head of our local Catholic church and the senior rabbi from our town's temple were also in attendance. Lastly, I was there to convince Senator Honeycutt to pursue marital counseling with Delilah.'

'They were having trouble?' Reade asked, although he and Tish already knew the answer.

'Yes, as I said, they were mainly living apart, with Delilah at Cypress Hollow with the children and the senator in Washington, DC. And, more recently, Delilah had begun to suspect that her husband was having an affair.'

'Did you believe that Benton Honeycutt was being unfaithful?'

'It wasn't my place to speculate, but I can say that the presence of a certain young lady at Cypress Hollow that weekend caused a goodly amount of tension.'

'Tell us about that day.'

'Not much to tell, really. It was another Honeycutt party, orchestrated flawlessly by Delilah.' He beamed. 'She really had a knack for creating a memorable gathering. Unfortunately, that particular gathering would become memorable for tragic reasons.'

'So you didn't notice anything out of the ordinary?'

'No, apart from the presence of the senator's aide, and the strange atmosphere it caused, it was a lovely afternoon. Even the weather cooperated, which, of course, it would.' He laughed. 'It wasn't just anyone's party – it was Delilah Dupree Honeycutt's party. The heavens wouldn't dare open up during her barbecue. They knew better.'

'Sounds as if Delilah was quite the perfectionist,' Tish observed with a smile.

'Not so much a perfectionist as someone who was overly concerned about other people's opinions. If Delilah was going to throw a party, she wanted people to rave about it for weeks. She'd have it no other way. I'm not sure if it was insecurity or the entertainer in her, but Delilah was a people-pleaser.' Dillard stared off at a point in the distance and frowned. 'Sometimes at the price of her own happiness.'

'You said you'd planned to speak with Senator Honeycutt about marriage counseling that afternoon. Can you tell us more about that?' Reade posed.

Dillard cleared his throat. 'Two weeks before the barbecue, Delilah had spoken to the senator about attending church-based counseling, but he wasn't very receptive to the idea, citing that I shouldn't be the person counseling them, despite me being their local pastor.'

'Why not?' Tish asked.

'He was displeased that I'd been accompanying Delilah to Daisy's recitals and spending, overall, more time with his family than he did. He felt that I'd be biased as a counselor and wouldn't see things his way.' The bishop smiled wistfully. 'I have to admit, he wasn't completely wrong. So I contacted a pastor friend from a neighboring county and asked if she would offer the Honeycutts impartial counseling. She agreed and I prepared to present the senator with the revised proposal the day of the barbecue.'

'Did you have a chance to make your presentation?'

'I did. It was a brief discussion because, once again, the senator wasn't very receptive to the idea, nor was he alone for very long. His aide had gone off to get a drink, but she was soon back at his side. I wasn't about to discuss the Honeycutts' marital issues in front of her.'

Tish nodded. 'What reason did the senator give you for refusing the second time?'

'He insisted that he and Delilah didn't need counseling. He told me he loved his wife, she loved him, and that their arrangement had been working out quite satisfactorily until I started filling Delilah's head with unreasonable expectations.'

'Unreasonable expectations?'

'Yes, I suppose he meant my active support of Daisy's singing,' the bishop replied.

Tish, however, wasn't convinced by the explanation. 'What happened after you spoke with the senator?'

'I broke the news to Delilah. She was a champ, as always. I could tell she was terribly disappointed, just as she was terribly upset that her husband had brought that woman to Cypress Hollow, but she never let on. She just went on with the party, doing her best to ensure everyone had a wonderful time. That's about all I remember of the barbecue. The party started breaking up shortly after dessert was served. I had the weekly coffee social and a wedding rehearsal scheduled at church the next morning, so I left at approximately twenty minutes after six. Maybe half past. I can't remember the precise time after all these years, but I'm sure it's in your records, Sheriff.'

Reade nodded. 'You didn't happen to be driving a blue sedan at the time, did you?'

'No, due to my profession I've only ever driven black cars. Watching the priest who's presiding over your father's funeral or paying a palliative visit to your dying mother drive up in a colorful vehicle could be extremely off-putting to many.'

'Do you believe that Delilah Honeycutt murdered her daughter?'

The bishop spent several moments in somber silence before answering. 'Sadly, I do. Delilah was . . . well, she was simply the most remarkable person I'd ever met – truly extraordinary – but she was under such stress that weekend, such strain. Daisy was a vivacious, healthy young girl. She loved her mother. She loved to sing. She was incredibly talented, but she was still only a child and children often misbehave. They don't understand when someone might be hanging on by a thread.'

'Did Delilah ever confess to you? Perhaps on her death bed?'

'No, the Episcopal Church doesn't believe in confession. We

believe that human beings can communicate their repentance directly to God. In addition, I was no longer in contact with the Honeycutt family. The day of Daisy's murder was the last time I saw any of them.'

'Where were you two evenings ago?' Reade asked.

'I was at home, reviewing candidates for the assistant bishop position. I had a salad for dinner, watched the news, and went to bed.'

'Can anyone confirm your whereabouts?'

'No, I was alone. My housekeeper left supper in the fridge for me as she does on weekdays.' Dillard brought his hands together in a prayer-like gesture and tilted his head down while he reflected. 'Daisy's death was such a tragedy. A tragedy compounded by Delilah's incarceration and subsequent death. It's difficult to make sense of these events, but if we search, and if we trust, we eventually find a reason, even if that reason is to remind us to hold our loved ones closer. Hold them close in our hearts and never let go.'

# EIGHTEEN

Reade's government-issued black SUV sped along the stretch of highway that linked Richmond to the small community of Ashton Courthouse, but this time it was Tish behind the wheel. 'Are you positive I'm insured?' she asked Reade, who was in the passenger seat, reviewing the floor plans of Cypress Hollow.

'Positive. You're an employee of the sheriff's department using the car for official police business.' Reade added, 'I also added your name to the policy.'

'Thanks. I want to get used to driving a bigger vehicle. My Matrix is getting older and I may trade it in for something with more storage when the time is right. That way I won't have to make several trips or rent a van every time I'm catering a larger event.'

'Feel free to drive this thing whenever you like. I could always use a break. I feel as though I've been driving all over hell's half-acre today.'

'That's because you have. It would make much more sense if we could schedule these interviews by geographical location.'

'As if anything in this case makes sense,' Reade grumbled. 'Except that Delilah Honeycutt probably killed her daughter. Which leaves us without a suspect for Gadsden Carney's murder.'

'I wouldn't go that far. We just learned that Benton Honeycutt might have been a violent man.'

'No, we learned that Gus Aldrich *believes* that Benton Honeycutt might have been a violent man. None of the other witnesses we've spoken to mentioned anything about the senator having a violent temper. Looking in someone's eyes and getting a feeling isn't proof.'

'Aldrich was deputy to Sheriff Carney. The same Sheriff Carney who told you to follow your gut. You can't discredit Aldrich for following his.'

'Touché,' he replied admiringly.

'We also learned that Walker James was having trouble dealing with his home situation.'

'Who wouldn't? Between his sister's incessant singing, his father's absence, and his mother's possible pill habit, there was a lot for the kid to take in.'

'Yet Walker James doesn't remember any of it. On the contrary, he calls his life at Cypress Hollow the happiest time of his life,' Tish countered.

'And while he forgets the true nature of his home life, he remembers being in the garage, when no one else recalls him being there.'

'We also learned from Gus Aldrich that there were two types of head wounds on Daisy's skull. One from a golf club and the other possibly from a croquet mallet – both of which were thoroughly cleaned. Children's skulls are rather thin, though, aren't they? Wouldn't using two different weapons be considered overkill?'

'It would.'

'Which weapon delivered the deadly blow?'

Reade scrolled through the files on his tablet. 'The golf club. The other injuries rendered her immediately unconscious and caused severe brain injury, which is why no one heard her scream.'

'Did Delilah address that in her confession?'

'Not that I can see, but I haven't gotten through all the case files yet.'

'You know what else we just learned? We learned that the then Reverend Ambrose Dillard was carrying a torch for Delilah. A very sizeable torch by the sound of it.'

'Yeah, I picked up on that, too. It's not often someone calls another person "remarkable" and "extraordinary." Benton certainly reacted to the idea of counseling like a jealous husband would, stating that everything was fine until Dillard came along and filled Delilah's head with nonsense.'

'The nonsense in this case being companionship and attentiveness. An example of how her marriage could be. I wonder if, during their many visits, Bishop Dillard ever told Delilah about his feelings for her.'

'Doubtful. Dillard's a man of the cloth.'

'Yes, but still a man.' Tish turned off the highway and on to Ashton Courthouse's main street. After driving through the town, she continued along the road for approximately five miles before turning on to Cypress Hollow Road – a gravel-lined thoroughfare just on the outskirts of town.

'Cypress Hollow should be near the end of the road on your left,' Reade directed. 'The original property incorporated over five hundred acres, which is why the road is named for it. Through the decades and multiple financial crises, Benton's grandfather and father sold off much of the land to developers.'

Following Reade's directions, she pulled through a set of wrought-iron gates and up the approximately 500-foot length of pavement to a 250-foot-wide circular driveway with an aging, cracked fountain surrounded by straggly hedges as its centerpiece. Within steps of the circular drive stood Cypress Hollow in all its white-clapboard and turquoise-trimmed majesty.

Just to the right of the front portico of the house, Officer Clayton sat waiting in his squad car, with Jules and Biscuit in the passenger seat.

Tish brought the SUV to a halt behind them.

'Gentlemen,' Reade greeted as the foursome – and Biscuit – emerged from their respective automobiles.

'The front door's open and the caretaker is making sure

everything else is unlocked.' Clayton then awkwardly added, 'Mr Davis is here because he has something to show us.'

'Jules, if you're looking for a scoop—' Reade began to warn, his arms folded across his chest.

'I'm always looking for a scoop, Sheriff,' Jules admitted. 'But I'd never go on air with anything without your permission. You know that. Anyway, that's not why I'm here. I have something to show y'all.'

Reade looked at Clayton, who explained. 'Mr Davis arrived at the office just as I was heading out the door. From the few seconds of footage I managed to see, it looks like he's stumbled upon something important.'

'OK,' Reade capitulated. 'Let's see it, but remember internet and cell service is extremely limited here.'

'Oh, I took no chances with this one, honey.' Jules tied Biscuit's lead to the front portico column and grabbed his iPad Air from the bedazzled messenger bag slung over his shoulder. 'Before I start, I checked into the background of the interview we watched at lunch. The Honeycutts weren't provided any questions in advance. The interviewer saw the segment as his big break – a chance for him to crack the case – so he arranged for the conversation to be as "off the cuff" as possible. The Honeycutts agreed because they felt the spontaneity of the format would depict them as "ordinary people" rather than wealthy, privileged citizens.'

'Ordinary people who rehearsed their answers to what they knew any interviewer worth his salt would ask,' Reade replied.

'Exactly. Now, moving on from that interview, this video shows Delilah in November 1996, post-confession, being taken into custody,' he described to the group huddled around him.

Jules pressed 'play' on the first of two clips uploaded to the iPad hard drive. The video screen opened to Delilah Honeycutt, dressed in a gray suit and matching overcoat, her blonde hair pinned back into an elegant chignon. She was being led by two unidentified officers through the snow and past a mob of shouting paparazzi into the sheriff's office. She looked straight ahead, not down, and never once turned to acknowledge the angry voices that surrounded her.

'Delilah's body language has changed drastically from what she exhibited during that first television interview,' Clayton analyzed.

'She's like a completely different person. Whereas, during the interview, she conveyed shame and guilt, here she's displaying none of that. Her shoulders are straight and slightly back, her chin is held erect, her eyes are looking forward instead of glancing around in search of escape, and her jaw is firmly set. These aren't illustrators of repentance; they're illustrators of defiance.'

'Now you know why I rushed over to show it to you,' Jules said excitedly.

'If I were to watch this video out of context, I'd conclude that this woman was going to trial after entering a not-guilty plea. Her body language isn't saying, "I'm sorry I did this." It's saying, "Go ahead and prove me wrong." I'd never, in a million years, guess that she's just confessed to a crime, let alone the murder of her child,' Clayton said.

'Now, here's the video from after Delilah's sentencing in January 1997,' Jules announced, launching another clip. This time, the clean-faced Delilah was dressed in an orange prison jumpsuit and her hair hung loosely about her face. Two unidentified officers led her, in handcuffs, down the steps of the Henrico County courthouse and into the back of a white van with tinted windows.

'We have a lot of the same body language that we saw in the post-confession video,' Clayton explained. 'Delilah's chin is up, her shoulders back, and she's looking ahead; however, her face is more relaxed. She looks like someone whose battle is over and – whoa, go back about five seconds.'

Jules complied and pressed the reverse button.

'There! Stop it.'

Again, Jules did as instructed.

'OK, now press play. Everyone, watch what Delilah does before stepping into the van.'

The foursome watched as Delilah paused and glanced over her right shoulder, the edges of her mouth slightly upturned.

'Is she . . . smiling?' Tish asked.

'Looks that way to me,' Reade concurred.

Jules reversed the video so they could watch the scene again. At the critical moment when Delilah turned, Clayton hit pause. 'There it is. It's there for a fleeting moment, but that's a smile if ever I saw one.'

Tish pointed to the image of Benton Honeycutt at the edge of the frame. 'She's smiling at her husband. But why? She's just been sentenced to life in prison.'

'That's what I was saying when the video first started. Delilah looks like someone whose battle has ended not with defeat, but victory. Her body language reads like someone who's won their day in court, and yet we know she didn't. It's extraordinary. Truly extraordinary.'

'You're not the first person today to use that word,' Reade noted.

'I really wish I knew what it all meant,' said an exasperated Clayton.

'We'll get to the bottom of it eventually. In the meantime, good work.' Reade glanced between the officer and Jules. 'Both of you.'

'Thanks. Does that mean I can take a look inside with y'all?' Jules asked. 'When – not if, when – you and Tish break the case, it might be handy to have some photos and video of the house to add to the live coverage.'

'So long as it remains off the record,' Reade stipulated.

'You have my word.' Jules crossed his heart.

'OK, let's go in.'

Leaving Biscuit tethered to the front column, Tish, Reade, Clayton, and Jules stepped through the turquoise front door and into the main foyer.

They may as well have been stepping back in time. The late-afternoon summer sun filtered through the windows and skylights bathing Cypress Hollow in swathes of dust-particle-laden sunlight. Tish narrowed her eyes to block out the peeling paint and wallpaper and imagined how the house must have looked and felt that afternoon twenty-five years before. The sound of children playing in the backyard, the smell of food cooking on a charcoal grill, the sense of excitement as guests mingled and drank and enjoyed summer at its peak. And then, at the end, a scream.

Tish felt a man's hand reach for hers. She turned around expecting to come face to face with the handsome countenance of Clemson Reade. Instead, she found herself nose to nose with Julian Pen Davis. 'Jules, what are you doing?' she asked in a lowered voice while she shooed away his hand.

'I'm scared,' he whispered. 'Is this not the spookiest place you've ever been in your life?'

'It's one of them,' she conceded.

Jules leaned in close. 'Any minute now, I expect to see the ghost of that dead little girl gliding down the stairs.'

Tish followed Jules's gaze to the steps, its handrail laced with cobwebs. Indeed, the setting was ideal for a haunted house movie, but more pervasive to Tish than the dust and disrepair was the home's atmosphere. Despite the bright and abundant sunlight, there was about Cypress Hollow an inexplicable heaviness.

'Hey, y'all,' a voice came booming from the top of the stairs, prompting Tish and Jules to jump and gasp in unison.

'Sorry to startle ya,' the man apologized as he came down the steps and into view. He was in his late thirties and dressed in camouflage shorts and a khaki-colored T-shirt. 'Just wanted y'all to know that I've unlocked all the doors, including the ones to the bedroom balconies. You need anything else?'

'No, that's about it. Thank you for all your help, Vernon,' Reade replied.

'No biggie. I look after most of the second homes in these parts, so I'm never too far away. You folks looking at that killing, ain't ya?'

'We're double-checking some facts, yes,' the sheriff confirmed.

'I still don't believe she did it. Ms Honeycutt, I mean,' Vernon clarified. 'She used to check in on my granny to make sure she had a good meal and some company. My mama was single and raising me so she couldn't always afford to help Granny as much as she'd have liked, but we needn't have worried. Ms Honeycutt would stop by a few times a week with food. I remember I was at Granny's for one of Ms Honeycutt's visits. She was beautiful and just as sweet as could be. She asked me my name and how old I was. Said she had a boy a few years younger than me. I had such a crush on her. I hate to think what they might have done to her in prison.'

'You said you didn't believe Delilah Honeycutt was guilty?' Tish posed.

'No, ma'am, I did not. Still don't. I thought it was the girl's daddy, to be honest. Granny said Old Man Honeycutt – the senator's granddaddy – had a wicked temper. He could be meaner than a wet panther, she said. I reckon the apple doesn't fall far from the tree.'

'Not usually,' Reade humored. 'Thanks again for your help.'

'Yeah, yeah, yeah. I'll be back in forty-five minutes or so to lock up. Till then, I'll be tooling around on my John Deere. With all these properties, there's always something to do. This here place is the only one that's vacant, though. Why no one's torn the place down and built something new in all this time is beyond me, but that ain't my business, is it?'

As Vernon went about his rounds, Tish wandered from the foyer and through the first doorway on the left. With its now-peeling hunter-green wallpaper, puffy, custom-made balloon-valance window treatments, and massive brass chandelier, the dining room was a study in 1990s home interior trends. With Reade, Clayton, and Jules silently in tow, she moved across the room and through the door that connected to the wood-paneled, bookcase-lined study, and again through the door that connected the study to the conservatory.

'This was where Priscilla was when she saw the car out front,' Tish said as she gestured out of the west door of the glass-enclosed space.

Reade opened the door and held it ajar. 'Let's take a look.'

Due to its shady location, the flagstone patio was covered with a thick cover of moss and lichens, but its vantage point over the front lawn and the fence beyond was undiminished despite over two decades of unchecked plant and foliage growth. What was also striking about the spot was its feeling of detachment from the rest of the backyard.

'Priscilla most certainly could have seen a car from this distance,' Tish verified. 'Yet it's far enough away that identifying the make and model of car might have been difficult.'

'When Priscilla saw the car, the sun would have been pretty much where it is right now,' Clayton added.

'Assuming Priscilla actually saw a car,' Reade added. 'Our buddy Aldrich thinks otherwise. Standing here, and seeing how isolated Priscilla was, one can imagine how easy it would have been for her to sneak into the house, make her way into the garage, kill Daisy, and then sneak back with no one the wiser.'

To illustrate the scenario, Reade led them back into the conservatory and along the route Priscilla would have taken. Once in the stiflingly warm garage, he and Clayton swung open the rear insulated and front barn-style garage doors for both light and ventilation.

'Where did . . . *it* happen?' Jules asked in a near whisper as he drew closer to Tish.

Reade pulled open the crime scene photos on his tablet and walked to a spot just a few paces shy of the center of the eastern wall. 'The body was found approximately here. The golf clubs and croquet mallets were piled on the floor against the wall, along with other sporting equipment.'

'So the weapon was already on the scene,' Jules summarized.

Reade nodded. 'That and the fact that the security system had been switched off and the security detail had been dismissed for the evening were the foundation of the Honeycutts' original argument that the murder had been committed by someone outside the household.'

Tish took note of a series of cracks near the center of the wall, approximately five feet and six inches off the floor. 'This is odd,' she said as she drew closer to examine it. 'Almost looks like a spider web.'

'I don't recall seeing that in the photos,' Clayton noted.

'Because it's not in the photos,' Reade responded as he scrolled through photo after photo of the garage as it was at the time of Daisy's death.

'Then this happened post-murder,' Tish presumed. 'Probably when the Honeycutts moved their stuff out.'

'Not necessarily,' Reade warned as he pulled out a pocket flashlight and inspected the cracks. 'This is a plaster wall. The stress to the wall might have been caused the day of the murder, but the cracks only developed over time and with exposure to cold, heat, and damp. Since this place has been vacant since the murder, we won't be able to pinpoint exactly when it occurred, but an expert should be able to discern what type of object and how much force was used to create it. From a cursory examination, the object was round, substantially sized – about twenty inches in circumference – and hard, but not so hard as to produce immediately visible damage.'

'So probably not a golf club or croquet mallet,' Tish guessed.

'Probably not, but, again, we need an expert's opinion.'

Jules leaned in and snapped several photos of the cracked portion of plaster.

As Clayton directed Jules as to what other elements of the

garage should be photographed, Tish wandered out of the back door of the garage. To the left, as depicted on the house schematic, was the now empty and cracked in-ground swimming pool where Louella Heritage had watched her children swim. To the right and north was the children's play area, its swing set now rusted and dilapidated. Beyond the play area, Tish could hear the sound of rushing water.

'The spot where Benton Honeycutt was standing when Delilah screamed that day,' Reade said, gesturing forty feet into the distance. 'From here, you can see where the water winds its way into the woods.'

Tish nodded. 'It was listed on the diagram as a brook, but this – well, this has a much stronger current than I expected.'

'Yeah, and it hasn't rained in nearly a week. Imagine the flow after a heavy thunderstorm.'

'So Benton was out there kneeling . . .'

'That's what John McIlveen said.'

'But Bishop Dillard told us that Benton wasn't a spiritual man.'

'Meaning he wasn't out there praying.'

'Meaning he was doing something else,' she answered before setting off for the creek. 'And I think I know what it was.'

Reade followed. 'You do?'

'There were no cleaning rags found in the garage, remember?'

'You think he got rid of them in the creek?'

'I do. Benton knew if he tossed them in the trash, the police would find them and test them for DNA, so he let the current carry them far away from Cypress Hollow.' Reaching the bend in the creek, she knelt down and tested the current with her fingertips. 'They would have moved quickly.'

'But he had to pass the Heritages and the McIlveens to get out here. How did he do that without them noticing what he was carrying?'

Tish stood up. 'What was the senator wearing that day?'

Reade's brow furrowed. 'What?'

'Does it mention anywhere in your files what Benton Honeycutt was wearing that day?'

'Not that I recall.'

'Gadsden Carney's notes mention it,' Clayton announced as he and Jules arrived on the scene. 'I saw it earlier this morning. The dude documented everything from that day – what people were wearing, how they were acting, the temperature. I thought it was weird, but I guess not. Anyway, the senator was wearing a blue denim shirt and tan shorts.'

'Plain tan shorts?' Tish questioned.

'Oh, um, no, cargo shorts.'

Tish turned to Reade and grinned. 'You can fit a bunch of rags in those and no one would notice a thing.'

'Well done,' Reade praised. 'But how did you know?'

'It was the nineties. Everyone and his brother had a pair of cargo shorts.'

'Ten ninety-nine a pair at Old Navy,' Jules reminisced. 'There was a pair for everyone – mom, dad, sister, brother, the family dog. Morgan Fairchild used to peddle them.'

'I'm pretty sure I had a couple of pairs,' Reade admitted.

'I didn't,' Jules boasted. 'I didn't want my butt to look saggy before its time. Now that I actually do have a case of pancake butt and an expanding middle-aged waistline, I admit those shorts do seem comfortably appealing. Kind of a summer riff on the Christmas dinner fat pants.'

'Um, Mr Davis,' Clayton interrupted. 'As they said back then, TMI.'

'So Benton had the opportunity and means to dispose of the cleaning rags,' Reade synopsized. 'What was his motive? Was he protecting his wife or was he protecting himself?'

'Or was he protecting Priscilla?' Clayton proposed. 'We all saw how easily she could have slipped in and out of the house. She's also the only one of those three people who could have murdered Gadsden Carney. She was even at the church that night.'

'She was, but if Priscilla had killed Daisy, why would Delilah have confessed?' Tish countered.

'Maybe she didn't know Priscilla was the killer. Maybe Benton took the blame so that Delilah would cover for him. Or maybe Delilah just gave up on life. She'd lost a child and her marriage was failing.' Clayton shrugged. 'People have given up for far less.'

'You're right, of course, but for some reason it doesn't seem to fit. If it's OK with everyone, I'd like to recreate the moment Delilah discovered the body.'

'Sure,' Reade replied. 'I think that could be useful for all of us. Where do you want everyone?'

'Someone needs to stay here, I think. We're far enough from the house for it to be questionable whether Benton actually heard his wife scream.'

'You're right. He may have returned to the garage to finish his clean-up job,' Reade agreed. 'Or to "discover" the body on his own.'

Tish nodded. 'On the other end of the spectrum, Priscilla said she didn't hear Delilah's screams. I'd like to test that. Maybe the real reason she was late coming to the garage was that she was inside the house, washing her hands.'

'OK, so someone needs to be on the patio outside the conservatory.'

'Someone also needs to be in Walker James's room. His memory of being at the scene doesn't fit with the whole narrative. I'd like to know what he could and could not hear. And lastly, I need to be in the garage, acting as Delilah.'

'Oh no, sweetie. Not you,' Jules contradicted. 'You do not have the lung power.'

'But I need to—'

'Nope. Remember back in college when we got a job helping out at that haunted mansion one Halloween? Y'all, I was the mummy who'd silently leap from his sarcophagus while Tish was a wraith who'd jump out and scream at people, only Tish's scream was so timid, folks laughed at her. Instead of letting Tish get fired, I switched spots with her. My screams were better than those of any B-movie queen.'

Tish frowned. 'The problem wasn't with my voice, but with my character. Sure, she was a wraith, but apart from that, what reason did she have for wanting to scream at people? Had she been more articulate, she may have gotten her point across better.'

'Seriously?' Jules folded his arms across his chest and screwed up his face.

'OK. You take the garage. I'll take the upstairs bedroom.'

'Was that really so hard?' he sighed before he and Tish took off for the house and Clayton trotted off for the east side patio.

Once inside the garage, Jules glanced at the time on his phone. 'I'll give you a couple minutes to get upstairs before I start. Be careful up there.'

'I'll be fine, Jules. There are no such things as ghosts, remember?'

Tish exited the garage, trekked across the massive extension that served as playroom and entertainment area, re-entered the main foyer, and scaled the steps to the second floor. As soon as Tish reached the upstairs landing, she regretted her last words for, in fact, it did feel as if the space might be occupied by malevolent spirits.

Whereas downstairs had been cleaned and emptied of all furnishings, the second floor remained a time capsule. A tall grandfather clock stood at the top of the steps, its pendulum and chimes visible through its glass case, but its face concealed by a white sheet. Next to the clock, a pair of wingback chairs in wine brocade – shielded in this spot from the sun's harsh rays – partnered a cherry plant stand, its plant long gone, for an otherworldly conversation area.

Remembering the plan of the house, Tish followed the hallway to the right, almost immediately coming upon a bathroom decorated in bright primary colors and featuring soft furnishings with a rubber duck motif. The children's bathroom.

Diagonally across the hall, Tish encountered what must have been Daisy's bedroom. Fifteen feet square and decorated in shades of pink, the wall opposite the door boasted a hand-painted mural of a castle set against a lavender sky. In the green grass surrounding the castle, pink trees grew and white horses pulled glass coaches. The carpet was thick plush in pale pink and the puffy window treatments were constructed of faded pink fabric with sparkling gold stars. A large dresser, nightstand, and two twin beds still remained in place, although their mattresses and bedding had long been removed.

Tish blinked back tears and focused on the task at hand, but catching a glimpse of the personality of the little girl at the heart of the case was gut-wrenching. *I'll find out the truth*, she silently promised as if Daisy might somehow be able to read her thoughts. *I'll find out what really happened.*

Next door to Daisy's room was Nanny Viola's sleeping quarters. Approximately ten feet by nine feet, the room was small and utilitarian in nature, featuring plain white walls and pinch-pleated drapes in a splashy Laura Ashley-style floral print of yellow roses on a blue background. As in the previous bedroom, a double bed frame and a nightstand remained, but the mattress and bedding had been removed.

Moving along the hall, she shuffled past a pair of floral-wall-papered bedrooms with an adjoining bath on her right, finally arriving at Walker James's corner bedroom on her left. A smaller room than Daisy's, the thirteen-foot-square space was decorated in a red-white-and-blue nautical theme replete with masculine dark-blue wallpaper, a coordinating border of various illustrated ships, and red carpeting with an anchor print. The bedroom boasted just one single bed frame and a massive built-in desk and bookcase combo which, given the presence of a rolling wooden office chair, must have been used for both schoolwork and video games.

Tish peered out of the window into the backyard. An adjacent door led to a spacious sheltered balcony that stretched the length of the three consecutive bedrooms – Walker James's, Nanny Viola's, and Daisy's. She could imagine Viola and the children assembled there the morning of the murder – Walker James sprawled upon a blanket, lost in the pages of a sci-fi or pirate tale, and Daisy, reading a story of princesses and castles aloud as Viola brushed her blonde hair.

The peaceful scene was interrupted by the muffled, yet fully audible, sound of screaming emanating from somewhere on the first floor. Tish opened the balcony door and stuck her head outside. From this elevated position, the source and location of the screams became abundantly obvious. If Walker James had the door open for air that evening, he would have known that something was wrong in the garage, but even with the door shut, he still would have heard his mother's cries for help.

Tish hurriedly retraced her steps back to the garage. Reade was already there. 'I heard the screaming just fine,' he announced.

With that, Clayton jogged through the garage door. 'Priscilla's telling the truth. I didn't hear anything out there except some birds and a passing car.'

'How about you, Tish?' Jules inquired.

'I heard everything. Muffled when the door to the balcony was closed. Distinctly when it was open. So the question remains: where was Walker James? The natural reaction in that situation is to find out what's happening, but, by all accounts, he never wandered downstairs to the garage to find out what was wrong.

Gadsden Carney's diagram has been highly accurate regarding the locations of everyone in the house at the time Delilah screamed for help—'

'Accurate except for the presence of Viola Tilley,' Clayton reminded her.

'Exactly,' Tish agreed. 'But what if Carney was right? What if Viola *was* in her room when Daisy's body was discovered? What if, fearful that what was happening might be too intense for Walker James, she insisted he stay in his room?'

'Sounds like a reasonable thing for a nanny to do,' Reade allowed.

'I agree, it does. But then why, after telling Walker James to stay put, didn't Viola go downstairs to see what was going on? Surely, if there had been a chance that Daisy was ill or injured, Viola would have been on the scene to help. She loved Daisy. She loved Delilah. She wouldn't have remained in her room when they may have needed her downstairs. But, for the sake of argument, let's assume that Viola *did* stay upstairs in order to prevent Walker James from investigating. Why deny being at Cypress Hollow? Why not tell police she was looking after Walker James? And, after all this time, why not tell us? Why does she still maintain that she was at a family barbecue all day?'

'Probably for the same reason Benton Honeycutt and his estate paid all her living expenses these past twenty-five years,' Reade surmised.

Tish nodded. 'Walker James's memory of being in the garage that day is so vivid. What if it isn't a false memory? What if he came down to the garage before his mother's scream? What if he wandered in here while his father was cleaning up? Benton wouldn't want anyone to know that he was in here disposing of evidence, so he carries Walker James upstairs, locks him in his room, and warns him not to open the door to anyone. Then Benton comes down here and finishes his cleaning and disposes of the rags. What if the real reason Walker James didn't come down to the garage that evening is because he already knew what was there?'

# NINETEEN

'Viola Tilley had a bit of a setback after our last visit,' Reade explained as he hung up the phone in his office.

Tish perched on the edge of his desk. 'Is she OK?'

'Yeah, the nurse says she'll be fine. Between her morning doctor's visit and a stint with the physiotherapist, the earliest we can meet with her is tomorrow at ten thirty.'

'Post-breakfast and pre-lunch,' she noted. 'I should be able to make that work with some juggling. Friday's one of my busiest days, though. Celestine will be helping me with breakfast – I'll see if she can stay on until Mary Jo comes in to help with lunch. I should probably ask her to stay a little longer, just in case I'm late. Are we arranging to meet Walker James again tomorrow, too?'

'Not yet. I want to see what Viola has to say first. Whatever she tells us can be used either to jog Walker James's memory or, if he's lying about what he remembers, as leverage to get him to open up.'

'You're right. It's probably not a good idea to confront Milla Lebrecht about a second interview until we absolutely have to. I just wish there was something more I could do right now.'

'You've done plenty. It's already six o'clock. Why don't you head home?'

'You sure?'

'Positive. I'll be here, debriefing my team first thing tomorrow morning, so I'll pick you up at the café at ten.'

'I'll see you then.' She hovered in the doorway for several seconds as she debated inviting Clemson to join them for dinner. Rejecting the idea on the basis that he'd probably seen enough of her for one day, she bid him goodnight and set off for the Thai restaurant.

Tish arrived at the café at six thirty, carrying a brown paper shopping bag filled to the brim with delectable-smelling goodies. 'Hey,' she greeted Mary Jo who was sitting on the front porch swing. 'This is an awful lot of food for five people. And why did you pay for the order? I told you it was my treat.'

'I didn't pay for the order myself,' Mary Jo answered as she led her friend inside, where Gregory, Kayla, Jules, Celestine, and, to Tish's great surprise, Sheriff Reade were waiting.

'What's all this?' Tish asked.

'A celebration of the last day of school and your first full day as a consultant to the sheriff's office. I know you and Reade celebrated privately, but we wanted to do something for you as well.'

'What a surprise,' Tish responded warily. 'What a . . . lovely surprise.'

'We're glad you like it, honey.' Celestine bestowed Tish with a hug and took the food to the series of café tables that had been pushed together to form a single dining surface.

'Why did you invite Clemson?' Tish whispered through a pasted-on smile.

'Because he's the man who hired you,' Mary Jo sang through an equally artificial grin.

'Is that the only reason?'

'Of course. What other reason could there possibly be?'

Tish wrinkled her nose and went off to congratulate Kayla and Gregory on their last day of school before greeting Clemson. 'You, sir, have quite the poker face.'

'Sorry, Mary Jo called me first thing this morning and gave me strict orders not to say anything to you,' he apologized and handed her a store-bought bouquet of Stargazer lilies. 'I hope these make up for it.'

'They're lovely,' she exclaimed. 'But you didn't have to do this.'

'Yes, I did. First, I was taught never to arrive at social functions empty-handed. Second, you deserve them. Well, you deserve better, actually, but they were the freshest ones the grocery store had to offer.'

'Sheriff Reade brought an ice-cream cake for dessert,' Jules interrupted and snatched the flowers from Tish's hand before buzzing off behind the counter.

'It was a one-stop after-work shop,' Reade went on to explain.

'It was very kind of you.'

'We'll see. Do teenagers even like ice-cream cake or are they too cool to enjoy it?'

'I'd hate to think there's anyone out there who's too cool for ice-cream cake.'

As the pair laughed, Tuna sauntered in from Tish's bedroom and rubbed the length of his body against her bare leg. She bent down and scratched his chin, which produced a purr as loud as a Geiger counter.

'Hey, I haven't seen this guy before,' Reade noted. Tuna responded to this acknowledgment by head-butting the sheriff in the shin.

'He's a stray who wandered in a few months ago. He usually spends business hours napping in the upstairs apartment or in my room.' Tish paused as Tuna allowed Reade to slowly stroke his fur, from head to tail. 'He's usually not this friendly, either.'

'What's his name?'

'Tuna.'

'I have a long-haired tuxedo cat at home just like him. Name's Marlowe.'

'Like the detective?' Tish guessed.

'No, the writer. I found Marlowe when he was a scruffy little kitten. I was driving back into town from a trip to the coast and pulled over to make a phone call. He was sitting on a pile of rocks on the side of the road. He didn't pay any attention to me. He was watching sheep graze on a farm in the distance. The whole thing made me think of a poem I had to memorize in grade school. "And we will sit upon the rocks, Seeing the shepherds feed their flocks, By shallow rivers to whose falls Melodious birds sing madrigals."'

'*The Passionate Shepherd to His Love*. Christopher Marlowe.'

'Is that the title?' Reade stood up and awkwardly ran a hand through his hair. 'I, um, I just knew it was Marlowe. If anyone from the department ever asks, though, the cat's named after the detective.'

Tish picked up Tuna and gave him a cuddle. 'Your secret's safe with us.'

Celestine called everyone to the table for supper. Naturally, the only two seats available for Tish and Reade were beside each other. Tish fired a glance at both Jules and Mary Jo and sat down.

Glasses of sparkling cider had been set beside each plate. Mary Jo lifted hers heavenward and rose from her chair. 'A toast to

Kayla and Gregory. Kayla has finished her last day as a high school sophomore—'

To this, everyone cheered.

'And Gregory has finished his last day of high school ever.'

Again, there were whistles and shouts to mark the occasion.

'I'm not sure how I got to be so . . .' An emotional Mary Jo broke into happy tears.

'Old?' Jules completed the sentence, instantly lightening the mood.

'I was going to say lucky.' Mary Jo laughed as tears still streamed down her face. 'I'm so very proud of you both. I'm extremely fortunate to be your mother.'

'Aww,' the group cried in unison as the clinking of glasses ensued.

'And to Tish . . .' Again, Mary Jo's voice cracked.

Jules stood up. 'Let me do this. To Tish, the woman who can do anything.'

The group cheered and drank to Tish before diving into platters of spring rolls, vegetable pad thai, papaya salad, beef with holy basil, green chicken curry, and fragrant jasmine rice, all to be washed down with cups of green tea and more sparkling cider.

Dinner was in full swing when Tish looked up to see a familiar face approaching the front porch of the café. She promptly excused herself and stopped by Mary Jo's spot at the head of the table. 'Hey, did you invite my dad?'

'Sorry, no,' Mary Jo apologized. 'I thought he was busy tonight, so I didn't bother.'

'Yeah, I thought he was busy, too, but here he is,' Tish explained before rushing out the door to meet him. 'Hey.'

'Hay is for horses, Letitia,' he replied as he had since she was a child.

She corrected herself. 'Hello.'

'Hi.' He nodded toward the group assembled in the café's front picture window. 'Looks like you're having yourself a party.'

'Just a small dinner to celebrate the last day of school. Why don't you join us? We have plenty of food and you would have been invited if we'd known you weren't busy.'

'I am busy. That's why I'm here.'

Tish must have looked as confused as she felt, for her father remarked, 'You look like your mother when you scrunch up your eyebrows like that. Anyway, I'm here to say goodbye.'

'Goodbye? Already?'

'Change of plans. Instead of driving all the way down to Hilton Head, my friend and I decided to take the auto train. The train rolls out first thing in the morning, so we're staying in a hotel room in Lorton tonight.'

Tish looked across the parking lot to where her father's car was idling. In the passenger seat, she could see the back of a woman's head. 'I see. So you're on your way there now?'

'Yeah, since we'll be right outside DC, we figured we'd hit up a nice restaurant and have a late supper before settling in for the night.'

'Sounds . . . yeah, sounds like a good plan. A ninety-minute drive is preferable to a seven-hour one.'

'Fourteen hours. We're taking the train both ways.'

Meaning that her father wouldn't be stopping for a visit on his way back home. 'Ah, I guess this is goodbye.'

'Yeah, I'll, uh, I'll call you when I get home in a few weeks.' Without as much as a hug or a kiss farewell, he turned on one heel to walk back to his idling automobile.

'Wait.' Tish stopped him. 'Why does it feel like you're always running from me?'

'I'm not running from you. I'm just . . . running. You know me. Never could stand still. I've been like this my whole life. Too late to stop now,' he joked. 'Now I'd better get going. There's a horse with my name—'

'I saw you,' she blurted.

He turned around. 'You saw me? What does that mean?'

'Back when Mom was sick, I saw you and the housekeeper. Together.'

'The housekeeper, huh? Which one?' He smirked.

'You know which one. You started giving me money and acting strangely after I saw you. It was the last housekeeper we had before . . .' She paused as the true meaning of her father's words dawned upon her.

How was it possible that she'd forgotten? Her family had gone through a seemingly endless stream of young, female housekeepers during her mother's illness. Some quit after the first day. Others left unexpectedly in the middle of their chores. And still others finished out a whole week and then never returned. Claiming that most housekeepers weren't accustomed to being around sick people, her mother changed domestic staffing agencies three or four times before finally finding Martha, an attractive brunette with a good work ethic and a sweet disposition. Martha stayed in the Lynch family's employ until Tish's mother's death four months after Tish had spied Martha and her father together.

'You,' she said in a near whisper. 'You're the reason we had so much trouble finding a housekeeper who would stay.'

'Letitia, you're a grown woman. I thought—'

'You thought what? That I'd already figured it out? No, I guess I'm a little bit naive when it comes to identifying someone I love as a sexual predator.'

'No, you've got it wrong. Look, I'm sorry for what I did, but you don't understand. It was difficult being in that house with your mother. I was lonely and starved for companionship.'

'There are support groups for people in that situation. Even back then, there were support groups,' she spat back.

'It wasn't as simple as that. When your mother and I got back together, it wasn't because we had some great big love story. It was so she could be on my health insurance plan. Your mother worked part-time so she didn't have insurance, and even though the two of you had been living with your grandparents, they didn't have the money to cover her expenses. When your mother got sick, I didn't want to see the two of you bankrupt, so I suggested she and I remarry.'

'OK, so you and Mom reunited for financial reasons. That doesn't excuse your behavior.'

'Maybe not, but you have no idea what it's like being looked at as a cash cow instead of a husband.'

'A cash cow? I'm sorry my mother was in too much pain to show you regular affection, but she loved you. She covered for what you were doing, so I wouldn't find out. And just before she died, she asked me to look after you.'

'Oh, yeah? How's that going?' he mocked.

'When you started bringing female friends to the house just two weeks after Mom's funeral, I decided you could look after yourself,' Tish stated coldly.

'You're mighty judgmental,' her father sneered. 'I thought your mother and I taught you not to criticize a person until you've walked in his shoes.'

'You did. And you're right – I haven't walked in your shoes, but I have walked in the shoes of those young women who lost a day's wages when they walked out on a job because their boss couldn't keep his eyes and hands to himself.'

'Well, then, if you're going to be high-and-mighty about things, I'd best be leaving.'

'Yes, I think it's time you did.'

Tish watched as her father walked back to his car, climbed into the passenger seat, and, after a few words with his companion, pulled out of the café parking lot without waving goodbye.

She stood in silence, startled by what she'd just learned and amazed at what her brain had chosen to remember and what it had chosen to forget: remembering Martha and forgetting all the others before her arrival. But of course she swept the memory of them under the proverbial carpet. She had no reason to tie a staffing problem to her father – not when her mother had insisted that the issue was the young women's aversion to her illness.

'Here I thought I was protecting Mom from the truth about Dad, when all that time, she was protecting me,' she thought aloud.

'That's what mamas do,' came Celestine's voice from the open doorway of the café. 'You OK, sugar?'

'Yeah.' She nodded, and then, upon consideration, shook her head instead. 'No.'

Celestine drew closer. 'You want to talk about it?'

'No. Not now. What I want is to go inside, finish my dinner, celebrate with those fabulous kids, and enjoy a lovely evening with friends.' Tish draped an arm around Celestine's shoulder and escorted her to the door.

'And a handsome man,' Celestine added.

'Not you, too,' Tish said with a sigh.

'I'm just sayin'. If you're not enjoyin' the proximity, then I'll happily swap seats with you. A woman my age needs to take advantage of every possible opportunity.'

# TWENTY

After a restless night and an unusually busy breakfast rush, Tish found herself back in the passenger seat of Reade's black SUV heading toward The Steeples for a second interview with Viola Tilley. Out of habit, she'd donned her usual café attire of black T-shirt and black capris, but at a quarter to ten, Celestine and Mary Jo reminded her to change, selecting for her a red dress with white polka dots and a blue denim jacket to wear when the forecasted rain showers struck at noon.

As Reade sped along, Tish applied a coat of red lipstick and then leaned back in her seat with a yawn.

'Trouble sleeping?' he asked.

'Yes, but nothing to do with the case,' she assured him.

'Good. I had a really nice time last night. I've known Celestine for years but I've really only spoken with Jules and Mary Jo at the café. I enjoyed getting to know them better. They're a lot of fun.'

'They are. We've had some good times. And we've been through some bad ones, too, but I know they always have my back.'

'Just like you have theirs,' he remarked. 'Speaking of which, I don't want to pry, but I saw you talking to your dad last night. Is everything all right?'

'My father stopped at the café to say goodbye. He and a female companion drove up to catch the auto train in Lorton last night.'

'That seems sudden. He only just got here. Did the two of you even have a chance to talk?'

'My father isn't much interested in discussing matters that don't involve women or horse racing,' she replied.

'I'm sorry, Tish.' Reade reached across the center console for her hand.

She didn't push it aside. 'I am, too, Clemson. I am, too.'

'Mornin', Ms Tarragon. Mornin', Sheriff,' Viola Tilley greeted them from her bed. 'Handsome as ever, I see.'

'How are you, Ms Tilley?' Reade asked.

'Tolerable.' She sighed, appearing to be in considerable pain. 'What brings you folks here this morning?'

Reade pulled over the two pink cushioned chairs reserved for visitors, and he and Tish took a seat. 'We wanted to ask you some more questions about the day of Daisy's murder. Specifically about Walker James. He claims to have been in the garage at the time his mother found the body. And yet no one remembers him being there. According to Gadsden Carney's files, you might be able to shed some light on Walker James's memory.'

Nearly a minute elapsed before Viola spoke, her voice trembling. 'I made a promise to Delilah and the senator all those years ago. I promised that I would carry their secret to the grave. As a woman of my word, I've kept that promise, but when you came to see me and told me there had been another killing, I started thinking that this is no longer between me, Delilah, and the senator. It's between me and my Maker.'

'You were at Cypress Hollow when Delilah found Daisy's body, weren't you?' Tish said softly.

Viola broke into soft sobs. 'I lied when Mr Carney asked me. I lied again and again because I thought it was all in the past. But it's not in the past anymore, is it? And now Mr Carney's dead because I lied to keep my promise.'

'Take your time and tell us what happened,' Reade gently urged.

'I went to my family cookout, like I said. Right before we were going to serve up supper, I realized I'd forgotten to bring my blood pressure pills. I always used to take them with my meal. So my nephew offered to drive me back to Cypress Hollow to fetch them. He'd just gotten his driver's license and would use any excuse to drive, so I took him up on the offer.'

'We got to the house and I told my nephew to wait out front near the gate with the car running. I didn't plan on taking very long. As I went upstairs to my room, I heard Delilah and the senator in the study, arguing.'

'Did you hear what they were arguing about?' Tish asked.

'No, just that Delilah was angry at something the senator had done – from the way she was talking, I imagined it had something to do with that girl he brought home. She was telling him that his behavior that day was insufferable or unbearable or something like that.'

'What happened next?'

'I went upstairs and got my pills. On my way out, I figured I'd peek in on Walker James, since he hated it when his mama and daddy argued. When I looked into his room, the video game console was on but he wasn't there. I didn't think much of it. He loved those video games but he'd often get bored and go off to look for his sister, so I turned the console off and went downstairs. As I passed the family play area, I noticed the door to the garage was open. If the senator had caught the kids leaving the door open while the central air was on, he would have had a conniption, so I went out to shut it, poking my nose into the garage first so I could scold Daisy and Walker James for their carelessness. That's . . . that's when I saw it.'

With shaking hands, Viola reached for a glass of water. Tish leaned over and helped the elderly nanny steady the glass while she drank. 'Thank you,' she said as Tish replaced the glass on Viola's nightstand. 'What I saw was Daisy, lying on the garage floor. Delilah was kneeling over her, crying, the senator was standing at her feet, and Walker James, at her head, was staring off into space. The way everyone was standing there and not running around calling for help or for an ambulance told me that Daisy was dead.'

'What did you do next?' Tish asked.

'I screamed – or tried to. Delilah jumped up and put her hand over my mouth and begged me to be quiet. Then she begged me to help her save Walker James. She begged me to save her boy.'

'How were you supposed to save him?' Reade posed.

'By not letting anyone know he'd murdered his sister.'

Reade leaned back in his chair. 'Did Delilah and the senator see Walker James kill Daisy?'

'No. They'd gone into the family area to continue their argument and noticed the door to the garage was open. Delilah popped her head in to see if anyone was in the garage because she didn't want them to overhear what was being discussed. That's when she saw Walker James standing over Daisy's body. It had been just two weeks since he'd threatened his sister with a golf club – it wasn't hard to figure out what had happened.'

'Did Walker James say anything? Did he confess? Apologize?' Tish asked.

'No, he didn't say a word. "What have you done?" Delilah asked him time and time again. But there was nothing. It was almost like he couldn't speak and couldn't hear. He just stared straight ahead. His little face was as white as could be and completely blank. Even when his daddy scolded him, there was no reaction whatsoever.'

'Sounds like shock,' Reade noted. 'What happened then?'

'We had to get Walker James out of that garage before anyone saw him, so the senator picked him up and took him to his room. He told him to stay there with the door locked and not come out until he personally got him. While the senator took care of Walker James, I snuck into the kitchen and got a bottle of spray cleaner. Using some old rags Delilah found, we cleaned the golf clubs and a croquet set that was lying nearby – just in case he'd used that instead.'

'Wait one minute,' Reade stopped her. 'You said you weren't sure what Walker James used. There wasn't a weapon in his hand?'

'No, Sheriff. We figured he got angry, hit his sister, and then dropped the club or mallet with the others.'

Reade frowned. 'Go on.'

'Delilah and I gave everything a good cleaning – as good as we could in the little time we had. The senator returned just as we were finishing up. I was about to toss the rags into the trash when he stopped me. If the rags were found in the trash, he said, it would be proof that we were covering up for someone, so the senator shoved them in his pockets and said he was going to dump them in the creek. A few minutes later, once he'd reached the water, he said, Delilah was to scream and pretend that she'd just found the body.'

'And you? What were you to do?'

'I was to leave Cypress Hollow as quickly as I could. The senator asked me if I had a way to get back to my auntie's house. I said I did. He told me to leave and never to tell a soul what I saw or that I'd been at the house that evening. And that's what I did. I got into my nephew's car, went back to my auntie's, and never said a word.'

'When asked, your family corroborated the story that you never left the barbecue.'

'They did, but that wasn't to protect Walker James. That was to protect my nephew. A rich little blonde girl was found dead in her home and a young black man in a beat-up car was parked just outside the front gate right around the time her body was found.' Viola looked Reade in the eyes. 'I'm sorry, Sheriff, but we both know how that would have turned out.'

Reade acknowledged the sad truth of Viola's statement with a nod of the head. 'Do you remember the car your nephew was driving that day?'

'I remember it well.' She smiled. 'It was my mama's car. When she could no longer drive, she turned it over to my nephew, who always drove it a little too fast for my liking. It was a four-door Chrysler LeBaron in light blue.'

'Well, that explains everything,' Tish stated as they got back into the SUV. 'It explains Walker James wanting forgiveness for his sister's killer. It explains Benton contaminating the crime scene, the threatening look he gave Deputy Aldrich, the family's lack of cooperation, and Delilah's reactions in those videos – guilt for the attention she lavished on Daisy to the detriment of Walker James and then, later, after she'd been sentenced to jail, victory. She and Benton could do nothing more for Daisy, but they could save their only surviving child.'

'Walker James was quite young. It's unlikely he'd have gone to a detention center, but he would have been mandated to undergo extensive therapy and rehabilitation. Plus, the murder charge would have remained on his record for life,' Reade explained.

'Not exactly the life the Honeycutts wanted for their son – nor their reputation. We know how much image played into their family dynamics.'

'After a revelation like that, it would have been difficult for anyone to view Delilah as the perfect mother,' Reade remarked.

'What about Benton? He was horrified at the prospect of having a daughter on the stage. Can you imagine how he would have felt to have a son who was a murderer? Why, he even stipulated to Priscilla that he didn't want any more children.'

'He probably couldn't stand the thought that he might produce another killer.'

A lengthy silence ensued as the pair ruminated over Viola Tilley's testimony and its implications.

'Are you going to arrest Walker James?' Tish finally asked.

'Not yet. We don't have sufficient evidence.'

'But Viola Tilley . . .' she began to argue.

'There's no doubt what she's told us changes the shape of the case, but it's still not enough to press charges. What we have is an eighty-six-year-old woman in a care home who, after twenty-five years insisting she was nowhere near the house, has suddenly changed her statement. It's like Harper Lee suddenly publishing a long-forgotten first draft a year before her death.'

Reade's reference to *Go Set a Watchman* made Tish sit up straight in her seat.

'You don't need a crystal ball to know what the district attorney and the press would do with that.'

'They'd assume you coerced Viola into changing her statement,' she surmised. 'However, Viola's story is substantiated by Priscilla's account of the blue sedan and by Walker James's memory of being carried upstairs by his father.'

'True, but even if I somehow managed to get the DA to take Viola's revised statement seriously, we're still lacking an eyewitness. No one in that garage actually saw Walker James commit the crime.'

'No, but Walker James tried to attack his sister with a golf club just weeks before the murder.'

'Circumstantial evidence. When Viola walked into that garage, she had no idea how long the boy had been there or what he was doing there in the first place. He wasn't even holding a golf club. I find it hard to believe that a kid that young and, by Viola's description, in an obvious state of shock would have had the wherewithal to put the golf club back where he found it.'

'You do believe that Walker James killed his sister, though, don't you?' Tish questioned.

'I do. It fits everything we know about the case. Delilah confessed before the police could speak with her son. She confessed to protect him.'

Tish agreed and yet Reade's observation about the golf clubs gave her pause. 'What about Carney's murder? We can't arrest Walker James for that either, can we?'

'Nope. Walker James has an airtight alibi in that he was with his attorney girlfriend at the time in question – an attorney who could be disbarred if caught fabricating an alibi. I'd also like to mention that given the information we have now, it would mean that Walker James killed Gadsden Carney to cover up a crime he doesn't even remember.' Reade shook his head. 'If we even approached the DA about making a case, he'd have me for lunch. And I won't even get into what Schuyler Thompson and those concerned parties would say.'

At the mention of Schuyler's name, Tish wrinkled her nose. 'Blech.'

'Sorry,' Reade apologized.

'Not as sorry as I am. I can't believe I ever put up with his nonsense.'

'I can't, either. Oh . . . sorry. Again.'

'It's OK,' she said with a smile. 'What do we do now?'

'I consulted with our staff psychologist this morning. She suggested I bring Walker James in for questioning so she can assess the situation. She thinks if we show him photos of the crime scene in the garage – not the body necessarily, but the scene – it might spark his memory. We'd originally scheduled something for early next week, but given this new twist, I'll see if I can bring him in today. Which is a big "if" while Milla's acting as watchdog.'

'You know, I thought of Milla last night.'

'So, you *did* lose some sleep over the case.'

'No, I only thought about the case because I didn't want to think about my father,' she explained.

Reade's eyes narrowed. 'You distracted yourself from family trouble by thinking about a murder case? I'd say that was crazy if I hadn't already done it myself.'

'Really?'

'It wasn't a murder case, but a string of burglaries and I wasn't forgetting a parent but an ex-fiancée. The premise is the same.'

'An ex-fiancée? I'm sorry.'

'Don't be. She broke things off because she thought being married to a small-town sheriff would be boring.'

Tish laughed. 'I think she may have miscalculated there.'

'I found out she married a physical education teacher in Ohio a few years back, so yeah, there was definitely some sort of judgment issue at play, but it's fine. There's someone out there who's right for me. I mean, I think . . . I hope there is,' he quickly added before clearing his throat awkwardly. 'You were saying about Milla . . .'

'Hmm?' Tish had been so enjoying their conversation (and privately wondering if she might be the right someone) that she'd nearly forgotten how the discussion started. 'Oh. Right. Um, do you remember when Milla pulled us aside after our meeting with Walker James and told us not to bother him again?'

'Yeah, of course I do.'

'You and I assumed that the concerned parties who sent Schuyler to your office were being influenced by Milla and Walker James, but, looking back, Milla's behavior indicates otherwise. Why all the posturing and legal threats when all she needed to do was make a phone call?'

'You have a point there,' he admitted. 'It's also been unusually quiet.'

'That's true. It's been over twenty-four hours since we left Walker James's and we've yet to be warned against a second meeting.'

'If that's the case, perhaps it won't be quite as difficult to get Walker James to the station as first anticipated.'

'You can always subpoena him, can't you?'

Reade started the engine of the SUV and backed out of the parking spot. 'I could, but it takes some time for a judge to grant a subpoena and I'd prefer to work with a cooperative suspect than a hostile one. For now, at least.'

'If Milla gives you a difficult time, you can take the angle that you're helping Walker James to uncover the truth and heal.'

'I'll try that, but I suspect it will stop working when they discover I'm trying to prove that Walker James is a killer.'

# TWENTY-ONE

With a promise to call her with an update after the café had closed, Reade dropped Tish at Cookin' the Books a few minutes before noon and just as the lunch rush was beginning. Tossing her handbag into her bedroom and tying a black apron around her waist, Tish set to work behind the counter and she, Mary Jo, and Celestine spent the next two hours serving up overstuffed sandwiches, rich soups, and rainbow-hued salads before cleaning up in preparation for the mid-afternoon trickle of customers looking for a pick-me-up of tea, coffee, lemonade, and Celestine's decadent baked goods.

Tish had just loaded the last of the lunch dishes in the washer when the café phone rang.

'I'll get it,' Celestine announced before picking up the cordless device near the cash register. 'Cookin' the Books Café and Catering. This is Celestine . . . Who may I ask is callin'?'

Ever since Tish received a threatening text message during the Virginia Commonwealth Bake-Off earlier that spring, Celestine had taken it upon herself to screen the café's phone calls. She placed a hand over the receiver and looked at Tish. 'A lady named Leah Harmon?'

Tish nodded and, stepping forward, warily took the receiver from Celestine. 'Hello?'

'Ms Tarragon, it's Leah Harmon, the psychic you spoke to the day before yesterday.'

'Yes, I remember. How may I help you?'

'I'm calling to give you an urgent message. It's from Delilah.'

At the mention of Delilah's name, Tish felt her heart begin to race. 'Um, if this is regarding the case, you should call the sheriff's department. Sheriff Reade would be able to—'

'I already tried there,' Leah interrupted, her voice rising in agitation. 'Sheriff Reade wasn't in. That's why I'm calling you. I have to get the message out *now*.'

'OK,' she replied tentatively.

'Delilah says you need to save her son. You need to save Walker James. She insisted that this is urgent. She said that something needs to be done before it's too late. She told me you will understand.'

Tish nearly dropped the phone. Apart from Reade and Viola Tilley, no one else knew the direction the investigation had taken that morning. 'But I . . . I don't understand. Save him how?'

'She didn't say. But when I couldn't reach the sheriff, she told me to call you. She told me that you will understand everything.'

'But I don't understand. I don't understand at all.'

'You will. That's what Delilah said. You will.'

The line fell abruptly silent. 'Hello? Hello?' Tish sighed and pressed the red button that switched off the handset.

'Who was that?' Mary Jo asked.

'The psychic on the Honeycutt case.'

'The one who gave you the message from your mother?'

Tish plopped down at one of the counter stools. 'Yes.'

'Oh, honey. You can talk to your mother yourself,' Celestine advised. 'I'm sure she's watchin' over you. Don't get mixed up with those psychics. They're just bad news. Several years back, my sister called that Dionne Warwick psychic company to contact her deceased pet potbelly pig, Jimmy Dean, and before you knew it, she was thousands of dollars in debt.'

'Jimmy Dean?' Mary Jo questioned in disbelief.

'Yep, my sister got him and his brother, Kevin Bacon, right after she split up from her second husband. Those pigs were nicer and cleaner and sweeter-smellin' than her two exes combined. Smarter, too. Kevin Bacon could open a box of Cheerios with his snout. My sister tried to get him on *Letterman*, but it just didn't pan out.'

After a bout of momentary speechlessness, Mary Jo asked, 'What did the psychic want, Tish?'

'To give me a message from Delilah Honeycutt.'

'A message from that murderer?' Celestine gasped.

'We're beginning to believe she wasn't a murderer,' Tish explained. 'We believe she might have confessed to protect the real killer.'

'What was the message?' Mary Jo inquired as she leaned her elbows on the counter directly in front of Tish.

'She wants me to save her son. She wants me to save Walker James.'

'Save him? Save him from what?'

'Clemson Reade, most likely. He's bringing Walker James in for questioning later today.'

'Well, there's nothin' you can do about that,' Celestine said. 'You were hired to help Clem, not stop him from doin' his work.'

'I know,' Tish acknowledged, 'but what if I'm missing something?'

'Oh, Tish,' Mary Jo sang. 'Let it go. I have no doubt that you and Reade covered every possible angle of this case. If he's bringing in Delilah's son, he has good reason.'

'He has very good reason,' Tish confirmed.

'There you go. Just let what that psychic said go right out of your head and relax. Maybe take a nap after we close today. You could probably use some sleep – I thought I heard you up and about last night.'

'I'm sorry if I woke you. It was a restless night.'

'That business with your daddy out in the parking lot kept you awake, didn't it?' Celestine guessed.

'Yes,' Tish confessed. 'I confronted my father about a memory I had and it turns out my memory was just a fraction of the picture. The situation was far worse than I'd ever imagined. I saw my father cheat on my mother with a housekeeper, but it turns out he tried it on – successfully and unsuccessfully – with just about every single housekeeper we ever hired.'

'Oh, Tish,' Mary Jo cried.

Tish shrugged. 'My mother knew. All this time, I thought I was protecting her by staying silent about what I saw; in truth, she was protecting me by not telling me what I should have already known. The signs were all there – the constant turnover of help, my father's reluctance to address the situation, my mother spending hours on the phone with different agencies, her waiting until I was at school to make those calls, even the "friends" my father brought home within weeks of my mother's death – it was all there and I remembered it, but not in its context. It's as if my brain chose to ignore everything but that single moment.'

Mary Jo plopped down on the stool beside Tish. 'It was a traumatic time in your life. Your mother was dying.'

'And you were young, honey,' Celestine added. 'Too young to be faced with everything you just described. Your young mind did what it did to cope.'

'Thanks, ladies.' Tish flashed a wan smile. 'I'm feeling a lot better now. Just talking to you both has helped tremendously. I think there's a reason three a.m. is called the witching hour. Any time I go to bed with something on my mind, that's the time I invariably wake up and start staring at the ceiling, my thoughts racing. Last night, I kept thinking about how my parents' relationship might have influenced mine. Mitch got out of a relationship to be with me, just like he did with his girlfriend before, but I married him without even questioning his fidelity. Then there's Schuyler and that whole disaster – why didn't I see how controlling or clingy he was? Now I've finally found someone who I *think* might be right and I'm too scared to—'

Tish stopped talking as she realized that between the patchy memory and a current relationship being influenced by the past, she might have been talking about Walker James as much as herself.

Mary Jo and Celestine leaned forward and urged, in unison, 'Yes?'

'Walker James,' Tish answered. 'I have to save Walker James.'

'Sugar, you were talkin' about how you met someone who might be right for you,' Celestine prompted.

'Never mind that, Celestine. This is important – I think I know what Delilah meant when she asked me to save her son. You see, Walker James has an amazing girlfriend, Milla – looks like a supermodel, has a law degree, fiercely loyal – but according to her, he won't marry her or commit to having children because of his family history. I don't think that's the case at all. I don't think his concern is about his family's past. I think he's uncertain about his own. He's uncertain because he remembers his parents finding him in the garage, but he doesn't remember anything that occurred prior to that or afterward.'

Mary Jo threw her hands up in the air. 'I thought you were having a breakthrough, Tish.'

'I am having a breakthrough, MJ.' Tish hopped from the stool excitedly. 'I'm having a breakthrough about the case. Today, we discovered that Delilah Honeycutt confessed to her daughter's murder in order to cover up for her son, who actually committed the crime, but I don't think that's true. I don't think Walker James did it. When his parents found him in the garage, he wasn't holding a golf club – the murder weapon – in his hand, but his parents behaved as if he was. They acted as if he committed the crime. His father carried him up the stairs to his room and locked the door. Soon after, he was sent away to boarding school and ordered never to speak of what happened—'

'Almost like he was being punished,' Celestine noted.

'Precisely. Then there's his mother's confession. He believes she committed the murder, and yet she wasn't in the garage when he arrived – but then why else would she confess, unless it was to protect him? Like you said last night, Celestine, mamas protect their babies, but, in this case, his mother's protection confused him, too. Walker James has probably spent the past twenty-five years wondering if he's guilty, while deep down believing that he's not.'

'How can you be so sure that Walker James just isn't afraid of commitment like a million other guys?' Mary Jo posed.

'Because he trusts Milla implicitly. He trusted her to be present during our interview, he trusted her to protect him if need be, and he trusts her to represent him and his video game empire as an attorney. He would never have let Milla get as close as she is if he were a commitment-phobe. He wouldn't have let her get that close if he thought he was the killer, either. No, there's something he knows, yet he doesn't realize that he knows it. It's why Gadsden Carney was killed. Gadsden Carney called Walker James no fewer than five times while reinvestigating the case. Carney suspected something, just as he suspected Viola Tilley was in the house that evening. Gadsden Carney was piecing together the truth about Walker James and someone didn't like it.'

'OK, but what are you going to do?'

'I'm going to review Carney's evidence wall and see if I can come up with something. Watch the café for me.'

Tish dashed off to her bedroom, leaving Celestine and Mary Jo to shrug at each other.

'I thought we were there,' Mary Jo said.

Celestine shook her head. 'I did, too. Talk about snatchin' defeat from the jaws of victory.'

As Mary Jo and Celestine lamented what they feared might be Tish's permanently single status, Tish knelt on the floor of her bedroom, extracted copies of the photos from Carney's visual display from a manila folder, and arranged them on the bed.

At the sudden activity, Tuna awoke from his napping spot beside Tish's pillow and, yawning and stretching, ambled across the bedspread – and photos – for a chin scratch. Tish reached out and repeatedly stroked the long-haired cat from head to tail, provoking a round of vociferous purrs, but her eyes remained fixed on the twenty or so photos before her.

Glancing between photos of the Honeycutts and the Heritages, school portraits, vacation snaps, and shots of holiday gatherings, she was uncertain what she was looking for and how it could possibly help with the case.

'OK, Delilah. You want me to save your son. What am I looking for?' she whispered, growing increasingly frustrated. 'What am I looking for?'

The question had only just departed her lips a second time when Tuna, tired of petting and ready to play, pounced on a nearby photo, picked it up in his teeth, and then sent it cascading down to the blue area rug beside the bed.

It was a photo of the garage taken from the front door, looking to the rear. The location of Daisy's body was marked with measuring tape, along with the location of the golf clubs and croquet mallets. Near the rear door of the garage stood the lanky figure of Gadsden Carney. He was in full uniform and, with his mullet and facial hair, he resembled a mustached Kurt Russell.

After giving Tuna a mild scolding for messing with evidence, Tish placed the photo back on the bed. As she did so, she felt her breath catch. Bishop Ambrose Dillard's words came rushing back into memory: *Tall fellow. No-nonsense type – clean-shaven, receding hairline, plain spoken.* The bishop's words didn't describe the Carney in the 1996 photograph, but the Carney found dead in the church cemetery.

Did Dillard kill Carney to cover up the fact that he'd murdered Daisy? Tish found the idea difficult to believe – Dillard was a man of the cloth, a friend to the family, and he loved Delilah deeply. Likewise, Daisy had shown no signs of ongoing abuse, so what possible motive did Dillard have to hurt the girl?

Tish's eye fell upon a faded color photograph labeled *Christmas Party 1995.* The image depicted, from left to right, Delilah and Benton Honeycutt, Dixie Dupree, and Frank and Luella Heritage posing in front of an ornately decorated and beribboned Christmas tree, the couples' four children lined up in front of them. Both families were dressed in their holiday finery – the women in black dresses and splashy, on-trend chandelier earrings, the men in classic dark suits, the boys in matching festive sweaters and corduroy trousers, and the girls in sparkly dresses with matching hair bows. Behind and slightly to the left of Delilah, looking like part of the group and yet decidedly alone, stood a man in a Santa suit.

Tish pulled the photo close and stared at Santa's face. Beneath the fake beard, the man's features were fine, even, and quite familiar, albeit far younger than the last time Tish had seen them.

The Santa was Bishop Ambrose Dillard.

That Dillard might dress as Santa and distribute gifts to parishioners and his friend's children was surprising – Tish thought him more inclined to teach about the birth of Jesus than to run around town in a beard and padding – but not altogether shocking. If Delilah had asked him to play the part, he certainly would have capitulated. However, the way he stood alone, behind the group – near Delilah, yet not with her – gave Tish pause.

She picked up a different folder and sorted through the group photos gathered in it. In every photo containing Dillard, he was standing near Delilah, his torso turned toward hers, but never physically touching her.

That the bishop had fallen in love with Delilah Honeycutt was obvious during their interview. She was willing to bet that he was still in love with her to this day. Although Tish doubted that Delilah would have asked her lover to act as a marriage counselor, had there ever been, in all those times they spent alone together, a moment when he might have acted upon his feelings?

Tish suddenly recalled how Leah Harmon had described Delilah Honeycutt's spirit as guilt-ridden. What if Delilah's guilt wasn't due to her placing Daisy in an unsafe situation? What if something Delilah had done had prompted the murder?

Tish's memory flashed back to Delilah's argument with Dixie the day prior to the barbecue. Delilah was insistent that she wasn't going to end her marriage over 'one stupid mistake.' Dixie assumed her sister had been referring to Benton's affair with Priscilla, but an ongoing affair with a twenty-five-year-old woman wasn't the product of a one-time lack of judgment. What if Delilah was referring to her own indiscretion? Had she, after her late-night phone call to Benton, told Reverend Dillard – her only true confidante – about the female voice she heard in the background? Is that why Reverend Dillard had offered his counseling services?

When Benton rejected the idea of counseling, had Delilah sought consolation in the arms of her good friend and advisor? Mrs McIlveen said he had paid a visit to Cypress Hollow the afternoon prior to the barbecue. Given Dillard's feelings for Delilah and Delilah's constant loneliness, it wasn't difficult to believe that such a visit might have led to something more – a long embrace, a kiss, a lingering touch. And, if it had, did Daisy, perhaps peeking around a doorway, happen to see it?

When Benton brought his 'friend' Priscilla home, Daisy asked if Priscilla was going to kiss her father. Was that because she'd witnessed another family friend kissing her mother just the day prior? Most importantly, if Daisy had witnessed Bishop Dillard kissing her mother, would she have told Viola or her father? Tish remembered Viola Tilley describing how Daisy sang about the things she'd seen, like her brother sneaking an extra candy bar for his lunch bag. Was it possible she might have sung about Bishop Dillard and her mother?

She felt a pit develop at the bottom of her stomach as she recalled what Daisy was singing the day she was murdered. *Christmas songs.*

With lightning speed, she moved to her dresser, extracted her cell phone from her handbag, and called Reade to discuss what she'd found. The call went straight to voicemail.

'Dammit,' she swore under her breath. Unearthing a business card from the bottom of her purse, she made a second call. This time, the recipient answered. 'Hello?'

'Hello, Mrs Honeycutt?'

'Speaking.'

'This is Tish Tarragon. Sheriff Clemson Reade and I saw you at your condo yesterday afternoon.'

'Ah, yes. How may I be of service?'

'I need to ask you a quick question about the day Daisy Honeycutt was murdered.'

'By all means,' Priscilla urged.

'Do you happen to recall the Christmas song Daisy was singing that afternoon?' Tish asked.

'I'll never forget it. I've been unable to listen to that song ever since. She was singing *I Saw Mommy Kissing Santa Claus.*'

For the second time in ten minutes, Tish nearly dropped the phone.

Priscilla must have heard the fumbling. 'Hello? Ms Tarragon? Are you there?'

'Yes, I'm here. Thank you for your help, Mrs Honeycutt.'

'You're most welcome. Is there anything else?'

'No, that's – that's all. You've been of great assistance. Thank you, again.' Tish disconnected and braced herself against the dresser as she visualized the events of that fateful day.

Daisy taunts Reverend Dillard by singing a song that indicates she's seen him and her mother kissing. The ambitious, guilt-ridden clergyman fears that alone with the family, the little girl will explain why she's chosen that particular song to sing – an explanation that would inevitably lead to Benton Honeycutt filing a complaint with the bishop and Dillard losing his parish.

Dillard is ambitious – he boasted about being the youngest rector in the diocese. He simply cannot take the chance of Daisy sharing her secret, so before he leaves the barbecue, he lures her to the garage in an attempt to quieten her. She refuses; after all, it's just a game to her and Dillard's a friend of the family who attends her recitals – he's not a threat. When Daisy ignores his demand, a desperate Dillard picks her up by the throat, shakes her, and pushes her against the garage wall. The blow is enough to cause injury and unconsciousness. Panicking, Dillard recalls Walker James's golf club incident. Spying the same set of junior golf clubs lying nearby, he picks one up and ensures Daisy is silenced once and for all and that Walker James will take the blame. Indeed, as the head of Walker James's troubled youth group, Dillard can attest to the boy's violent temperament which Dillard would no doubt state – sadly and inaccurately – had grown acutely more severe with the deterioration of his parents' marriage.

When the deed is done, Dillard wipes down the golf club, replaces it with the rest, escapes through the front garage door, and drives off for home. Because he said his farewells to the Honeycutts and the Heritages well before the discovery of the body, he's not even considered a suspect.

Fast-forward to Gadsden Carney's investigation – after a quarter of a century thinking he'd gotten away with murder, Bishop Dillard was being questioned again. It must have been a nightmare, because now Dillard had far more to lose than a parish. He had the bishopric and a life's legacy at stake. Carney was incredibly astute and the bishop rather unguarded about his affection for Delilah Honeycutt. Once Clayton had a chance to go through all of Carney's notes, it would be clear just how far Carney had gotten in the investigation. For now, suffice to say he'd gotten too close to the truth.

Dillard needed to deal with Carney, and quickly. Promising new information, Dillard places an anonymous call to the retired sheriff and arranges to meet him at the Honeycutt gravesite on Tuesday evening. As his former parish, St Jude's Episcopal Church of Ashton Courthouse offers Bishop Dillard a distinct advantage over Carney. He knows which hiding place offers a clear vantage point of the Honeycutt family plot, plus he has access to the church schedule so he can choose the perfect moment to strike – during an extremely loud ladies' charity supper where his and Carney's vehicles would blend with the other seventy-odd vehicles parked in the lot and along the road. In addition, if anyone did happen to witness him on church grounds at the time, they'd hardly remark upon the presence of a man dressed in black and a clerical collar.

Unaware of Carney's medical condition and therefore not in a position to make Carney's death look like it is due to natural causes, Dillard murders the man with a sharp blow to the back of the head. Launching a surprise attack from behind not only minimizes the chance of Carney crying out, but having already attacked Daisy in a similar fashion, Dillard has a good idea of precisely where on the back of the head to land a fatal blow.

With Carney dead, all that's left for Dillard to do is to dispose of the body so that his death isn't connected with Daisy Honeycutt's. Once again, the choice of time and location gives Dillard the upper hand. As former rector of St Jude's, Dillard is well-aware of the groundskeeper's idiosyncratic schedule. Comprising primarily middle-aged to elderly women, the members of the Junior League are unlikely to stray from the well-lit gravel path to roam through the tall grass of Tuesday's un-mowed churchyard – especially after a heavy dinner and a few tipples of punch. Likewise, following the late evening function, the church gates will remain unlocked at least until dawn. And so Dillard leaves Carney's body with a plan to return in the wee hours and dispose of the corpse under cover of darkness, confident that his crime would remain undiscovered during his absence.

Or so he thought . . .

Tish recalled Jules and Celestine's account of a dark sedan driving slowly through the sleepy town and past the churchyard as they waited for Reade to arrive. Did that dark sedan belong to the bishop? Or did he return to St Jude's later that night only to find a sea of fluorescent light and a team of forensic experts scouring the Honeycutt plot? Either way, Tish was grateful she'd chosen to cut through the cemetery that night, otherwise Carney's murder might have gone undetected.

Her heart pounding, Tish again tried phoning Reade. Once again, the call was sent directly to voicemail. *Where is he?*

Growing concerned over Reade's whereabouts, Tish called Officer Clayton. 'Jim? Hey, it's Tish.'

'Hey, what's up?'

'I've been trying to call Clemson, but there's no answer.'

'He went out to bring Walker James in for questioning, but he's had trouble finding him. Walker James wasn't at his home or his office.'

'What about Milla?'

'She was at their place but said Walker had gone out wandering or something like that. She says he does it every now and then when he's stressed. Weird, isn't it? The guy's a recluse who doesn't show up for conventions, but when you search for him on a random Friday, he's nowhere,' Clayton said.

'That is weird,' she agreed, but there was another important matter at hand. 'Look, I really need to talk to you. I think I've solved the Carney murder and the Honeycutt case.' She described the photo of Carney and the song Daisy was singing.

'Wow. The bishop? That's crazy.'

'Yes, but what are we going to do about it? Can we arrest him?'

Clayton drew a deep breath. 'It will be tough. First, he's a priest – we need proof he's our guy before we rile up that kind of public sentiment. Second, I need to clear his arrest with Richmond Police since it isn't our jurisdiction – we've already got the OK to question witnesses in the case, but filing charges is completely different. It's going to be difficult to get the go-ahead if the only evidence we have is an old photo. I'll look through Carney's files here to see if I can find something else. Is there anything you can think of?'

Tish stepped away from the dresser and surveyed the photos sprawled across the bed. Holding the phone in her right hand, she stroked Tuna with her left, just in case he had some other surprises in store for her. Apart from a contented purr, he did not. 'No, I can't think of any—' She turned around to see Schuyler Thompson standing at the café counter, ordering afternoon coffee for the mayor's office staff. 'Wait,' she urged. 'I might have something. Hold on a second, would you?'

'Schuyler,' she addressed him, as she stepped from her bedroom to a spot behind the counter.

'Tish,' he greeted with more than a touch of frost in his voice.

'I need your help.'

'That's a new one. You never needed my help with anything.'

'Please. This is important.'

'OK.' He sighed. 'What is it?'

'I need to know who directed you to stop the reopening of the Honeycutt investigation.'

'I told you, the board—'

'Higher than the board. Who put the pressure on the board to stop the case?'

'I'm afraid I can't tell you.'

'This is a matter of life and death—'

'It always is with you,' he replied snarkily.

Tish rolled her eyes. 'OK. Let's try this the other way around. I'll tell you who it is and all you need to do is nod.'

Schuyler folded his arms across his chest and said nothing.

'When you made your plea to us, you said the Honeycutt case brought great pain and suffering to the Ashton Courthouse community,' she said. 'I heard those exact words uttered yesterday afternoon by Bishop Dillard. He's the one who contacted the board, isn't he?'

Schuyler remained silent, but he swallowed hard and looked the other way. She'd seen him make that exact gesture before – it was as good as a yes. 'I have all I need,' she said triumphantly before putting the phone to her ear. 'Jim? Yes, it's Tish again. The bishop was the party trying to interfere with our investigation.'

'That's obstruction,' Clayton replied. 'That should be enough to hold him until we can get him on the murders. I'll go talk to

the deputy sheriff and see what she says. Then we'll get the ball
rolling with the Richmond Police.'

The two disconnected and Tish, relieved to have almost
brought such an odious case to a close, wandered to the sink
and poured herself a glass of water. Her respite, however, was
short-lived. There was still the matter of the missing Reade.
How she wished she could have shared the news about the bishop
with him directly.

And where was Walker James? Where on earth had he wandered
off to? He didn't strike Tish as the outdoorsy type.

Suddenly, Tish heard Walker James's voice play inside her head.
*I go there often . . . in my dreams. Sometimes I feel like part of
me will always be trapped there, doomed to rattle around the
hallways and the grounds like the ghost in some Gothic novel.*

He'd gone to Cypress Hollow.

It was at Cypress Hollow that Walker James said he was the
happiest in his life. He'd fashioned his new home to resemble it
– right down to the turquoise shutters and door. Visiting the real
thing would be like visiting a second home. If Walker James did
indeed rattle along its hallways – not as a ghost, but in human
form – that would explain why the property had been taken off
the market and the house maintained.

Whether he was looking to rekindle the happiness he found
while sunning himself on the old balcony outside his childhood
bedroom or struggling to find answers in the dank, dark garage,
he was as haunted as everyone else whose lives had been touched
by the death of Daisy Honeycutt.

Tish put the water glass down on the counter. Hard.

*The garage. The garage and Ambrose Dillard.*

Ambrose Dillard had gone out of his way to destroy Walker
James in order to save himself. Only the Honeycutts' quick thinking
and Delilah's confession had saved the boy from being accused
of the crime of murdering his sister and all the ramifications that
would stem from such charges.

*And now Ambrose Dillard had Walker James's phone number.*

Clemson had given him Walker's business number, but his staff
would have told him that the bishop had been in contact. No doubt
Walker would remember Reverend Dillard and agree to meet an
old family friend.

That's what Delilah meant when she instructed Tish to save her son. He needed to be saved from Ambrose Dillard.

Tish picked up her phone and frantically dialed Reade's number. For the third time in a row, she was redirected to voicemail. Had Clemson deduced Walker James's whereabouts? Was he on his way to Cypress Hollow, where there was no cell or Wi-Fi service?

'You all right, honey? You look a bit peaked?' Celestine asked, snapping Tish from her fugue state.

'No, I'm not all right.' She tried Clayton again, but this time there was no answer. 'Clemson might be in trouble.'

'Trouble? What kind of trouble?'

'I think he's on his way to Cypress Hollow and I think the killer might be there, too.' Tish raced to her bedroom, collected her purse and car keys, and dashed back into the café, where Schuyler had launched into a tirade.

'You think you're so clever, Tish. You always think you're so clever, but just wait until that little trick you pulled on me comes out in court. It will never stand because I neither confirmed nor denied your statement. You—'

'Oh, shut up, Schuyler,' she shouted and sped off for the front door.

'Wait.' Celestine, untying her apron, followed. 'I'm not letting you go there by yourself. I'm going with you.'

Tish didn't argue, but directed Mary Jo to call Clayton. 'If he doesn't answer, then call the sheriff's office direct line and tell them what's happening. See if they'll send someone over.'

'I will. And Tish? He'll be OK.'

Tish blinked back tears and sprinted off across the parking lot to the red Matrix.

Mary Jo, meanwhile, was left with a fuming Schuyler. 'So . . .' She smiled awkwardly as she pushed his order across the counter. 'Considering you didn't receive our usual high standard of customer service, that's, um, that's on the house.'

Tish drove hell-for-leather along the westerly road that connected Hobson Glen with the neighboring community of Ashton Courthouse, prompting Celestine to lean forward in her seat and clutch, white-knuckled, at the dashboard.

'Don't you think you should slow it down?' the baker prompted. 'You can't be sure he's there.'

'If I've figured out that Walker James has been visiting Cypress Hollow, then Clemson has, too.'

'You're right. Clem's a smart fella. Too smart to be caught in a trap.'

'This isn't a trap for Clemson, Celestine. This is a trap for Walker James. The bishop has been questioned twice now about Daisy's murder. In order to throw us off the scent, he needs to make it look as if Walker James committed both crimes. Getting him alone at Cypress Hollow is the perfect place to make that happen. If Clemson is there, it's to take Walker James in for questioning. I'm not sure he realizes he might be walking into something more.'

They arrived at Cypress Hollow to find the front gates open and Reade's SUV parked near the entrance. It was empty.

'What do we do now?' Celestine asked.

'We're going up to the house,' Tish announced. 'We have to.'

Tish steered the Matrix along the pavement and pulled to a halt in the circular driveway, feeling somewhat relieved. 'There are no other cars on the property. Not even one belonging to Walker James. I must have been wrong about him being here. Clemson must be here alone, checking the house and the grounds.'

The two women stepped out of the car to hear the sound of a running engine.

'Sounds like a motor,' Celestine whispered.

They rushed to the garage to assess the situation. The engine was operating at high gear and wisps of exhaust occasionally escaped from beneath the door. Celestine and Tish exchanged knowing glances.

Someone – possibly Clemson – was inside.

Tish tried the garage door handles, but they didn't turn. Like a shot, she took off around the house and tried the back door. As expected, it, too, was bolted shut.

'The outside doors are all locked,' she reported, jogging back to the front of the house.

'On the count of three,' Celestine instructed, walking several paces back. Tish followed her lead. Within seconds, the two women were hurtling toward the doors, throwing their combined weight at the center latch. The doors flexed inward slightly, but the lock didn't budge.

'It's no use,' Tish stated, her voice trembling. 'Go to Clemson's car and see if you can use his radio to call for help.'

'No problem. Lloyd and I were members of a CB club in the seventies. What are you going to do?'

'I'm going to try the door inside the house.'

'No!' Celestine clutched Tish's arm.

'I have to. If there's someone in that car, we don't know how long they've been there. And we don't know if it's . . .' Tish's voice broke. 'I have to get in the garage.'

Celestine nodded. 'Be careful.'

While Celestine took off for the SUV, Tish dashed to the hatchback of the Matrix and, lifting the bottom panel of the trunk, extracted a tire iron, which she wielded over her head as she approached the front doors of Cypress Hollow. Thankfully, they were unlocked.

Leaving the door open behind her, Tish stepped into the foyer and listened for any sound that might indicate another human being was on the premises, but the building was eerily quiet. Padding through the foyer, she stopped outside the family entertainment area and peeked around the doorframe. The space, as well as the playroom beyond, appeared vacant.

Hastening through both areas, Tish arrived at the small mudroom adjacent to the garage and tried the door. Like all the other entrances to the garage, it was locked, the key nowhere to be seen.

Her heart racing, Tish carefully retraced her steps to the front door. She couldn't stand by and wait for help, not when every second could mean the difference between life and death. Sprinting to the Matrix, she jumped behind the wheel and drove along the driveway to the garage. Aligning the front bumper with the garage doors, she slipped the transmission into reverse and backed as far as she could on to the front lawn. Then, after whispering a prayer, she pressed the accelerator to the floor.

The Matrix sped across the lawn, down the strip of driveway, and collided with the garage doors with a ground-shaking crash that sent glass, metal, plastic, and wood hurtling into the air.

After taking several moments to orient herself, Tish fought her way out of the air bag's suffocating embrace, hoisted herself from the driver's compartment, and rushed to the garage to examine her handiwork. The doors had been busted in, but the latch was still loosely hinged.

'Tish! My God, girl, are you out of your mind?' Celestine scolded as she arrived at the garage.

'Probably.' Tish took the tire iron she'd carried into the house and swung it down, severing the latch in two.

Moving quickly, she and Celestine pushed the doors inward and scrambled to the bright green Alfa Romeo Giulia idling in the center of the garage. Walker James Honeycutt sat unconscious behind the steering wheel. A white sheet of paper lay on the passenger seat beside him.

Finding the doors of the vehicle locked, Tish, wielding the trusty tire iron, smashed the driver's side window of the automobile and reached a jacket-sleeved arm through the broken glass to unlock the door.

Swinging it open, she then reached inside and shut off the engine.

'Walker James,' she called, the exhaust fumes inside the car causing her to cough. 'Walker . . . James.'

Walker James didn't respond.

'Let's get him out of there,' Celestine rasped.

Tish and Celestine grabbed the young man by the torso and endeavored to pull him out of the vehicle. It was a difficult task.

'What the devil's going on in here?' came a shout from outside the garage doors. It was Vernon, the caretaker.

'Help us,' Tish implored.

Vernon, wearing the same camouflage and work-boot ensemble as he had worn the previous day, rushed to their aid. 'Oh my God! It's Mr Walker James.'

Reaching past Tish and Celestine and into the car, he easily hoisted Walker James out by his upper body and then instructed the women to each grab one of his legs. The trio then carried him from the garage and out on to the lawn. As they stretched him out in the sun and checked his vital signs, Walker James coughed and sputtered before drawing a deep breath.

The screech of sirens sounded a close distance away. Help was coming, but where was Clemson?

Tish gazed up at Cypress Hollow. Was Clemson trapped somewhere inside? Or worse, had the bishop killed Clemson before staging Walker James's suicide? She needed to find out.

Steeling her nerves, she started for the front door, but the caretaker, grabbing the back of her denim jacket, pulled her back. 'Whoa, now. If you're looking for that sheriff fella you were with yesterday, he should be comin' up from the hollow any minute now.'

'The hollow?'

'Yeah, I spotted a black sedan parked about a quarter mile from here on the service road that leads to the stables on this property. I met your sheriff at the front gate and stopped him before he even made it up the drive. He called for backup and hopped on the back of the mower. I drove him as far as I could down the trail to the hollow – can't drive a car down there and horsepower's faster than foot power. He told me the car belongs to some fella disguised as a priest and up to no good. Can you believe it? Anyways, your sheriff sent me back up here to check the house. Good thing I did, too.'

'I'll say,' Celestine agreed. 'Woulda taken Tish and me a lot more sweat and tears to get the poor young man out of that car.'

As police cars and ambulances flooded the property, Tish watched as Clemson Reade emerged from a copse of trees to the far left and front of the garage and handed a handcuffed Bishop Dillard over to Officer Clayton for processing.

She flew to him and threw her arms around his neck.

'Hey, now,' a surprised Reade said with a chuckle. 'What's all this?'

'I thought—' She buried her face in his chest.

'Hey, it's OK. We got him.' He slid an arm around her waist and smoothed her hair. 'I know it's been a tough case, emotionally and—'

Reade's voice fell off as he took note of the destroyed Matrix and the trashed garage door. 'What's all that?'

'Walker James was in there. Bishop Dillard tried to make it look like suicide. Celestine and I broke down the door to get him.'

'My God.' Reade pushed Tish away slightly and looked her up and down. 'Were you driving? Are you OK?'

'I'm fine. I just – I thought you were in there,' she said with tears in her eyes.

'No, I was on my way here when Clayton and the deputy radioed with your tip about the bishop. I'd only just arrived when Vernon, the caretaker, told me about a mysterious black sedan parked down near the stables. I went down to check it out, thinking it might belong to the bishop, and found out I was right. I'm such an idiot – I had no idea anyone was in the garage. Walker James might have . . . you might have—'

Tish embraced him again. 'I'm fine, but if anything had happened to you, I don't know . . .' She suddenly pulled back. 'The night I was shot, you said that, didn't you? You said that if anything happened to me, you didn't know what you would do.'

'I did,' he confessed. 'I can't believe you remember that.'

'I didn't until now. So you . . .?'

'Loved you even then?' Reade filled in the blanks. 'I've loved you ever since you confused my sousaphone with a tuba.'

'Since then?' Tish gasped and drew a hand to her mouth in surprise. 'Then why did you leave?'

'Because I felt like a failure for letting you get shot. And because you were on track to becoming Mrs Mayor and I wasn't sure I could be near you and watch it happen.'

'What made you come back?'

'Celestine told me you were available and said if I didn't come back, she'd slap me to sleep and then slap me for sleeping.'

'So all this was going on behind my back and I didn't have a clue about it?'

'I'm afraid so,' Reade frowned. 'I'm sorry.'

'Some detective I am.' She laughed and then, throwing her arms around Reade's neck again, she leaned in for a kiss.

He did not disappoint her.

# TWENTY-TWO

Eleven a.m. on the following Saturday saw Tish, in a black dress, and Reade, dapper in a dark suit, returning to Cookin' the Books following Gadsden Carney's emotional funeral.

'Hey, chickens,' Celestine greeted from the kitchen.

Mary Jo and Jules, meanwhile, issued their hellos from the counter, where they'd been using the downtime before lunch to huddle together and scroll through the most recent photos of Biscuit who, blissfully unaware that his owner had aspirations of registering him in an online pet beauty contest, slept peacefully at Jules's feet.

'My, my, you do clean up well, Sheriff,' Jules noted.

'Down, Jules,' Tish jokingly ordered.

'Yeah, one of two suits I own for court appearances,' Reade explained. 'I can't remember the last time I wore them for a social event, let alone two social events on the same day.'

'Well, Gregory's graduation party tomorrow is strictly informal,' Mary Jo advised. 'So you'll still have your backup suit in the closet while that one's at the cleaners. Tomorrow's all about good friends, good food, a wonderful son moving on in his life—'

'And trying not to punch your estranged husband and his new girlfriend in the face,' Jules reminded.

'Yeah, that, too.' Mary Jo nodded. 'I've been practicing meditation techniques to help me cope, but I can't promise I won't slip.'

'I'll be sure my riot gear and first-aid kit are in the trunk,' Reade teased. 'Is there anything else I can bring?'

'Wine. Lots of it.'

'Got it,' he said with a smile.

'I know it's a strange question, but how did the funeral go?' Celestine asked.

'It was a beautiful service,' Tish replied.

'Carney would have been happy,' Reade said. 'It was hard on his family, of course, but they have a sense of pride knowing he went out a hero.'

The group fell silent for several seconds.

'And now we have a wedding for which I need to change,' Tish announced before giving Reade a kiss and heading off to her bedroom.

'But you look great as you are,' he argued.

'I can't wear black to a wedding. It's bad luck. I won't be long.'

'I'm glad that young man is gonna marry that girl,' Celestine opined. 'It'll be a fresh start for them.'

'Yeah, it will be a small wedding – just his future in-laws, his aunt, his former nanny, and us, all in the backyard of his house

– but it should be nice. Walker James has also decided to tear down Cypress Hollow and turn the grounds into an arts camp for underprivileged and at-risk youth,' Reade explained. 'He's already hired Leah Harmon to head the visual arts team – a thank you for all she's done – but there will be staff on hand to teach singing, dancing, digital arts, writing, you name it. He's naming the camp for his sister and mother.'

'Aww. Well, he probably doesn't remember me, he was so out of it, but you make sure to give my best to him and his bride.' Celestine beamed.

'Oh, he knows who you are. He emailed me to say that when he and Milla get back from their honeymoon, he wants to get together with you, Tish, and Vernon to discuss a suitable reward for saving his life.'

Tish emerged from her bedroom wearing a peach, floral-printed, V-neck chiffon dress with flutter sleeves and a pair of nude strappy sandals. She'd run a crimper through her normally straight, bobbed blonde hair and accented the wavy style with a pair of delicate, chin-length diamante earrings.

Reade literally took a step back. 'Wow. And to think I said you looked great before. This is . . . just wow.'

'Thank you.' She curtseyed.

'You two look fabulous together.' Mary Jo took out her phone and snapped a photo.

'Y'all better not do anything I wouldn't do,' Jules advised with a wink.

'Oh, and what's that?' Tish challenged.

'When I find out, I'll text you.'

'Deal.' Tish turned to Reade. 'We'd better get going if we want to be there before noon.'

'Whose vehicle are you taking?' Jules asked.

'In these heels? I'll give you one guess.'

'Well, you need to get that new van of yours out on to the streets. Now that it's all lettered up, it's a great way to get your business noticed.'

'The thing's cherry red and as big as a billboard. I don't need to take it out. It can be seen from Mars,' she quipped as she led Reade to the door.

'You'd better not be catchin' any bouquets,' Celestine shouted after them. 'Not until we get this place cleaned up from Gregory's party.'

Reade and Tish laughed and shook their heads. Stepping on to the front porch, they were met by an intimidatingly large man in a striped button-down shirt and gray slacks. 'Ms Letitia Tarragon?'

'Yes.' The use of her formal first name surprised her.

'This is for you.' The man presented her with an envelope for which she needed to sign.

'I wonder what it is,' she said aloud after the man had left. Opening the missive with anxious fingers, she held the enclosed document to her face and read.

Within moments, her rosy complexion went ashen.

'What is it?' Reade asked.

'It's from Schuyler. It's an eviction notice.'

# JULIAN'S RHUBARB AND RASPBERRY CORDIAL

Makes approx 4 cups/1 litre

INGREDIENTS:
- 2 ½ cups/600g white granulated or golden caster sugar
- 2 ½ cups/600ml water
- zest 1 large orange
- zest 1 large lemon
- 3 tablespoons lemon juice
- 6 tablespoons orange juice
- 1 ½ cups/200g raspberries, fresh or frozen
- 2 lbs/900g rhubarb, chopped
- 2 thick slices fresh ginger, peeled

METHOD:
Put the sugar and water in a large saucepan with the orange and lemon zest.

Bring to a simmer then add rhubarb, raspberries and ginger slices.

Cook the mixture over a medium heat until the rhubarb is soft and falling apart.

Pour the mixture through a colander, pressing out as much juice as possible then strain the liquid through a sieve lined with cheesecloth or muslin.

Pour the cordial into a large, sterilized bottle with airtight lid and store in the fridge for up to 1 month.

Serve approx 2 tablespoons/30ml of cordial per 2/3 cup/150ml of soda water or a blend of soda water and white wine for a refreshing summer beverage.

# TISH'S "ENLIGHTENED" AMBROSIA SALAD

Makes 6 servings

Although Tish adores traditional Ambrosia, she doesn't always enjoy the extra fat and calories brought by the sour cream, whipping cream, and marshmallows. This version retains the coconut and canned fruit of the original, but lightens it up with fresh berries and grapes and creamy, calcium-rich yogurt.

INGREDIENTS:
- One 20 ounce/435g can pineapple chunks, drained
- 1 ½ cups/200g green seedless grapes
- One 11 ounce/300g can mandarin segments, drained
- 1 cup/100g flaked coconut
- 1 cup/144g fresh strawberries, sliced
- ¾ cup/184g vanilla yogurt
- ¼ cup/37g chopped, toasted pecans

METHOD:
In a large serving bowl, mix together the pineapple, grapes, mandarin segments, coconut, strawberries, and yogurt. Cover and refrigerate for at least one hour. Just before serving, mix in the pecans.